Slow Hands

LYNNE KAUFMAN

Slow Hands

MIRA®

MIRA

ISBN 1-55166-718-5

SLOW HANDS

Grateful acknowledgment is made to Wesleyan University Press for permission
to print lines from Antonio Machado's poem, "Last Night As I Was Sleeping,"
from *Times Alone: Selected Poems of Antonio Machado,* translated by
Robert Bly.

Visit us at www.mirabooks.com

Printed in U.S.A.

First Printing: June 2003
10 9 8 7 6 5 4 3 2 1

For Steve:

Thank you for all those years of listening to
"I'd never let my wife do that."

And did you get what
You wanted from this life, even so?
I did.
And what did you want?
To call myself beloved, to feel myself
Beloved on this earth.
  —Raymond Carver, "Late Fragments"

Why is it that even the most clear-eyed monk
Cannot sever the red thread of passion
Between his legs?
  —Zen Koan

Whoever said money can't buy happiness
didn't know where to spend it.
  —Bo Derek

Bad things come in threes. I looked out the window of my office at the Family Therapy Center just in time to see the rain begin. It wasn't just a drizzle, either, the way the perky TV weather girl had predicted, but a piercing downpour. Unseasonable weather for San Francisco but appropriate to my mood. It was early December, supposedly the season of good cheer, but Mom was in the hospital, my client, Grace, had attempted suicide and my car was in the shop. Granted the car was a minor annoyance but I had just heard from the mechanic.

All in all a bad day. I dialed Harry's number. Ruth-Ann, his dental assistant, answered the phone. "He's got someone in the chair," she informed me.

"Tell him it's his wife," I said. "I need to talk to him."

And he was on the line in a minute, leaving his patient mid-cavity. I could always count on Harry; our daughter, Wendy, and I were the most important people in the world to him. "That man is good husband material," Mom had said when she first met him, and the material had gotten stronger over time. I had already given him an update on Mom and on Grace so I told him about the car, my ten-year-old Honda.

"It needs a new radiator," I said. "It's covered with lime."

"Can't they clean it?"

"No, it's plastic. You can't clean plastic." My voice rose in exasperation. "Why do they put in parts they can't fix?"

Harry is a pragmatist; he deals in *hows* not *whys*. His response was comforting yet annoyingly predictable. "How much do they want?"

"Nine hundred and ninety nine dollars."

"Wow, why don't you get a new car?"

"Because I don't want to figure out all those new dials. And I don't want to wait for the first scratch. And the new cars are never as good as the old ones."

"And it's raining," he commiserated.

"And I forgot my umbrella."

"And I still love you," he said.

"Thanks." I blew him a kiss. "I hope you win tonight. And remember no more than three sets or you won't be able to walk tomorrow."

"That's tomorrow," he said cheerfully and hung up.

There was just time to call the hospital before my Group arrived. Now that HMOs had changed the face of psychotherapy, reducing the number of approved sessions, I was doing less individual and more group work. My clients actually preferred it as they could avail themselves of more sessions and it was helpful for them to hear each other's problems as so many of them were shared.

Like food. What woman didn't worry about her weight? The exception was Esme, darling Esme, the angel of the Cardiac Care Unit. I dialed Moffitt Hospital; Esme answered on the first ring.

"How's Mom doing?" I asked.

"Hanging in there, darlin'." Her soft New Orleans patois wafted past my ear like a warm breeze.

"Can she talk?"

"She's resting quietly."

"Well, don't disturb her. I've got Group in five minutes. Coralee and I will be there at nine unless you think we should come sooner." My sister and I had visited every night since Mom had been admitted last week with a serious heart attack.

"Now, don't you be agitatin' yourself, darlin', your mama is in good hands. See you then."

"Can I bring you anything?" I asked.

"A latte would be nice," she suggested.

"Anything else?"

"Ohhh, I wouldn't say no to a piece of pecan pie. And don't be forgettin' that whipped cream. Thank you, darlin'. You take care, now." She hung up the phone.

Why can't more women be like that? I envisioned Esme's generous body poured into her nurse's uniform, breasts and belly billowing like the sails of a clipper ship. Rear round and rolling as a tidal wave. Her body was bountiful, bodacious. And she displayed it. There was no shame there, no cover-up. She ate when and what and how much she pleased. Black women seemed to have an easier time of it, I thought, at least with their bodies, with their appetites. It came of living in a matriarchal society, strong, lusty women and fade-away men.

Esme had proudly shown me her rogues' gallery of ex-lovers—each man better-looking than the one before—and even more proudly the three children they had sired: bright-eyed children who now lived with Esme and her mother.

Esme seemed to have solved the three nagging problems of every woman client I had ever had. Weight, aging and men.

"How do you do it?" I had asked.

"It's all about love, honey. I love my job. I love my kids. I love Jesus. And I love my jelly roll. It keeps me cheerful, girl." She had laughed, a free and full-throated laugh. I'm sure Esme had her problems but I would give a lot to hear that kind of laughter in The Group.

The women would be here any minute. I glanced about my consultation room; it looked inviting. I had redecorated it just last year in Southwestern style dusty pinks and greens, bleached wood and Georgia O'Keeffe prints. I loved the economy of her paintings; they matched my own style. Today, as usual, I was dressed in soft earth-toned colors highlighted by a favorite silver-and-turquoise Navajo necklace. My dark hair was kept short and my major extravagance was a top-flight trim every six weeks. I straightened the pile of *Ms.* magazines, checked the hot water in the urn, made sure the stoneware mugs were clean. Disposable cups were easier but Laura objected. They were not kind to the environment. Fluorescent lights gave her migraines. Air-conditioning kicked up her allergies. Laura was a sensitive soul who worried about everything, but to her credit, since she always allowed for disasters, she was invariably early. That was her knock on the door now.

I rose and let her in. "Good evening, Dr. Russack." She rejected my offer to hang up her coat and hurried to the softest, largest chair she could hide in. Laura, the youngest of the group at thirty, was a graduate student in art history and a blond bulimic who seesawed dangerously from a size three spandex to her current elephantine muumuus. She filled her mug to the brim with herbal tea, wrapped her hands around it, inhaled the steam and closed her eyes.

The next to arrive was Terry. With her gray curls, granny glasses and matronly bosom she looked the prototype of the kindly kindergarten teacher she was, except that she had just been laid off work, was menopausal and had decided to quit smoking. She immediately flung open the window, undid the top three buttons of her blouse and picked up a magazine to vigorously fan herself. It was the *Ms.* anniversary issue with Virginia Woolf as its cover girl. The juxtaposition of Terry's broad shoulders and Virginia's Bloomsbury sunken-cheek pallor was arresting.

The last was Mary Ann, who breezed through the door, chose the chair with the straightest back, opened her Louis Vuitton briefcase and started punching buttons on her state-of-the-art Palm Pilot. Mary Ann, a corporate attorney, usually on the road and always on edge, seemed to subsist on the olives in her martinis. She was never hungry; the others would have hated her if she weren't equally as miserable. "I have no life of my own," MaryAnn had confessed. "I just depose others." She stared at me impatiently. We were five minutes past the hour and Mary Ann billed her own clients by the minute. She tapped her manicured fingernails against her cashmere slacks. "Can we get started or what?"

"But we're not all here yet," Laura demurred softly.

"That's right," Terry said as she mopped her damp brow. "Where's Grace?"

I rose and poured myself an extra strength coffee. "I'm afraid I have some bad news."

I could see the women prepare themselves. Laura downed her apple blossom tea. Terry reached for her placebo cigarette. Mary Ann leaned forward, pencil poised, ready to take notes.

"It's about Grace," I began.

"Oh, God," Laura cried, "I knew it. I just knew it." She began rocking back and forth, holding herself. Terry, ever efficient, ever solicitous, brought the younger woman a fresh cup of tea, which Laura clutched gratefully. Tea was a blessing, warmth without calories.

How did Laura know? Perhaps because she had been so close to utter despair herself. Laura had been hospitalized twice when she had starved herself below the eighty-five-pound mark. Looking like a skeleton, she had still complained about being fat. Women were their own worst critics, I thought. At least the women in this room were.

"What happened?" Mary Ann asked.

I decided to lead in slowly. "Grace has had an accident. Her ankle is broken."

"Poor thing," Terry sighed.

"How did it happen?" Mary Ann asked.

"She fell," I said.

"From what?" Mary Ann probed.

"The bridge," I said.

"Which bridge?" Laura whispered.

"The Golden Gate. No one jumps toward Oakland," Mary Ann said.

"She tried to kill herself?" Terry exclaimed. "Why? That woman had everything."

"Everything but Maurice. The pig," Mary Ann spat.

Maurice, Grace's husband of forty years, had left her for his twenty-five-year-old secretary. How unfair, we had all thought, for elegant, witty Grace to be the victim of such a cliché. Fortunately she had a loving family a wide circle of friends and a huge settlement. If anyone could get through this humiliation intact, we had agreed, it would be Grace. And The Group had applauded her decision to leave her husband. If he had shown some remorse and asked to be forgiven, it might have been different, but the bastard wanted to have his cake and eat it, too. Although Grace had wryly quipped, "I would have been happy to be his cake. He thought I was his Pepto-Bismol." That humor must have deserted her in her plunge off the bridge. Her daughter had called me last night. She and Grace had been watching a TV movie and, after a typical bittersweet girl-loses-boy ending, Grace had run from the room shouting, "What's she got to cry about? She's thirty years old." Grace had driven her

BMW to the Golden Gate Bridge and tried to jump off. Fortunately she had landed on a safety railing. Oh, Grace, I thought, why didn't you call me?

"I know why she did it," Laura whispered, holding out her empty cup to Terry who rose to fill it. "I wish I had her courage. You know what life is...a long road to getting tired. And I'm tired...I'm tired of fighting. Tired of trying to be happy. Life is the pits. I'm never going to have a boyfriend."

"What about me?" Mary Ann said bitterly. "I haven't had a date in six months."

"You think that's bad," Terry cried, "my roommate is gay and he's dating my ex-husband. There are no straight men in San Francisco." She reached into her purse and pulled out a cigarette, this time the real thing.

"Hey, just a minute, this is a no-smoking zone," Mary Ann protested.

"How about a special dispensation?" Terry asked. "We're in crisis, here."

The three women looked at me. It seemed important to hold my ground, to stick to the rules. Terry had vowed to kick the nicotine habit and this was California—secondhand smoke was the new bubonic plague. "No smoking," I said firmly.

Terry stabbed the air with her unlit cigarette, pointing it angrily at me. "Life's a losing battle against age and despair. Everything runs down. You start dying the day you're born. Peggy Lee got it right. 'Is that all there is?'"

Even Mary Ann, that bastion of practicality, of Churchillian fortitude, nodded in agreement. "Yeah, it's clear that talking doesn't work. It's too slow. It's too soft.

We need drugs. We need Prozac." With this she reached into her coat pocket for a package of bite-size Milky Ways and passed them around.

Each of the women took a handful, including me. For a few minutes there was only the sounds of ripping paper and vigorous chewing. Sugar and carbs...a little hit of love.

I pried a bit of caramel from my molar with my tongue. "You know how I feel about Prozac. It masks the symptoms and doesn't cure anything." And it kills your sex drive, I thought.

"But it makes you feel better," Laura said, devouring her last Milky Way. "Even my mother's on it." She licked the empty candy paper. "I want some meds."

"But Sara can't prescribe them," Mary Ann said as she passed the bag again, "isn't that right?"

Of course Mary Ann knew that was right. Half her practice was suing doctors.

"Only an M.D. can prescribe drugs," I said. "And in my opinion, they prescribe far too many and mostly to women."

"Please, Dr. Russack, you don't want what happened to Grace to happen to all of us," Laura cautioned.

"I feel terrible about Grace, just the way you do. But I don't think medication is the answer," I protested.

"We've given up on answers," Mary Ann countered. "How about just getting through?"

"It could save some time," Terry added reasonably.

"We can talk about it," I conceded. "I could refer you to a colleague, a psychiatrist, for evaluation and he could prescribe the drugs if we thought it was necessary."

"It's either that or booze," Mary Ann said.

"I understand how you feel," I said , "but can we move on? We're all here now and we do have our two hours. Who'd like to start? How was your week?" Silence. Heavy silence. Long silence.

Finally Laura, the gentlest of them, patted my hand. "It just doesn't feel right, Dr. Russack. Not tonight. You know, opening all those wounds. Sometimes you just want to forget."

"Absolutely. How about a movie, ladies?" Terry suggested. "There's a new romantic comedy at the Kabuki."

"Great," Mary Ann said, "let's go watch other people kiss." She stuffed the remaining candy in her purse. "Let's face it, Doc. It's not your fault. The one thing we really want, you can't get us." They all began to get up and gather their things.

"Drugs?" I said.

"Meds or a man." She paused at the door. "Want to come to the movies and sublimate?"

"Thanks, but I can't. I already have plans."

Terry smiled and waved. "Nothing personal, Sara. You're a great therapist. Maybe it's just time for a break."

"It's the holidays, anyway. So why don't we take off a month or so?" Mary Ann suggested. "We can start again in the new year. Is that okay with you, Sara?"

No, it wasn't okay with me. I was their therapist. I wanted to be needed. Needed to be helpful. But this wasn't about my needs, I quickly reasoned. At least it wasn't supposed to be.

I mustered a smile, almost as genuine as if the suggestion had been mine. "Sure, we'll start again in January."

They put on their coats, gathered their handbags and headed for the door. And they were gone. I sat for a moment, stunned. Well, at least they had asked me to join them. I didn't think it was me they'd abandoned, just therapy. I walked to my desk, studied my wall of diplomas, my master's degree in psychology, my certification as a licensed marriage and family counselor, my professional awards. I had been practicing psychotherapy for twenty years, read all the professional literature, took postgraduate seminars to keep up with the latest methods. I prided myself upon being a competent and caring therapist. I had a full practice and most of my patients got better. Why was this happening? I was deeply shaken. After all, therapy was not an exact science. It depended on intuition, on rapport. What was wrong? Was it the world? Or was it me? I forced myself to sit down and write my usual post-therapy notes. I recorded what happened succinctly and unflinchingly. *Rebellion among the troops. The Group questions the usefulness of therapy. They want drugs. Or a man. Grace attempted suicide. Why didn't I see it coming? I feel responsible.*

Elsa, help! What would you have done? I thought about my supervising therapist, the woman who had trained me. Elsa was gone now but the memory of her patience and common sense still burned bright. Back when we were working together, I would report some therapeutic frustration or failure and she would smile and pat my hand. "Rome vasn't built in a day, Sara. Ve do vat ve can." And I would feel better. It wasn't the words. Platitudes, really, even with the Viennese accent. It was the touch of those violet-scented fingers. It was her touch that healed. And I was afraid I was losing mine.

I turned off the lights and sat for a long time staring out at the growing darkness.

CHAPTER 2

By the time I left my office, the rain had turned into a light mist. I was to meet Coralee at Ovations, a small French restaurant at the top of Nob Hill we both liked; I for its soft lighting and crisp linen and Coralee for its robust Burgundian fare. I checked my watch. It wouldn't take much longer to walk than to ride the bus. The exercise might do me good, clear my head, and Coralee had never been on time for anything in her life, including the day she was born. I had been there, waiting. Ralph, my own father, was long gone and Sam, our new dad, was serving in Vietnam. Sadly, Sam never came back; and from then on we were a troika...the three mouseketeers as Mom called us. I was ten, a plump precocious fourth grader, when she had placed the tiny red-faced bundle in my arms. "This is your new best friend, Sarie. What shall we call her?"

I had looked down into the baby's sky-blue eyes. And

as my new little sister returned my gaze with steadfast curiosity, I said "Coralee."

"Coralee?" Mom had asked. "Where did that come from?" I had brushed my cheek against the baby's fuzzy scalp. The name was in honor of my second favorite grown-up, Coralee Davis, the children's librarian, who had led me from Grimms' Fairy Tales to the Bobbsey Twins to Nancy Drew to William Shakespeare. Coralee Davis had opened my world to romance and adventure and meaning.

When I reached the restaurant, I was in a much better mood despite my damp hair and shoes. "If you're depressed," Carl Jung said, "it means you're too high in your head." Exercise had helped and so did the warmth with which the young maître d' greeted me. He was new, tall with a thatch of sandy hair, and his "Good evening, madam" revealed a plummy English accent. He helped me out of my coat and led me into the dining room. To my surprise, he stopped in front of one of the few leather banquettes, an absolutely choice table. That happened so rarely. The usual table offered to an unescorted woman was next to the kitchen or by the door. It seemed to be some unwritten restaurant code. Offer the worst table first. Then it would become some sort of character test: would the patron protest or rise above it? And which was the more admirable? Happily, for once, I didn't have to decide. I was being well treated. Bravo Ovations!

"Thank you... um," I said, pausing for his name.

"Simon," he supplied.

"Simon," I said, noticing his eyes were jade green.

"And would madam like an aperitif while she waits?"

I looked at him blankly. The Group session had taken its toll; I wasn't up to choices.

He leaped into the breach. "May I suggest the house special? Kir royale?"

I nodded gratefully.

"A good pick-me-up when you've had a hard day." He unfolded my napkin and laid it upon my lap as solicitously as if it were an ermine wrap. I settled into the cushioned chair and noticed for the first time the Vivaldi playing in the background. I closed my eyes and listened. "Music is like a naked woman running madly through the forest." Who said that? García Lorca or some other passionate Latin. I imagined myself running naked in the forest; it had to be more fun than churning in the gym on a stationary bike. I had never been a fitness maven. Indeed, I had managed to tolerate the little blobs of jelly that increasingly appeared on my stomach and thighs and to conceal them through artful dressing. Tunics for the tush was my dress code. But last month, when I turned forty-five, and my upper arms continued to wave long after I had stopped, I gave up desserts and bought a membership to the Jewish Community Center gym.

Harry and I had discontinued our membership at the synagogue after Wendy's bat mitzvah but somehow it was comforting to *schvitz* with my own kind. Let's face it, Jews aren't naturally thin or fit, especially women and especially my generation.

Simon arrived with my drink and placed it before me with a flourish. "A bit of bubbly with a hint of blush." He stood by my side as I took my first sip. "How is it?"

"Excellent."

"Not too sweet?" he asked.

"Just right."

"Well, then, cheers."

"Cheers," I said. Then, "Where are you from?"

"New York," he said.

"Originally?"

"Oh, you mean the accent," he said with mock surprise. "England."

"Where in England?" I asked.

"You know the U.K.?"

"A little."

"Oxford," he said.

"Everyone knows Oxford," I said. "What did you do there?"

"Got my degree."

"In what?"

"Think of the most useless pursuit you can."

"Computer science?" I ventured.

"I didn't say tasteless. I said useless."

I was beginning to enjoy this: the banter, the bit of flirtation, all heightened by Simon's exotic accent. I busied myself with my drink, looked up at him through my lashes. "What then?"

"I'll leave you guessing," he said as he walked to the door to greet the next guest.

I watched as Coralee shook the rain off her honey-blond hair and handed Simon her red silk poncho. My gorgeous colt of a sister, her mile-long legs clad in black velvet tights, her torso wrapped in a silver mesh leotard, walked toward me turning heads in her wake.

As Simon pulled out her chair, he carefully appraised us. "You two must be related."

"Now how did you know that?" I said, "We don't look at all alike."

"Au contraire," Simon insisted. "The family resemblance is unmistakable."

"In what?" I persisted.

"Style," he said. "Now what can I get you to drink?"

"I'll have whatever she's having," Coralee said.

"What did I say?" Simon smiled and walked to the bar.

Coralee draped her purse over her chair and in turning caught a glimpse of Simon's retreating form in his well-fitting black pants. "He's rather dishy."

"Really? I hadn't noticed."

"Don't act coy with me." She grinned. "I was standing at the door for ten minutes before you two noticed me."

"Just making small talk while I waited for you."

"Now, listen, you don't have to cover to me, for God's sake. We all like a little male attention. Even you, Sadie, Sadie married lady."

"Especially after a tough day," I admitted.

"For me, too. And we're going to talk about it. But first give me a hug."

I leaned forward across the table but Coralee was already on her feet. This was not to be a token hug. This was to be a let's get real, full-body embrace. I stood up and was pulled in firm and close. My sister gave great hugs.

For the rest of the meal, Simon was a comforting presence who brought food and cleared plates as we filled each other in on our days.

"How's Mom?" Coralee asked.

"Esme said she was resting comfortably," I reported, "and the cardiologist said the scans look good. She's recovering."

"That was a massive heart attack, though," Coralee said. "It left a lot of damage."

"Apparently there was damage before. Lots of little strokes."

"That she never told us about," Coralee said. "Yvonne the independent."

"I don't think she can go on living alone, though." I sighed. "Not after this. She needs to come home with one of us."

"Kicking and screaming all the way," Coralee said. "My apartment is small but I'm happy to have her."

"Me, too. We'll just have to convince her."

Coralee nodded. "Now tell me why today was such a bad day. Harry okay?"

"He's fine. He just got a new laser drill."

"State-of-the-art Harry." She smiled. "And my adorable niece?"

"Wendy's great. Her skin's clearing up."

"Then what's wrong?"

"My practice," I said and told her about Grace's suicide attempt and the response of the group.

Coralee's color rose as she listened. "Those women don't realize what a great therapist you are. I mean, all you can do is listen and give advice...you can't change their lives."

"I wish I could," I said.

"Sounds like they're lonely," she reflected. "I can empathize. It can be tough without a guy. Even roll-over-right-after-it's-over Bruce."

Before I could question her further, Simon appeared
with the dessert menu and Coralee seized it. "Now hear
this, we are not sharing an order of low-cal biscotti. We
are each ordering our own dessert," she said. "We need
it."

"All right, then. I'll have a lemon sorbet."

"I said a real dessert," Coralee said, signaling Simon.

"Make that a double chocolate mousse," I conceded.

"Now you're talking."

"And pecan pie and a whole-milk latte," I added.

"You go, girl." Coralee grinned her approval.

"To go, girl," I amended. "They're for Esme."

"Too bad," she said, grinning. "I thought you were finally getting down."

When the check arrived later tucked in its discreet
brown leather wallet, Coralee grabbed it.

"It's not your turn," I protested.

"It may be the last one I pay for a while. I'm officially
unemployed."

"Since when?"

"Today."

"What happened to Festive Fare?" I asked. I thought the
upscale catering service that Coralee ran with her boyfriend
Bruce was thriving. They had just done the opening for the
Picasso show at the Legion and their clever cubist food displays had hit all the society pages. Coralee had face-painted
the waitresses to look like Dora Maar and the waiters wore
bulls' heads. Her phones had been ringing off the hook.

"I'll tell you about it in the car." Coralee signed the bill
and added a whopping twenty-five percent tip. I raised my
eyebrows, but Coralee just shrugged. "It's only money."

And as Simon held the door open for us, I added, "'Money's like manure, it's only good if you spread it around.'"

Simon nodded in recognition. "Thornton Wilder," he said.

"Ah, so that's it," I cried. "You're a lit major."

"With a specialty in romantic poetry," he added.

"Divinely superfluous beauty," I said.

"Nothing more essential than the superfluous. Thank you, ladies, and have a good night."

"Now what was that all about?" Coralee asked as we walked up the steep incline of Nob Hill to her car. The rain had stopped and it was a crisp, clear evening.

"I was just trying to guess who he is."

"He's a waiter, right?"

"That's not who he is, that's what he's doing."

"Ohhh, heavy," she said, linking her arm through mine. "Comes of all that analysis. Me, I'm a simple soul. All I peel are onions. Now will you look at that moonlight," she commanded.

I gazed upward, admiring the full moon as it illuminated the vaulted roof and stained-glass windows of Grace Cathedral. "Listen," Coralee said, and in the silence, I heard the bells of the cable cars as they followed Tony Bennett's directive, and "climbed halfway to the stars." It was December, I thought, and in most of the country people were digging out their driveways. It was good to be in California. "When we're depressed, it is because we refuse to praise." I thought of my favorite Machado poem:

Last night as I was sleeping
I dreamt—marvelous error—

That I had a beehive
Here inside my heart
And the golden bees
Were making white combs
And sweet honey
From my old failures.

I loved poetry, loved knowing something by heart so it was always with me. Simon had recognized my quote from *The Matchmaker*, the play they'd later made into *Hello, Dolly!* Somewhere in America, Carol Channing was probably making an entrance right now. But Simon knew the source, knew it was Wilder.

"Where's your car?" Coralee asked.

"In the shop," I said. "It's a sad story, it's got lime disease. Now tell me about Festive Fare."

"Festive Fare is a child of divorce. I gave Bruce custody."

"You broke up with Bruce? Why? You were doing so well."

"In business," she said.

"As a couple, too," I persisted. "You were together for two years—that's the longest you've been with anyone. You had the food thing in common. And he was crazy about you."

"I know," she said, "he wanted to get married."

"Would that have been so bad?"

"Yes," Coralee said unlocking the door of her sun-flower-yellow sports car and rolling down the canvas top.

I climbed in, shaking my head in puzzlement. "I don't get it. I thought you two were good together."

"We were," she said flinging her head back to look at the stars. "Good and boring."

"That's called stability, Corrie, it makes people live longer."

She gunned the motor and peeled out of the space. "No, big sister, it just makes it feel that way."

CHAPTER 3

When we arrived at the hospital, Mom was sitting up, propped against three pillows. She was dressed in a mauve satin dressing gown, her red hair freshly brushed, her mouth and cheeks a brave crimson. But despite Esme's careful ministrations, she looked weary and fragile.

She perked up when she saw us, though. "Darlings, welcome." She held out her newest pot of rouge. "Rose petal rain, pretty fanciful. Do you know how much money women spend on this stuff every year?"

"Not a clue," I said. Mom collected droves of what she called her "useless bits of information." Conversation starters, girls, she would say, good for business.

"Eight hundred and seventy-five million dollars," she supplied. "Isn't that amazing? If I knew that I would have gone into cosmetics, not real estate."

"You did just fine with real estate," I said.

"Well, you couldn't go wrong with land in the seventies."

"'Land...the one thing they're not making more of.'" I quoted the slogan of Right Way Realty, Mom's former employer.

"That's it, darling," she said.

Not to be outdone, Coralee quickly added, "And, Mom, do you know why red is the color of romance?"

"Why?" Mom asked.

"It suggests the aroused genitals."

Mom started to laugh, but her familiar throaty chuckle immediately turned into an alarmingly loud choking. Three monitors began buzzing.

Esme quickly moved to her patient's bedside and lifted Mom's frail arms high above her head until she could catch her breath. Mom collapsed against the pillows, breathing hard but managing a smile. She gestured toward the glass of water. Coralee held the straw to her lips as she took a tiny sip.

She struggled to swallow the water. "Oh, you girls are a tonic," she whispered, "that's for sure." She turned to Esme. "Aren't I lucky having these two?" She held out her hands. "Come close. You are the best things in my life. And I am so proud of you." Clasping my hand and then Coralee's, she brought them to her cheek. We stayed that way until Esme announced it was time for Mom's sleeping pill and pain medication. Mom kissed each of our hands. "And Sara, make sure you tell Harry and Wendy how much I love them."

My throat tightened in alarm. "Now, Mom, let's not get

melodramatic. You can tell them yourself. You're going to be home in no time."

"Home," she sighed, "that sounds good." She released our hands. "Goodbye, darlings...I'm tired now, I need to sleep. Remember to be good to each other."

As we edged out the door, I looked back for a last glimpse, but she had already turned her face to the pillow.

"How about a cup of that great hospital coffee," Coralee suggested and I quickly agreed. Neither one of us was ready to leave the hospital just yet. It was as if by keeping vigil, we could fend off danger. We took the elevator four stories down to the dreary pea-soup-green cafeteria and found a table far in the corner, avoiding both the uniform-clad groups of chattering nurses and doctors, for whom it was just another day at the office, and the subdued clusters of families who were as confused and troubled as we.

Coralee and I drank the tepid coffee down to its muddy dregs as if it were a shaman's potion, and by some sympathetic magic, it could make Mom better.

"She's going to be all right," Coralee said. My sister, ever the optimist.

I unraveled the edge of my disposable cup. "I can't imagine life without her."

"Don't say that," Coralee admonished.

"Remember the story about the Taoist priest." Mom loved Chinese lore. " 'When it comes time for Taoists to leave this earth, girls, they can just will themselves to die. That's the way I want to go.' "

"Stop it. You're being morbid," Coralee said.

"Sorry, it must be the decor."

But as Coralee drove me home all I could think of was why then had Mom said goodbye instead of good-night. And why did I have this granite boulder sitting in my chest and why when I hugged Coralee good-night, did she cling to me like a child?

The lights were out when I got home but Harry was still up when I climbed into bed. "How's Yvonne?" he asked.

"Not so good." My voice broke. I nuzzled into his chest, feeling my fatigue.

His stroked my hair, kissed my forehead. And in typical Harry fashion, did not try to talk me out of my feelings. He held me until I fell asleep.

I slept fitfully, struggling through confused and fragmented dreams. Mom was placing a baby Coralee into my arms. She was wrapped in a blanket, a mauve satin blanket, and it was slipping. But it was no longer Coralee in the blanket. It was Mom and I couldn't hold her.

The phone woke me at 4:00 a.m.

It was Esme. "Your Mom passed, darlin'. Peacefully. In her sleep."

"When?" I asked.

"A few minutes ago. Hour of the wolf, love, that's when a lot of them let go. She told me not to wake you if anything happened , to wait until the morning." She imitated Mom's throaty voice, "'My Sara has got to get her eight hours or—'"

"'She's a bear.'" I swallowed hard.

I hung up the phone. Bear...nobody would call me that again. Not in that way. Not ever. I remembered winter mornings, rainy and cold even in California, Mom waking me for school. I hated to get up; I still do. Coralee would have already finished breakfast and I was still buried under the covers. Mom would sit on the side of my bed, patiently play with my hair, rub my back although she was already late for work. "Come on Boo Boo Bear," she would croon, "time to rise and shine." Mom. I sank to the floor still cradling the phone.

Harry climbed out of bed and knelt beside me, his back stiff, knees creaky from last night's tennis match.

"How many sets did you play?" I accused tearfully.

"Four," he admitted.

"I told you not to do that," my voice rose. "Why don't you ever listen!" I began to sob. He drew me close and I buried my head against the springy gray hair of his chest and breathed in the familiar fragrance of Old Spice, the same aftershave he had worn since college, since the first time we kissed. Familiarity was an underrated comfort, especially in times of trouble. I needed to remember that when marriage seemed a burden or a cage. I thought of Elsa, my wise old therapist, shaking her head over the latest divorce statistics. "Ven vill people realize marriage isn't about having a dance partner? It's about having a partner to circle the vagons ven the Indians attack."

"But Mom was supposed to come home," I insisted to Harry. "She was getting better."

"There's often a second heart attack after the first. It's a dangerous time and there was a lot of damage."

"But she was strong and she wasn't old, Harry. God, she was only sixty-three."

"We never know how long we've got. That's why we've got to make the most of it." He hugged me hard. "Go and call Coralee. I'll make some coffee."

I dialed my sister's number. She picked it up on the first ring. "Sarie. I can't...I just can't believe it. How can she not be here anymore?"

I had seen a documentary once about Jane Goodall and her chimps. A baby chimp had died and its mother wouldn't put the body down. Wherever she went, she just kept carrying it. She couldn't understand what had happened. Neither could we.

"Corrie, can you drive?" I asked.

"I think so."

"Then get in the car. Harry's just put up some coffee."

When Coralee arrived, red eyed and bedraggled, we cried. Cried hard. But in a while, after long hugs and steaming mugs of Harry's industrial-strength brew, we were telling Yvonne the Invincible stories. By that time Wendy was up. Her dark hair was tangled, her olive skin still flushed from sleep; she seemed much younger than her sixteen years. As she entered the kitchen, she looked from one to the other of us.

"What happened?" she demanded.

I told her.

"Oh, no!" She clutched her terry cloth robe tightly around her slender frame. "I wanted Nana to come to my graduation. She was my last grandparent."

Harry's parents had died in an auto accident when Wendy was still a baby.

"Some kids still have all four. It's not fair."

"It's not," I agreed and poured her some coffee.

She examined it skeptically. "I thought I wasn't allowed to have coffee."

"Today's an exception. Drink up."

"As Mom used to say, 'Here's to small comforts.'" I topped up my coffee and we four clinked mugs.

"I'm really going to miss her." Wendy's voice broke.

"We all will, sweetie, but you know what we need right now," Coralee said, springing up, "food." She headed for the fridge pulling Wendy with her. "Come on, girlfriend, I'll teach you to crack eggs with one hand." Harry and I watched as Wendy carefully opened the eggs; Coralee added cheese and herbs, then expertly cooked and folded the mixture into golden-brown omelets which we ate with surprising appetite. Harry left for the office; Wendy for school. Coralee and I did the dishes then drove to the hospital to sign the necessary papers and collect Mom's things.

We drove through the familiar streets in silence. How could everything look the same yet be unalterably changed? How could the first face we ever touched be gone?

When we arrived, Esme gave us a warm collective hug. "Do you girls want to view your Mom's body?" she asked.

I shook my head.

"That wouldn't be her," Coralee said.

"Have you thought about burial plans?" Esme inquired gently.

"I'm not sure what she'd want," I said, "but we're going to her apartment, she may have left some instructions. And Esme, this is something from all of us." I handed her an envelope.

"That's not necessary," she protested.

"It's for the children's educational fund," Coralee added.

"All right, then." She smiled and tucked the gift into her uniform pocket. "Thank you, girls. Be well."

We left the hospital and drove through Golden Gate Park to the Marina where Mom had lived in a small rent-controlled apartment ever since she had sold our old house in the Mission. Coralee parked the car and we climbed the four flights of stairs to Mom's roof-top apartment. "It's too inconvenient and too far to carry groceries," I had told Mom when she had first found the place. "The exercise is good for me," she had proclaimed, "and just look at this view." And, indeed, as we opened the door, the picture window offered a panorama of the sun-spangled waves of San Francisco Bay, the rainbow spinnakers of the darting sailboats and the white wings of the soaring gulls.

"If she left instructions anywhere," I said, "they'd be in the honey box."

The honey box was a permanent fixture of Mom's household, a miniature cedar hope chest that she had been given on her high school graduation. It was where she kept her important papers and any stray money the household had. When all else failed, there was always a little something left in the honey box. It resided on the dining room sideboard.

The flat was dusty after a week's disuse but the decor was vintage Mom. Every surface was covered with Chinoiserie, a reflection of her love affair with the Far East. Ever since reading Pearl S. Buck, Mom had longed to go to China. The closest she had come was Grant Street's Old Shanghai Restaurant, but she had created her own miniature world in this one-bed apartment. There were photos of the Great Wall, translucent porcelain rice bowls, ivory chopsticks, rosewood carvings of dragons, framed brocaded textiles, brass incense burners still smelling of sandalwood. The coffee table held a stack of her favorite reading material, glossy travel brochures of trips to China. One was open to a cruise of the Yangtze River. "I'd better get my act together," Mom had told me just last Christmas, pointing to an article in *National Geographic.* "They're building a dam and the old cities are going to be flooded and lost forever."

"Why didn't we get her a ticket?" I cried. "Why didn't we go with her?"

"We were waiting for the perfect time," Coralee said with an ironic smile, "when we had the money, when we had the vacation days, when we thought we deserved it." She held out her little finger. "Let's make a vow, Sarie. We will not postpone pleasure."

I hooked my little finger around hers and nodded solemnly. It would be a more difficult vow for me than for Coralee. When we broke apart, I asked, "Ready to open the honey box?"

Coralee walked to the sideboard, gently picked up the box and carried it to the dining room table. The box was unlocked as usual. I lifted the lid. On the top was a large violet envelope. Purple, in any shade, was Mom's favorite color.

To my darling daughters, it said, in Mom's generous looping script. I gazed at the inscription, remembering all the birthday and holiday cards, the chatty, trivia-studded letters I had received every week when I was away at college. The valentines—Mom still sent them to us every year. To Harry and Wendy, too. It was last Valentine's Day when three of my patients hadn't received a single card that I had formed The Group. I thought of them now and wondered how they were doing on their sabbatical. Holidays were hard on the psyche.

Coralee picked up the envelope and sniffed it: Mom's lilac scent. "Remember how she used to put a drop of that perfume on every letter? 'Fragrance, my darlings, the quickest route to memory.'" Coralee handed me the envelope. "You open it."

I lay the envelope on the table, the oak refectory table where we had taken all our ceremonial meals. And with Mom, many nights were ceremonial. We celebrated all the Jewish holidays, for that was her upbringing, all the Christian holidays, for the two departed dads, and various other Midsummer Night's Eves, Groundhog Days, April Fool's Days, whatever would inspire costume and revelry and spice-laden foods. Coralee reached for my hand and for a moment we bent our heads in prayer. I was surprised to find the words that came "...and if I die before I wake, I pray the Lord my soul to take."

"Every night," Coralee said, "when she put us to bed. And God bless Mommy and Daddy and every sentient being." She smiled. "How many kids got a little dose of Buddhism at bedtime?"

"Ah, the Far East." I broke the gold leaf dragon seal on the violet envelope and pulled out the two heavy sheets. The paper was handmade with tiny violet petals pressed into the fibers. I read the first page aloud.

"'To my own dearest bear and bumblebee,

"'By the time you open this, I will have left San Francisco, left California, left the United States, the planet Earth, the galaxy. But you will never leave my heart and I will never leave yours. For love is stronger than death.

"'So, smile, my darlings. This return is not a sad time. I move from temporal life to eternal life. At least that's what the Buddhists say and who am I to argue? I would like my body to be cremated and the ashes spread on Mount Tamalpais on the Dipsea Trail, the part where you come out of the forest and catch your first glimpse of the Pacific. You know, that expansive aha of blue.'"

"That's where we walked with Mom last Mother's Day," Coralee said softly.

"And you brought that great lunch," I said. "Every course had some exotic fungi in it."

"'Shroom heaven." Coralee sighed. "I'm glad we did that."

"Me, too. Celebrate first, Mom always said, then find the occasion." I returned to the letter.

"'The apartment, the furniture, the tchotches are to be divied up. Keep what you want and give the rest to the charity. Maybe the Salvation Army. I've always loved *Guys and Dolls*.

"'Now, here's the surprise, darlings. Look down in the bottom of the envelope and you will find a key.

It will open a safe deposit box in Wells Fargo Bank
on Grant Street. In the box you will find stock certificates in Great Wall Software. On the current market they are worth one million dollars. Bet you never
knew your old mom was so clever. Well, I wasn't,
but Lionel Chu was. Remember Lionel?'"

"Lionel Chu," Coralee recalled. "He was that student
from State that Mom let live in the basement of the old
house."

"Rent free," I added. "And he was always blowing the
fuses." I returned to the letter.

"'Remember how he was fiddling around with those
keyboards and screens long before anyone had ever
heard of the Internet? Well, thanks to Lionel, you two
have a nest egg. A very generous nest egg. I have
only two conditions. One, that you share it equally.
Two, that it takes you someplace you've never been.
My lawyer John Duffy will provide the details. And
here, my darlings, is the mood music for the trip.'"

I unfolded the second sheet. It was a yellowed photo-
copy from *Reader's Digest* dated twenty years ago.
"Your turn, sweetie," I said and handed it to Coralee.
She read it out loud, slowly and carefully.

"'If I had my life to live over, I'd make more mis-
takes this time. I'd be sillier. I'd take more chances.
I would climb more mountains and swim more

rivers. I would eat more ice cream and less beans. I would have more actual troubles and fewer imaginary ones. You see, I'm one of those people who lived sensibly and sanely day after day after day.'"

"Mom took risks," I protested.

"But she wished she'd taken more." Coralee continued reading.

"'Oh, I've had my moments, but if I had to do it over again, I'd have more of them. In fact, I'd have nothing else. Just moments, one after another, instead of living so many years ahead. If I had my life to live over, I would start barefoot earlier in the Spring and stay that way later in the Fall. I would go to more dances. I would ride more merry-go-rounds. I would smell more roses.'

"That's beautiful." Coralee wiped her eyes.

"Mom always had a weakness for kitsch."

"You are a goddamn snob."

"Consider the source," I protested. *"Reader's Digest!"*

"What does it matter? It's true," Coralee sobbed. "And she never got to China."

Despite myself, I felt my own tears well. "She never saw the Great Wall."

"The only man-made object you can see from the moon." Coralee blew her nose hard. "Maybe that's where we should take her ashes?"

"Get real, Corrie." I inadvertently started to giggle. "Mom wanted to walk on the Wall, not litter it." We were both laughing now; it was as if I were channeling Mom's voice. Our loved ones never leave, I thought, they just talk to us from farther away.

"A million dollars," Coralee said, her eyes wide with amazement, "I can't believe it."

"That's a lot of money," I agreed. "I had no idea Mom had that kind of savings."

"And she lived so simply." Coralee stood up and began pacing the small dining room. "She could have gotten a bigger apartment. Gone on that trip."

I sat fixed in my chair watching Coralee go round and round the table. "Mom loved seeing her investments appreciate."

"Jesus saves—" Coralee smiled "—but Moses invests."

It was Mom's favorite axiom; she had had it printed on her business card in three languages. When she was warned that it was politically incorrect, she responded with her one sentence of perfect Mandarin, which translated into, "Screw 'em if they can't take a joke."

"Corrie, stop it, you're making me dizzy."

"How can you just sit there?" she said. "Don't you see our whole lives are going to change?" She hugged herself in excitement. "What are you going to do with your half?"

"Invest it," I said. "And you?"

"Spend it," she said. "Nothing but moments. Mom said. Remember."

"But this is her legacy to us. It's special. And she said it needed to take us someplace we've never been."

"Tibet. Sulawesi. Uzbekistan," Coralee offered.

"I think she meant it more as an inner journey. Something that could really change us."

"Sara, dear, you are free to do whatever you like with your half." She picked up the envelope, held it to her heart. "Thank you, Mom, for this opportunity. We will each do the right thing." She turned to me for agreement.

But my eye was caught by a drama outside the window. A gull flew by with a crust of bread in its beak. Another gull attacked it and tried to snatch the bread. They battled with loud cries and flapping wings, each desperately trying to stay aloft and win the prize. I watched, mesmerized, when in the heat of the struggle the bread fell into the Bay and was lost to both.

CHAPTER 4

I put a short notice in the *San Francisco Chronicle* announcing Mom's death and that the family would be holding a memorial service at The Hall of Flowers the following Sunday at ten in the morning. When we pulled into the parking lot at nine-thirty, all the spaces were filled. There must be another service, I thought, but when I entered the designated room, I saw that they were all there for Mom. There were nearly two hundred people. A few Coralee and I recognized, neighborhood people, shopkeepers, Esme with her three spanking-clean children, Mom's doctor and dentist. But there were a dozen men and women in hiking boots, Mom's Sierra Club Trailblazers, and her Great Book Club and her Gardening Group and a pack of Right Way Realtors. The large cluster of black-clad Chinese elders chatting away in Mandarin were her tai chi group. Harry and Wendy were waiting for us up front. Harry was wearing the dancing tooth tie that Mom had bought him for Chanukah and Wendy had red roses for each us. We pinned the flowers next to the black mourning ribbons the rabbi gave us, which he had slit with a razor blade to commemorate our loss.

A folk-singing trio sang a medley of protest songs that Mom loved, including every verse of "We Shall Not Be Moved." Coralee and I grew up on Peter Seeger and Woody Guthrie albums; we could sing harmony with the Weavers and Peter, Paul and Mary. A crimson-robed chorus from the John Coltrane Memorial Church sang some rousing gospel, including Mom's favorite, "In the Upper Room." A rabbi intoned the Kaddish, the Hebrew prayer for the dead. The Chinese chanted Buddha's name and burned incense. Then it was over. Mom had requested that there be no eulogies, no speeches, only music and song.

It was time for the buffet. Coralee's face was stricken. "I didn't prepare enough food." There is no greater fear in the Jewish heart than the threat of an inadequate supply of food. A true hostess sets a table that looks as full after the guests leave as before they arrived. "Who knew Mom had so many friends?" she sighed.

"Apparently, there's a lot we didn't know about Mom," I said. We grow and change, I thought, why don't we realize other people do, too? Then, "Don't worry, Corrie, it'll work out. Think loaves and fishes. There's always enough food."

And of course there was. Not just with Coralee's carefully prepared bite-size morsels of stuffed mushrooms and bacon-wrapped shrimp but with the added hampers of dim sum and platters of pita and hummus and sides of corned beef that the other mourners had brought. The party spilled out on the lawn where Mom's acupuncturist set out a barrel of rice wine and her hairdresser two kegs of homemade beer.

Coralee and I made the rounds of our guests, thanking them for coming, sharing in loving anecdotes and fond memories of Mom. Hours later, the party was still going on, the rising voices a happy Tower of Babel, when Coralee and I made our exit. I kissed Harry and Wendy as they harmonized on "Kumbaya" and climbed into Coralee's car.

Once we were out of the city and across the Golden Gate Bridge, the traffic lightened and Coralee was able to drive at her normal breakneck speed. Even though the little sports car handled the twisting road to the Dipsea Trail well, I still had to hold on tight to Mom's urn on the hairpin turns.

Coralee parked at the trailhead and we changed our clothes in the car. After shedding our decorous black dresses and pumps for jeans, sweatshirts and tennis shoes we began the steep ascent. Coralee slowed her pace so I could keep up with her, and we walked in a silence that was for me both reflective and breath saving. The thick fog that had blanketed us as we began our ascent lifted as we climbed until when we reached the summit, and the sun shone in long rays like those in a Tintoretto or a Turner, turning the clouds pink and gold. An earthly depiction of Heaven. "Nobody makes anything up," Mom had once said, showing us a classic Chinese landscape drawing and then a photograph of the actual jagged limestone mountains of Guelin. "See, it's all already here. All we have to do is pay attention."

So Coralee and I paid attention. We walked through the wet grass to the very edge of the cliff and sat down, hips touching, legs dangling into space. "Are you ready?" I asked. She nodded. I lifted the top of the urn, reached in and as I took a handful, I gasped.

"What's wrong?" she cried.

I opened my palm revealing the bits of white shards. "There are bones."

"Bones and fingernails," she said, "they don't burn."

"How did you know that?"

"I spent a year in Bali, remember? There's a cremation every day." She reached forward and scooped up a handful of Mom's ashes. She closed her eyes for a moment, then placed a dab of ash on her forehead and then on mine. "Who will be our teacher now?" she asked softly. "Who will tell us that we already know everything we need?" Coralee gestured to me to release my handful of ashes. I leaned forward but my arm was frozen.

"Goodbye, dear one. Happy landings." She flung open her hand and the white-grey ashes flew into the sun. I watched them until they disappeared and then was finally able to open my own hand.

When the urn was empty, we sat like bookends supporting each other's back. We sat there for a long time, weary as if from heavy labor. Coralee broke the silence. "Do you remember the Raisinettes," she asked, "the ones we used to buy at the movies every Saturday?"

"Twenty-five cents a box. Now you buy them loose and shovel them in a designer paper bag for four dollars a scoop."

"Mom used to buy us each a box," Coralee said. "I

would eat mine before the credits had rolled and you, Miss Flawless, rationed yours so they'd last till the very end of the double feature."

"I don't remember that," I said.

"You used to eat them one at a time. God forbid if two were stuck together; you'd separate them. You'd hold each one between your fingers, rotate it and lick off all the chocolate before you'd pop it into your mouth. And then you'd chew it slow and hard like it was sirloin. You used to drive me crazy."

"I was a slow eater."

"You'd rattle that box and make me beg."

"Well, you shouldn't have been so greedy. I was trying to teach you impulse control. And it's been borne out. Did you read about the marshmallow test?"

She started plucking at the grass. "No, and I hope this isn't going to be a lecture."

"Just a fascinating finding. This researcher took a group of four-year-olds and put a marshmallow in front of each of them and told them he had to go out to do an errand. If the kid could wait and not eat the marshmallow while the researcher was out, he'd give the kid two when he came back."

"I would have scarfed it down before the door closed," Coralee said.

"Two-thirds of the kids did just that. The others, though, covered their eyes, sang songs, even tried to nap. Anything to exercise some impulse control."

"To get two marshmallows and please the boss. Big deal."

"The big deal is that twenty years later, following up

on these kids, the one-third who practiced impulse control graduated from college with honors, had good jobs, good relationships and—"

"The others became serial killers?" she said.

"No, they just pay eighteen percent on their credit cards."

"Sara—" her voice rose angrily "—I do not regret my life for one goddamn minute and I would not change it for anyone else's...including yours."

I was surprised by the intensity of her response. I thought we were just bantering. Granted that our choices in life had been very different. I was the stable one, long-term everything, and Coralee the free spirit: many ports, many jobs, many men. Different choices but not necessarily right or wrong. Still I had been thinking about the inheritance and felt that I ought to reintroduce the concept of investment before we saw the lawyer. Coralee and I needed to come to some agreement. That was why I hadn't told Harry or anyone else about the money yet.

However, this was not going at all the way I planned. This was supposed to be a gentle inquiry. "Corrie, I think you've had a great life," I said quickly. "You've been all over the world. How many women have crewed on a Greek yacht, hiked the Inca Trail, kayaked in the Trobriands—"

"And have nothing to show for it," she countered.

"Continuity isn't everything."

"Don't you patronize me," she said.

I could see the color rise on Coralee's neck. Storm warning. When Coralee's temper flared, words were useless. I held out my hands, but she refused. "I'm really sorry," I said. "Please." Relenting, she offered her hands and I clasped them in mine. "Breathe," I said. We took four deep breaths in silence, one for each of the cardinal directions. Our decades-old ritual of truce. We stood for a moment, palms touching, fingers interlocked before we slowly drew apart.

"I guess I'm still upset," she said. "Mom was so alive. I can't believe she's gone."

"She isn't, Corrie. She'll be with us forever. And then there's the stock."

"Is that what this was all about...the marshmallow manifesto? Coralee, the spendthrift, blowing her half mil before the ink dries."

"It's about using our money wisely. And maybe even together."

"What do you mean together?" she asked.

"Well, invest in something...a business maybe."

"But you're already in a business," Coralee said, "the helping business."

"I could do something on the side. Something new," I said. "I told you the story of Grace's suicide attempt and how The Group reacted. The world is getting tougher. The stress. The pace. Maybe 'the talking cure' just doesn't do it anymore. Hell, maybe I need a break, too."

Indeed it had been twenty years since I had gotten my Marriage and Family Counseling Certificate right after my M.A. It was the same year Harry finished orthodontist training and we got married. Three years later Wendy was born and now our only child was filling out college entrance applications. Soon the nest would be empty, if you could call it a nest. It was more like a motel room.

All three of us were on separate schedules, and frankly, Harry and I weren't billing and cooing very much anymore. Not that we weren't close. Not that we didn't still love each other, but I was getting pretty good at pretending to be asleep before he turned off the eleven o'clock news. Apparently we weren't alone. One of my clients had given me a list of the top ten excuses wives use to refuse sex. My favorites were, "Sorry, dear, I'm tired of faking it." And, "Not tonight, hon, I've run out of triple A batteries."

I had shown the list to Mom at one of our last lunches. She had smiled but said it was too bad that so many people weren't having good relationships. Then she had changed the topic to Coralee and her venture into the catering business with Bruce. Mom had floated Coralee a sizable loan for kitchen equipment. "Someday I wish you'd go into business with her," Mom had sighed. "With your head and her heart, you'd be great."

"Don't I have a heart, Mom?"

"Yes, of course you do, darling," she said patting my hand. "I'm just talking about good partnerships."

Okay, Mom, I thought. I picked up her empty urn, tucked it under my arm, and pulled Coralee to her feet. "So what do you think?" I asked Coralee. "If we did go into business together, what would it be?"

"I don't want to go into business, Sarie. Not with you or anyone. I want to be free. I want to take that money and play."

"Well, then let's play," I persisted, "right now. How about 'What If?' Indulge me. Okay?" It was a game I had invented when we were children to wile away the time

waiting for Mom to come home. What if you could fly?
What if you were a dog? What if you could eat rocks?

"If you insist," Coralee said. We walked slowly down
the trail, the sun warm on our backs, the sky a cloudless
blue, the sweet scent of jasmine perfuming the air.

"The Halprin Sisters Book Store," I suggested.

"The Halprin Sisters Lace and Leather Boutique," she
said.

"The Halprin Sisters Interior Design Studio."

"The Halprin Sisters Mighty Mud Baths." She picked
a long spray of purple jasmine and set it behind my ear.

We continued our walk as I spun out other possibili-
ties: The Halprin Sisters Detective Agency, The Halprin
Sisters Software Emporium, The Halprin Sisters Tooth
Whitening Salon.

Coralee stopped to point out a grove of wild daffodils.
"Hey, Sarie, enough with what might make money. How
about what would be the most fun? Something that
doesn't feel like working at all. Something that feels like
the opposite of working? That feels like the best thing in
the world?"

"Chocolate," I said.

"Better," she said.

"Okay, chocolate and red wine," I offered.

"And a massage," she said closing her eyes. "I'm coming back as a Kobe cow."

"What's that?" I asked.

"Japanese cattle bred to be the most tender and most
expensive beef in the world. They're fed beer and massaged all day."

"Sounds great. I wouldn't mind a bit of pampering

right now," I said looking at the steep hill ahead. "I'd like to snap my fingers and be carried in one of those boxes with poles. What's that called?"

"A palaquin," Coralee said. "Like the Empress of China. And those four buffed guys wouldn't be hard to take, either."

"Those old gals with power called their own shots, all right," I added. "Take Catherine the Great. She would commandeer a new soldier for her bedroom every night."

"Wow, every night!"

"She was a woman of great appetite and she rewarded those men big time and especially her purveyor."

"She probably liked them young and hung." Coralee laughed.

"Who doesn't?" I agreed. As we rounded the last curve, I was relieved to see the parking lot emerge. Hiking up was hard on the lungs but hiking down was hard on the legs. Life was a trade-off. "Do you want to hear one of Harry's jokes? I'll make it short. He tells it better."

"Men do tell jokes better," Coralee mused. "It must be genetic."

"It's just practice. Men can tell the same story over and over. Our threshold for boredom is lower."

"And so is our attention span. What's the joke?" Coralee opened the car door.

"Mom loved this one," I said as I carefully placed Mom's empty urn at my feet.

"There's this sheikh who has a loyal retainer named Hiram and each night the sheikh calls Hiram to his chamber and commands Hiram to bring him a different woman from the sheikh's harem. 'Hiram, bring me Fatima.' And

Hiram runs out to the harem and brings in Fatima. The next night he says, 'Hiram, bring me Scheherazade,' and Hiram runs out and gets him Scheherazade. The following night he says, 'Hiram, bring me Jasmine and then Lachme and Tanya,' and so on for years. Until one night poor Hiram drops dead. The sheikh, of course, is flourishing. The moral of the story...it's not the sex that kills you, it's the running after it."

Coralee laughed her full rippling laugh. "Not much point in running after it in San Francisco. Between the gays and the twenty-somethings, it's slim pickings."

"That's what I hear," I said. "In fact, that was the challenge Mary Ann threw out during that last session. 'You can't get us meds and you can't get us a man.'"

"She's got a point." Coralee eased the car into the busy traffic on Highway 101. "You can sublimate all you want but, hey, as Mae West put it, a hard man is good to find."

"So what about Bruce?" I asked. "How good was he?"

"Bruce? He read cookbooks in bed."

"Well, Harry reads medical journals and falls asleep with the light on."

"At least he's there for you, Sara, every night. I envy you that."

"Yes, he's there *every* night...and that's wonderful... but..." I pondered the enormity of the word *every*...every night, every week, every year, and thought of the flip side. "How about this for a wedding vow? Do you, Sara, promise to have sex with Harry, and no one else but Harry, for the rest of your life until one of you drops dead?"

"Well, when you put it that way that explains why I'm

still single." She looked at me quizzically. "Do you wish you were?"

"Of course not," I said quickly. "I love Harry, it's just that right now my life's a little stale." If I couldn't tell the truth to my own sister, to whom could I? There was something about death and birth that cast a blinding light on platitudes. Something demanded the truth. Something demanded you own up to the complexity of your own experience, face the confusions and live the questions.

"You know what Mom told me once," Coralee said. "That the only things worth keeping are memories, and when she was a little old lady in an oxygen tent, she was going to do a replay of all the men she had ever made love to."

"Mom said that? How many were there?"

"She didn't keep track," Coralee said.

"I bet she did. Sooner or later every woman adds them up."

"Do one-night stands count?" Coralee asked. "If they do, I could set a new world's record."

"Braggart," I chided.

"It was in my salad days. You had to fend them off with a stick. And I didn't...maybe I should have."

"Don't be hard on yourself. 'When we look back on our lives, it will not matter who we loved but that we loved.'"

"Who said that?"

"Graham Greene. Hard left, sweetie. I just spotted a Dairy Queen. I feel the need to sublimate."

Coralee spun a screeching wheelie and we bounced to a stop in the parking lot. She turned to me, her eyes like lasers. "I've got it. There's only one thing I would consider doing if we had to start a business. Not that we're going to, of course."

"What?"

"Just think of that Kobe cow." She grinned wickedly and moaned a deep-throated and lascivious, "Mooo."

CHAPTER 5

The next day Coralee and I met in the offices of Mom's lawyer, John Duffy. It was an old-guard law firm, and Duffy was a senior partner with a mahogany-paneled corner office that boasted an expansive city view. He was in his fifties, trim and impeccably turned out in a gray pinstriped suit, maroon silk tie and custom-made Italian shoes. He rose to greet us, taking first my hand and then Coralee's. "Your mother was a wonderful woman," he said. His face looked genuinely stricken.

"So you knew Mom?" Coralee asked.

"Oh, yes," he said, "very well. So strong and honest. Such a good heart. She will be missed." His voice choked and he removed his gold wire glasses to dab at his eyes.

I glanced at Coralee in puzzlement. I wasn't aware that Mom knew any lawyers, but from the depth of John Duffy's response they may have known each other in ways I hadn't fathomed.

Then in true legal fashion, he was all business. "Did you bring the stock certificates?"

I opened my purse and handed him the thick envelope. He counted them as quickly as a bank teller. I noticed that each bore a logo of The Great Wall as seen from the moon. "They are worth one million point four on today's NASDAQ."

"That's great," Coralee said. "Can you cash them in for us?"

"Certainly."

"When would that be?" she asked.

"As soon as I see your business plan," he answered.

"What business plan?" her voice rose in surprise.

"Didn't Yvonne tell you?" John Duffy reached into his desk and removed a large manila folder. He scanned our blank expressions. "I guess she left it up to me. She was a bit concerned about your response." He opened the folder, removed a document and passed it across the desk. It was a very short statement in Mom's hand and duly notarized.

"Well, ladies," John Duffy said as we read it, "as you can see, your mother's will expressly stipulates that her legacy be divided equally between you and be used solely for a joint venture."

"How did you know that, Sara?" Coralee accused.

"I didn't. It's just that Mom and I sometimes talked about—"

"What a flake I was. How irresponsible. Of all the nerve!"

"Be that as it may, you still need to open a business together." John Duffy deftly slid the envelope back into the manila folder. "And you need to present a business plan before any of the money can be released."

"And what if we don't?" Coralee stood in agitation. "What if we don't present a stupid plan? If we don't open a goddamn business?"

"Then the money stays in trust for twenty-five years," he said calmly.

"You mean I can't spend that money until I'm sixty." Coralee gasped. "And Sara will be..."

"Never mind," I interjected quickly.

"Sorry," he continued, "I'll be the custodian of the stock until I see proof that you have established a business."

"What about the dividends?" I asked.

"Unfortunately, they accrue to the estate," he said. "I therefore urge you to embark on your venture with all due haste." He rose and saw us out. As we passed through the hall, I noticed a framed poster of The Great Wall inscribed at the bottom in Mom's distinctive hand, "Some things are made to last."

"I can't believe it," Coralee cried, as we exited the building. "Leaving us the money but tying our hands. It's not like Mom."

"I think she wanted the best for us, Corrie. We just need some time to think it over. Come on, let's do lunch. On me."

"All right," she said grudgingly. "Ovations. And this time I'm ordering the foie gras. To hell with delayed gratification."

On the drive over, we speculated about Mom and the lawyer. Not her type. She was an ex-Socialist, a red diaper baby. He was a fat cat in a three-piece suit. Yet he teared up when he said her name. And hadn't she stopped telling lawyer jokes several years ago?

As we entered the restaurant, we were greeted at the

door by Simon, our Oxford waiter. "Mrs. Russack. Ms. Halprin. How nice to see you again. Let me show you to your table." I was impressed that he remembered our names. He must have gotten mine from last time's reservation and Coralee's from her credit card. Clearly, he had made an effort. He handed us each a menu and then in obligatory California style, ran through the specials. The ingredients fell upon my ear soft as flower petals...radiccio, shitaki, confit, ganache.

Coralee smiled into his sea-green eyes and cut him off sweetly. "White asparagus. Baked foie gras with truffles. And a bottle of Crystal."

"Make that a double," I said.

"Including the champagne?" he asked.

"Maybe," I said, "but bring it one bottle at a time."

When Simon brought the frosty bottle, gently popped the cork and poured the effervescent wine, we lifted our glasses in a toast.

"To Mom," Coralee said.

"And to us," I added. "We're going to work this out."

Coralee drank down her first glass moodily. "Still, a gift is a gift. It shouldn't have strings."

"I think it was out of love, not control, Corrie." And I told her about Mom's admonition about using heart and head. "She wanted this money to help us grow, to bring both of us into balance."

"But I could buy the sweetest boat, Sarie. I could sail it around the world. It's what I've always wanted to do. And then I could sell it when I got back."

"If you didn't wreck it. Mom wanted you to invest in something permanent, something that would appreciate."

Simon brought the first dish.

"Appreciate this," Coralee said, holding out a buttery spear of asparagus.

It tasted like the first day of spring. I could always count on Coralee to bring me back to the moment. Otherwise I might have shoveled away this ambrosia as if were a Big Mac. "Fabulous," I agreed. We finished the dish and returned to the conversation in a more benign mood.

"What would you have done with your half if you were totally free?" she asked.

"Oh, maybe a week in Hawaii with Harry and Wendy, if we could convince her to leave her friends. And then... I'd renovate the house, add another bathroom, landscape a bit—that would raise its value. And I'd invest the rest."

"In the safest thing you could find."

"Right. Risk-phobic, that's me." On the roulette wheel of life, I play only red or black. And even then I'm nervous. "But it's a moot point, sweetie. We have no choice. We're in this together. The money must be spent on a mutual venture. So what's it going to be? Come on, you had this great idea, what was it?"

"It was just a joke," she said as Simon brought our foie gras. We paused reverentially as we took our first intense creamy bite. The senses, I thought...we don't give them enough air time.

I took a sip of champagne and let the flavors mingle in my mouth. "Heaven."

"Almost as good as sex."

"Better," I said.

"No," she said, "there's nothing better than great sex."

I feigned surprise. "Was it on the menu?"

"Not yet," she said. "But it will be. Prix fixe and à la carte."

"What are you talking about?"

"That's our business," she said grinning broadly.

"What's our business?"

"Sex," she said.

"Sex?" I repeated.

"Selling sex," she said loudly, louder than she intended. Simon, standing by to refill our champagne glasses, guffawed. Conversation stopped. Heads turned. Two dowagers sitting at an adjacent table choked on their coffee. Simon rushed to their aid, ready to do a Heimlich, but all they needed was a gentle back patting. He gave us an amused look and left for the kitchen. This time we both watched his exit. He filled those tight black pants to perfection.

Coralee waited until order had been restored in the restaurant then she leaned closer. "Okay, big sister. We are going to play a jackpot round of 'What If?' Are you ready?"

I nodded in agreement and for the rest of the meal, through profiteroles, mango meringues and double espressos, we played "What If?"

"It would be a bordello for women. A private club where their every sensual and sexual desire would be catered to. By gorgeous. Expert. Professional. Studs."

"Would women want to pay for sex?" I exclaimed.

"Why not? Men have paid throughout history."

"Men are different. They have different needs. Different standards."

"Well, our bordello would reflect that," she said. "It would cater to a woman's desires. Do things a woman's way. We could buy a beautiful, elegant house and set it up like a spa."

"It's immoral," I protested.

"So is sexual deprivation."

"It's illegal," I said.

"Only if we're caught," she countered. "And, anyway, we're just playing here," she chided. "Remember, 'What If?'"

Okay, I thought, willing suspension of disbelief. It was the prerequisite of any fiction, of any dream. Never mind ethical caveats, reality constraints.... What If? thinking could make it so. I was the former lit major, the lover of Shelley and Keats. Why not play along? Use the real joy-stick: the human imagination. Enter the magic kingdom. Never mind virtual reality on a computer screen. My own erotic musings could top any software programming.

"So," Coralee teased, her voice a honeyed purr, "if you could have anyone, anyway, anywhere...who would it be?"

"Guilt free?" I asked.

"Oh, Sarie, guilt free is like fat free...bland and synthetic. Got to have a little guilt. Got to have a little risk. Got to pay a small price or there's no adrenaline rush."

This was coming from the girl who had gone bungee jumping on Mount McKinley and hang gliding in the Grand Canyon. Coralee knew from adrenaline.

I toyed with the lemon strip in my espresso. "Oh, someone tall, dark and debonair. Like Cary Grant or Hugh Grant." I spooned up the last of the mango sauce. "But I'd say there is only one thing in a man that's indispensable."

"His gazilkes?" One of our pet names for the male anatomy.

I shook my head no. "His hands."

"His hands?" She seemed puzzled. "Smooth, hairy, big, what?"

"Slow," I said. "Just ...real...slow." And I began to sing the Pointer Sisters' song . When was it popular, ten years ago? Longer? I remember the first time I heard it; I was driving a car pool of little girls when it came on the radio and I had pulled over and turned up the volume, despite their squeals of protest. I hadn't wanted to miss a word.

" 'You want a lover with a slow hand
You want a lover with an easy touch.' "

Coralee chimed in, her soprano true and sweet. " 'Believe me baby, I understand, when it comes to love, you want a slow hand.' "

Just then, Simon was at my elbow. He laid the check gently on the table. "Is this slow enough?" He grinned and sauntered off.

I flushed. "He heard everything."

Coralee shrugged, her face beaming with delight. "That's what we'll call it. Oh, God, Sarie, you are a genius. Once a song...now a bordello. The Halprin Sisters Present...Slow Hands."

"Just a minute, sweetie, we are just playing here. No way am I getting involved in a project like that. I am a respectable married woman. I'm a licensed therapist."

"Well, I'm not waiting twenty-five years to change my

life." She crossed her arms high on her chest, stuck out her chin, Coralee defiant.

"Look, I'm not ruling it out," I said quickly. "It's an interesting idea. Very creative. Maybe even socially useful. It's just that it's pretty radical. I need to think about it."

"That's your way of saying it'll never happen."

"Not at all," I said, stalling for time. And then inspiration hit. "Let's start with the house. That's a great idea. Real estate is a terrific investment. How about if we open a bed-and-breakfast?"

"A B-and-B?" she said wrinkling her nose in distaste. "Boring!"

"We can decide its function later. Mom would be delighted. I'll call the Right Way office tomorrow and we'll start looking. And you can put the business plan together for John Duffy. What do you say?"

"What about Slow Hands?"

"First things first," I said. "Duffy's not going to fund a bordello."

She gave me a long hard stare but unfolded her hands. At the very least, I had bought some time.

CHAPTER 6

True to her word, Coralee promptly whipped together a business plan for our projected bed-and-breakfast and, as expected, John Duffy agreed to advance the money as soon as we put an offer on a house. The next step was finding the house. That was expedited by Mom's real estate connections. Right Way Realty matched us up with a smart cookie of a broker, and within a week we had seen all the best houses in the Bay area. We went out every afternoon with Sophie, in her ruby-red Right Way blazer, her three-inch fuck-me heels, and her shiny red Chrysler convertible. I cleared my schedule and Coralee was officially at liberty.

I set the criteria for the house. It must be in a good neighborhood. I had not been Yvonne Halprin's daughter for nothing. She had schlepped me around for years as she checked out properties. "Only three things matter in real estate, baby bear—location, location, and location.

Everything else you can change. What you want to buy is the cheapest home on the best block."

In addition to Mom's cardinal rule, I added the caveats that the house be in good shape, have lots of street parking and that it be zoned for multiple occupancy. When, a week into the search, Sophie showed us the Maybeck mansion in the Berkeley Hills, not far from the UC campus, it felt perfect. Granted it needed more work than I had wanted, but the place had such charm. The brown-shingled Victorian sprawled on a double lot framed by massive old oak trees. In the back garden, cherry blossoms were in bloom and a magnolia was just about to bud. Upstairs there was a rabbit warren of small bedrooms, at least six of them, and several full and half baths. And downstairs—and this is what sold me on the house—there was a wide sunny living room with enormous windows that offered a view of the Bay that Mom would have loved. It was furnished with a grand piano, a bevy of fine, though worn, Oriental rugs, several over-size sofas and a number of vintage arts and crafts pieces which Sophie assured us came with the house. The wainscoting, the leaded glass, the window seats were all out of some childhood I never had. Harry's tastes run to Swedish modern and since I had always wanted easy maintenance, our home looked a lot like our offices. But this was the sort of place in which to throw fringed shawls on the couch and harem pillows on the floor, to light a fire and drink absinthe.

I had a sudden picture of myself, in floor-length red velvet, a cigarette flaming in an ebony holder, a beautiful young man or two at my feet as I held court. I shook my head to dispel the image. It did not fit with my plans for the house.

"It's perfect," I said. "You can live on the first floor, Corrie, and we can rent out the rest. There's always a shortage of housing in Berkeley. Let's do the numbers, Sophie."

But Sophie, being a Right Way veteran, had already done them, not only for the down payment and mortgage but also renovation costs for the dry rot and the water damage she had already spotted. It was manageable. We could meet the down payment easily, take out a loan for the renovation and pay it off on the interest from the mutual funds we would buy with the rest of Mom's legacy. Mom would have approved. "Make money on other peoples' money."

I remembered the first economics lesson Mom had given me. I was in second grade and had set up my first business venture, a lemonade stand. Mom asked me why I was doing it. "To make money, of course," I'd replied.

"Fine, darling, and what else?"

I thought hard. "To give people something good to drink."

"And when would they want that the most?" she probed.

"When they're really, really thirsty."

"Very good, baby bear. And when would that be?"

"When they've worked hard."

So I moved my stand to the bus stop and raised my prices from a nickel to a dime.

Coralee was equally pleased with the house. It was the expansiveness that really appealed to her. She was currently living in a cramped studio apartment over a North Beach pizza joint. "The only thing I'll miss is the smell of pesto in my hair," she said. "And it will be wonderful to live rent free. I can go back to my photography."

Coralee had a closet full of photographs she had taken on her around-the-world journeys. She had a particular gift for catching emotional moments between people, especially portraits of lovers. Nothing overt as kissing or sex but the look. She knew how to capture the look of love, the sideward glance, the softening of the eyes, the secret smile. Her photos made me remember the way my heart leaped when I was in high school and saw that special boy. Once Harry was that special boy.

It's not supposed to last; that's what evolutionary biologists tell us. Four years and the sexual itch begins again. Few species mate for life. Even the supposedly monogamous birds have been discovered to play around as evidenced by the range of DNA in the eggs the female is hatching. I could just picture those scientists, invading nests, snooping around with their microscopes. Now even the birds were having paternity tests. Next step would be prenuptial worm declarations.

I was quite the student of animal couplings. As if that could tell me something about my own sex life. Cranes courted for months in elaborate choreographed displays, then closed the deal with a mere cloacal kiss, just one momentary brush of the genital openings and conception would happen. Quite an anticlimax after all that dirty dancing. And then there was the white rhino, whose daffodil shaped member expanded when inserted and he was trapped in there for hours. My favorite were the bonobos apes, our closest genetic relatives, who had sex whenever and wherever and with whomever they pleased. They especially liked to have an orgy when they came upon a new cache of food. Defused competitive feelings, the primatologists reasoned.

I left Coralee and rushed to the grocery store. That evening I cooked stir-fry chicken, making sure I kept the asparagus out of Harry's portion and the portobello mushrooms out of Wendy's. The things we do for love. We exchanged the day's news. Wendy had gotten an A on her English essay and a C in trig. "Spot quizzes," she said, "I hate them."

"Me, too," Harry commiserated. "I'm glad I'm through with surprises."

"How about good ones?" I grinned. Now that Coralee and I had agreed about what to do with the money, it was time to break the news to my family, first about the inheritance, then about the house. Harry listened carefully as I filled in the details, whistling with admiration at the half million, nodding with approval at my financial plan. I have always handled the money in our family. Harry vacillates between a savings account and his barber's wild hunches. Wendy wanted to know if she could buy a car.

"When you start college," I assured her.

"But I was going to get it then, anyway. How about now? I've got my license."

"It would just distract you. You need to study."

"It distracts me more having to ask for rides. And you never know how they're going to drive."

She had a point. My daughter always had a point. I

think she'd make a good lawyer. "Okay, how about if you wait a year and we get you an SUV."

"Wow. Cool. Rad. Evil. Thanks, Mom." She leaped up from the table to call her five best friends.

"Blackmailed yet again," Harry teased.

"Hardly, it's safer. And the resale is good."

Harry and I took our coffee into the living room. "So you think running a bed-and-breakfast with Coralee is going to work out?" he asked.

"Sure, why not?"

"Well, you should pardon the expression but you two are like apples and oranges. I know you love each other but you have never been known to see eye to eye."

"We don't have a choice, Harry." I told him about the stipulation in the will. "We have to be in business to-gether." I didn't tell him about Coralee's notion. Although I must admit ever since she had brought it up I'd been looking at men differently. The brawny butcher who boned my chicken breasts; the crew-cut bagger who ran my credit card; the Latino policeman with the pearly smile monitoring the broken traffic light. What if?

"Good old Yvonne, speaking up from the grave," he continued. "It's my way or the highway."

Sometimes Harry's reliance on clichés drove me mad. Other times it was a comforting shortcut. Today as I un-folded the *Chronicle* and handed him the news and sports sections as I took the business and entertainment, it felt good. I always knew where I stood with Harry as opposed to my dealings with my dear sister.

A case in point was our meeting to sign the papers the following week. As I pulled up to the Victorian on Grove

Street, I spotted Sophie's convertible, its top down despite the damp fog, and Coralee's yellow sports car. The two were sitting in the living room sipping the lattes Sophie had provided and eating the muffins Coralee had baked. That was the first thing that tipped me off. Coralee only bakes when she can't sleep, and these moist apricot-pecan morsels were a testament to her late-night ruminations. Was she having second thoughts? I wondered. Was this scheme too sensible for her? Too fiscally sound?

I was reassured when Sophie presented the contracts and, after I did, Coralee signed them with a flourish of her vintage Waterman pen. Coralee, who would dress in ubiquitous jeans and T-shirts, chose a few material objects with great care. These needed to unite form, function and beauty, and these she was careful with.

Sophie left with the signed papers promising to send us her list of contractors, carpenters, tile men, decorators, etc., and leaving us alone to walk through the house again. I whipped out my tape measure. "For window treatment," I said. I loved trade lingo. Not just curtains...but treatment. Not just makeup, but product. Not just movies...but the industry. It made everything seem important and inside. Suddenly I felt a surge of excitement. Maybe this was just what I needed. New possibilities. New vistas. I reached out and gave my adventurous baby sister a big hug.

CHAPTER 7

It took two weeks for the house to close and another month for the renovations to be finished. Fortunately both the dry rot and water damage were minor. Sophie had advised us well. The furniture from Mom's apartment fit nicely into the house, and her chinoiserie added a touch of the exotic. We found a great sale on beds and dressers, and we were ready for the next big step: opening our B and B.

I met Coralee at the house on a clear crisp morning. She had moved into the large first floor bedroom and painted the walls a soft violet. As the sunlight streamed through the newly washed windows, it was like living inside a giant blooming orchid. I settled myself on her purple velvet settee. "So where do you think we should advertise?" I asked.

"Not to worry," she said. "I've already done it." She handed me a copy of the alternative newspaper, the *San Francisco Guardian,* opened to the personals.

I have scanned them upon occasion. A therapist needs

to keep up with what's happening in the culture, and sometimes, I admit it, I like being titillated. I glanced down the page. The usual...phone sex ads, nasty girls, horny high school seniors, passion princess. Massage services. Males seeking females. Males seeking males. Males seeking couples. And then the others, becoming ever more explicit and finely specialized—ads for S and M, B and D, for bi-sexuals, transvestites and transsexuals.

"Listen to this," I said, "'Fetish and fantasy...Mistress Jezebel...foot adoration and exotic storytelling. I'll let you worship me.'" I turned the page. "'Hottest dominatrix in town. Smothering discipline. Full-body worship. Forced Greek and French.' What do you suppose 'forced Greek and French' is?"

"Having moussaka and eclairs stuffed down your throat?" Coralee seized the paper and pointed to the section headed Help Wanted Adult. And there amid the requests for actors in adult films and nude models, I saw the ad.

The headline was two inches high and read, Men Wanted. The text was simple: "Wanted four men who love to please women. Must be attractive, intelligent, sensitive and have slow hands. Send photo and letter to P.O. Box 333, the *Guardian*."

"That's us," I gasped. So while I was only fantasizing Coralee had put the rubber to the road. "You took an ad?"

"Not bad, huh? Got it all into two lines."

"I thought we'd agreed to open a bed-and-breakfast."

"Too much work, and way too bourgeois. And anyway, I wanted to give your scheme a chance."

"My scheme!" I cried.

"You're the one who wanted the house."

"As an investment," I protested.

"It's just a lark, Sarie. Aren't you the least bit curious who'll turn up? I put in your big condition...must have slooow hands."

I smiled despite myself. "Honestly, Corrie, what kind of guy would answer an ad like that?"

"We're going to find out." She led me out to her car and popped the trunk. It was overflowing with letters and parcels. "Audiotapes, videotapes, testimonials from satisfied customers. One guy even baked some brownies. They're not half-bad." She grinned, handing me one. "Now grab this box and let's start reading."

I took a bite of the brownie. My favorite, marshmallow and walnut. "I'm not going along with this. I'm just curious about the letters."

"Yeah, yeah," she said and handed me the largest box.

The letters were a hoot. We hadn't had such a good time since Mom made her first commission and took us to Disneyland. I had ridden each attraction in turn while Coralee went straight for the biggest roller coaster and had never gotten off. It was little surprise, then, that we had different favorites among the men's applications. I favored subtlety, and Coralee, by her own admission, went for the rush. By mid-afternoon, however, we had filibustered, negotiated and compromised the entries into three piles: for sures, maybes and no ways. For sure meant definitely worth an interview. When we added up that pile, the number was impressive. Twenty-five! We had found twenty-five men who could do the job or at least who were eager to try.

There were all sorts of guys, many of whom sounded great, perfect for Laura or Mary Ann or even for Coralee. I held up a photo. This one looked just like James Garner in the early *Rockford Files*—rumpled, lived-in face, wide, amused mouth, broad shoulders. And then his letter: "Hi, ladies. Saw your ad. I hope I'm your man. My wife died two years ago, and I would sure like to apply what that wonderful woman taught me about pleasuring the female sex. I've learned it's not all about what's in the sack. It's about listening, and talking and touching. But I hope you won't hold it against me that I can last all night."

We were like kids with an F.A.O. Schwartz Christmas catalogue. And despite my stated indifference, I found myself grabbing for the photos first. Some of them were as sedate and impersonal as passport shots, but others were full-length eight-by-ten glossies of men...men... men. Men with moustaches, men with beards. Men with buzz cuts, men with ponytails, men with shaven heads. Men with baseball caps, men with cowboy hats, men with earrings. Men in tuxedos, men in tight jeans, men in wet suits, business suits and birthday suits. Couldn't help noticing those. A few were in profile sporting major arousal.

The accompanying letters varied just as much, from a scrawl on a legal pad to elegant calligraphy on embossed stationery to faxes and e-mail and an enterprising candy gram. That one caught our attention. It was a five-pound box of Schaffenberger hand-dipped dark truffles, top of the line. The card read "To the Halprin Sisters, toward a sweet launch."

"Now who blew our cover?" Coralee asked. "Our ad just had a post office box."

"It's signed, 'Love, Simon,'" I said.

"Simon who?" Coralee turned the card over. "'It's always a pleasure to serve.'" She held the card out, pointed to the discreet gold lettering, Ovations and a phone number.

"That maître d'," I exclaimed.

"He overheard us, remember? Do you suppose he's applying?" she asked.

"What else?" I said. "That's not the number of Ovations."

"You're right." She stood up and walked toward the phone.

"Hey, wait a minute," I said. "There are three more boxes to go."

"Save them for later, he's a keeper. I've been thinking about that guy ever since our dinner."

Although I hadn't realized it until that moment, so had I. Something about Simon's height, those piercing green eyes and open vowels added up to memorable. The other men's applications had been interesting, but his was truly compelling. It would be exciting to get to know him better. Suddenly the idea of Slow Hands seemed a bit more viable. Not for me, of course. I had no intention of sampling the merchandise, but the enterprise could be a financial security blanket for Coralee and a psychological aid for my clients. And the thought of seeing Simon again was extremely appealing. I felt a twinge of guilt as the bed-and-breakfast transformed, at least hypothetically, into a bed-and-whatever establishment. What would I tell Harry? Fortunately my husband wasn't innately suspicious or overly observant. And if things came to pass, I trusted that I would think of something.

Coralee put the call on conference, and I listened in eagerly. Simon picked up on the first ring. "Bartlett here."

"Halprin Sisters here," Coralee said.

"Does that mean I've made the first heat?"

"It means you get an interview," Coralee said.

"When?" he asked.

"How soon can you make it?"

"How about now? See you in twenty minutes."

"I haven't given you the address yet," she said.

"It's 69 Grove," he provided. "I saw it in the real estate sales. Cheers." He rung off.

"He may be our man," Coralee said, "attractive, intelligent and...highly motivated."

He proved to be all three when he arrived at the house half an hour later carrying a huge bouquet of mauve peonies, a box of sushi tied in an antique obi and a bottle of top-grade sake. "I thought we might require a bit of nourishment," he said as he unfurled the obi, an extravagant length of sea-green silk embroidered with golden cranes. He laid it on the dining room table and placed the food upon it. He arranged the peonies artfully in a celadon jar. Simon had clearly mastered the art of gift giving; his choices were elegant, extravagant and sensual.

As Coralee and I ate the delicate slivers of fish, Simon wandered about the house, pacing off floor lengths, tapping the walls for weight-bearing beams, looking for all the world like a prospective owner.

It was getting me nervous. "Come and have some sake," I said, pouring a small cup of the clear but potent wine.

He seated himself opposite us, tipped his head back and downed the cup in one swallow. "Samurai style. I could breathe fire."

"So could I," I said. "You eavesdropped on a private conversation."

"And a lucky day it was for me that I did. I don't usually peruse the sex personals. And I would have missed this golden opportunity."

"For what?" Coralee prodded.

"To follow my bliss," he said, smiling.

I recognized the reference. It was from Joseph Campbell, the eminent scholar of mythology. I had heard him speak, and it had changed my life. He had championed the need for ritual, for beauty and for the sacred in the everyday. And for a time, I had honored that search in my own life. "Do you know Campbell's work?" I asked.

"I wore out two sets of the Moyers tapes," Simon said. "He changed my life."

There were only two reactions to Campbell's work: either you didn't get it or it changed your life. I had switched my career from teaching to psychotherapy.

"'There is no part that doesn't see you. You must change your life,'" I said, quoting Campbell's favorite Rilke poem.

"Aesthetic arrest," Simon added. "Once you see into the heart of things, you can't float on the surface anymore."

I noticed Coralee's blank stare. "What Campbell meant," I said, "was that we each have to find our own path. A path with a heart. A path that uses all of you."

"I see," Coralee said, but from her uninflected tone, I could tell she was feeling left out. She hated literary quotes. "It's just secondhand experience masquerading for the real thing," she had chided me more than once. She rose and busied herself by reheating the sake.

I could almost read her thoughts. *Why can't you talk like a normal person? Why do you always have to quote someone else?* But everyone used some frame of reference, I thought. If you didn't read poetry, you'd use a sitcom or a Spielberg movie or the Yankees score. Or the sale at Macy's. Some fragment of fact wrapped in an opinion offered in hopes of eliciting a comment, of engendering a connection.

Coralee returned to the table with the warm sake and refilled our cups. I smiled my thanks and sipped the fragrant wine.

So Simon liked poetry, I thought. How wonderful. I had just finished the collected Rumi, and there was a new biography on Emily Dickinson that said she was really in love with her sister-in-law. I realized that I was looking forward to many conversations with him. But what about Coralee? Would she go for an intellectual?

I looked up from my reverie to find Coralee lifting the last sliver of tuna in her chopsticks. She dangled it inches above Simon's waiting mouth, teasing until he seized her hand and snared the morsel. Their eyes locked as he slowly chewed.

Coralee turned to me, her eyes bright. "Do you know that Simon made the sushi himself?"

"Really?" I said. "Where did you learn to do that?"

"Picked it up in Kyoto," he said, "but Provençal cuisine is my specialty."

"Listen to this." Coralee reached for his résumé. "Diplomate de Cuisine, Cordon Bleu; Maître d' Design Interior, Musee d' Louvre; Master of Fine Arts, Cortauld Gallery, London; Oxford D. Phil."

I gave him an appraising look; he must be close to forty. "Guess you couldn't make up your mind?" I teased.

He smiled. "It took me a while to find a field that combined everything I was interested in."

"And what was that?" I asked.

"The thirteenth century. The invention of love."

"It took them that long?" Coralee said. "Weren't people getting it on in the caves?"

"The invention of *romantic* love," Simon amended, "and all its accoutrements. It was an accident of history. The time of the Crusades. Most of the men were off fighting the infidels, but a few lucky ones got to stay home and guard the women."

"Eleanor of Aquitaine founded the courts of love," I said to Coralee. "They had these mock trials on how a lover should behave."

"And the subject of my dissertation recorded it all. A young monk called Andreas Capellanus. He wrote the first book on courtly love."

Coralee polished off the remainder of the sake. "And just what is so great about courtly love? In one sentence and no big words."

"It's all about the adoration of women," Simon said.

"And foreplay that doesn't stop," I blurted. "Blame the sake," I demurred.

Simon gave me a playful smile. "Then we'll order it by the crate."

CHAPTER 8

We hired Simon on the spot. It was a very informal agreement, for although Coralee and I had put together a business plan for John Duffy, that was for a projected bed-and-breakfast. We had no concept of a budget for Slow Hands as yet. But Simon was happy enough to move into the largest upstairs bedroom for the time being, rent free. And since he would continue to work the lunch shift at Ovations, a small stipend would suffice until the enterprise was on its feet, so to speak.

The next step would be hiring our staff. We weren't even sure what to call them. Escorts? Gigolos? Studs? Ladies' men? I thought it interesting that none of the nomenclature was derogatory, unlike the terms for their female counterparts: like sluts, whores, tramps. But we still couldn't find a name that felt right for our *boys,* and what would be the equivalent of *madam* for Simon? *Mister* didn't quite do it.

Simon moved in the following week, and we met at the

house for a strategy session. He produced a bottle of chilled white burgundy from a voluminous picnic basket and a package of king-size pistachio nuts, which he insisted upon shelling for us, one by one. It would get us in the proper mood, he said, accustomed to being pampered.

"Perhaps we're having trouble knowing what to call our men because we haven't figured out their job description," I said.

"Exactly," Simon concurred. "Now open wide," he commanded. As I did, he popped a plump pistachio into my waiting mouth. As I happily crunched, I wondered if this constituted incipient infidelity or outright hedonism.

"It's simple." Coralee took a deep swig of her chilled wine. "The men are there to pleasure our women."

"In what ways?" Simon asked.

"'How do I love thee...let me count the ways?'" I quoted Browning.

"'Every way but loose,'" Coralee quoted Clint.

"So I take it," Simon said, "we will be providing both sensual and sexual services."

"Sensual," I amended. "I don't think women would want to pay for sexual services."

"Why not?" Coralee asked. "We pay for everything else."

"It's too commercial. Too impersonal," I said.

"Sarie, we pay to get our hair cut, our nails polished, our legs waxed, our bodies massaged."

"But that's maintenance. It's not affection."

"What about therapy?" she persisted. "You lie someone down on the couch and act interested in their piddling life for a hundred bucks a throw."

"We don't pretend to love them."

"But you pay attention," Simon said. "Isn't that what it's all about?"

"Well, yes," I agreed, "the heart of the service is paying attention. That feels okay. That feels like something you could pay for. It's the buying of the sex that doesn't feel right."

"Why not?" Simon asked.

"Call me old-fashioned, but I still remember men wanting it and women withholding. I remember men having to court women, to seduce them. If a woman pays for it, it's like shooting fish in a barrel. Where's the sport? And it's important for a woman to feel wanted, desired. If you're whipping out your gold card, where's the conquest?"

Coralee and Simon were silent for a long moment weighing my point.

"Well, then," Simon suggested, "we have to work in an element of suspense. Does he or doesn't he?"

"You mean he can reject her?" Coralee said.

"Not exactly reject, but not make it a sure thing, either. Like life. But with better odds."

"What do you mean?" she said.

"Some connection will happen. That's guaranteed," he explained. "But just what and just when will be negotiable."

"And the amount of money you pay does not control what happens," I added.

"Unlike the male counterpart...so much for straight sex, so much for oral sex, so much for half and half," he said.

"Exactly," I agreed, my ideas coming in a rush. "It'll be a club. A private club with monthly dues. A social club. You can use the facilities one day a week, have a massage, a conversation, a dance and..."

"A romance," Simon said.

"Yes," I said, "a little male attention."

"Agreed," Simon said smiling. "So which of our applicants would be the most attentive?"

"We're going to turn that task over to you, Simon," I said. "At least for the first round. It'll be a test of your skills."

"I would be delighted to vet them for you. Are there types that you would like to see represented?" he asked.

Coralee thumbed through the keepers. "I think variety is the key. We want women to be able to play the field, to have the man they've always lusted for but never had."

"Yes," I agreed, "the real thing but heightened."

"Tell me more." Simon got out a legal pad and pen and proceeded to take notes.

I lifted one of his gift peonies from the vase. They were still vibrant. "Let me see. How about passion?" And to emphasize it, I plucked a peony petal, and let it fall to the floor.

"Muscles," Coralee said, and joining the fun, plucked a petal.

The traits and the petals came raining down...a great smile, a sense of humor, tight buns, soulful eyes, rough edges, imagination, tenderness, cultivation, naturalness, mystery, communication, all man, strongly developed feminine side.

"Ladies, ladies." Simon flung down his pen. "Tender

and rough, all man and sensitive, communicative and mysterious. Don't you think some of these traits are contradictory?"

"That's the idea," I said drawing the curtains open upon the dazzling blue bay and the glistening white skyline beyond. "Take San Francisco. The city began with the Gold Rush, and the bordellos of the Barbary Coast, and now it's the home of dot.com millionaires, and more Chinese restaurants than Shanghai. That's what makes it interesting."

"Something for everyone," Coralee added, "one-stop shopping."

"Call us when you've got the cast," I said tossing the naked peony stem into the trash.

Coralee scooped the discarded petals from the floor. She walked to Mom's urn, which we had placed on the mantle, and piled the fragrant petals before it. "Om shalom, Mom. We're on our way."

I expected that Simon would be efficient, but I was amazed at how quickly he combed through the applicants. It was just a few days later that he called me at the office, and asked if we could meet that evening. Coralee was free, he said, and how about Zuni's for dinner? His treat.

It was a Tuesday, and that was usually a family dinner night. In fact, in was my turn to cook. But I didn't want to postpone the meeting; I was dying of curiosity. So I called Harry, told him something had come up at the last minute with the bed-and-breakfast Coralee and I were setting up, that we had hired a manger, and needed to go over the requirements for the guests. If you're going to lie, I had read somewhere, keep the details as close to the truth as you can. Not that this was the first time in our twenty-year marriage that I had colored the truth, but somehow it felt different. Like the proverbial slippery slope. And yet, I reasoned, no hard and fast decision had yet been made about the purpose and function of the house. So, technically, it could be true.

"Don't worry about it, sweetheart," he said, "I'll bring home a pizza. See you tonight."

I had a good thing in Harry. And I knew it. But I wouldn't have missed that dinner at Zuni's for the world. Zing went the strings of my guilt. I've felt it ever since I was a little girl, anytime I wanted to do something just for me. The dry throat, the queasy stomach, but this time it wasn't going to stop me.

Luckily, I always kept another outfit at the office for those days when there was no time to go home. So, off came the utilitarian pants suit, and on came the short black skirt, the pumps. I checked myself out in the mirror. Not bad for an old lady. Was it the change of clothes or was it expectation that brought the sparkle into my eyes, the spring in my step? Adventure. Risk. The unknown. And an attractive man. There was no substitute for it.

Parking near Zuni's was the usual urban nightmare. The restaurant was trendy, a great place to people watch, its clientele ranging from evening-dressed opera goers to body-pierced Gen X slackers, and it served fresh and eclectic food. Its whole leaf Caesar salad, pasta con sugo, and chicken with Tuscan bread stuffing were famous; its

wine list global and ever-changing. And the décor was
perfect for San Francisco: brick walls, bright contemporary paintings, crisp white linen and the centerpiece a
large log-stoked open oven. The staff was friendly and
attractive, neither servile nor snooty, just there to help.
In all, the place was casual, comfortable and provided
great service. A good model for Slow Hands.

After I circled the block four times I surrendered the
keys to my newly fixed car to the valet, reminding myself that I could afford these little luxuries now. All I had
to do was think I deserved them. It was a relief not to
thread my way through the gauntlet of the homeless
camped out in nearby doorways with their sleeping bags
and overflowing shopping carts. I vacillated between giving them a handout and ignoring their pleas. I knew my
money would just go to alcohol and drugs, but refusing
to recognize them hardened my heart. After all I was
going to Zuni's to spend eight dollars on a glass of wine.

I opened the carved wooden door, pushed aside the
heavy velvet curtains that shielded the restaurant from the
Market Street breezes and smiled at the hostess. "I'm a
bit early," I said, scanning the bar. She was a twenty-
something Eurasian, beautiful despite her bleached-blond
crew cut.

She checked her book. "Your party is here, Mrs. Russack. I'll show you to your table."

She led me into the central room of the restaurant,
swaying on high golden wedgies. Simon and Coralee
were sitting next to each other, cozily ensconced at a
corner table. I saw them before they saw me. They were
leaning towards each other; Coralee was talking, Simon

listening. Heads tilted, hands folded, their body postures identical; they were intent upon each other. The space between them seemed charged. Not for nothing was I a student of body language. There was a powerful communication going on here, and I felt a painful twinge of jealousy, of being left out. Oh, come on, I chided myself, it's just that they're both young and single and living in the same house. I was probably reading far too much into this.

Nevertheless, I was glad to see them move apart as I came near, and Simon graciously stood and offered me his seat. I took it and sat next to Coralee while he took the chair opposite us. I was definitely happier with that arrangement. They had ordered a bottle of Sancerre and Simon poured me a glass. "My favorite white," I said.

"Mine, too," he agreed, "crisp and fragrant." He gave me a warm smile. "And it goes beautifully with our first course."

Right on cue, the waiter arrived with the dozen oysters Simon had ordered. The presentation was elegant, very Parisian, the oysters nestled in a bed of crushed ice and dark-green seaweed. The waiter rolled off their exotic names...pacific angels, rocky point, blue point triton toed. Coralee reached for a large shell and happily slurped away. Simon did the same. I reached for some crisp Acme bread instead. "Sara, which one can I get you?" Simon asked.

"I'm going to pass," I said. "I've never developed a taste for oysters."

"I cannot let you go another day without them." Simon selected a tiny bivalve and held it out to me.

I didn't want it; it smelled fishy even from there, but I didn't want to be a bad sport, either. "All right," I relented, "how do I eat it?"

He squeezed a bit of lemon juice onto the oyster, then held the shell up to my lips. "Now when I tilt, just swallow. You can chew once if you like, but swallowing it whole is better. Okay, here goes."

I felt the salty fluid in my mouth and then the squirmy little creature. I gulped and sputtered. It was like swimming in a tropical sea. Or more precisely like...a blowjob. I turned bright red. So that's why oysters are considered an aphrodisiac. Simon ordered another dozen, and while we waited for them to arrive, he took out a large manila envelope.

"It was hard to make the choices," he said. "I was matching our personality profile, and, of course, looking for the best of class. But I was also looking for an ensemble. And I think I have it, an array that will please the most discerning of women. All awaiting your approval, of course."

I lifted my glass. "Here's to man, in his infinite variety."

"I've selected four rather broad categories, I'm afraid," Simon said, "but customer research bears it out."

"What customer research?" Coralee asked, scarfing down the last enormous oyster.

Simon ticked off his research sources on his fingers, "Women's sexual fantasies as recorded by Shere Hite and Nancy Friday. The most requested routines of the premiere troupe of male strippers, the Chippendales. Favorite male nudes from *Playgirl*. And the bestselling titles of soft and hard core porn at Deep Sensations, the leading women's sex shop."

"You have really done your homework," Coralee said. "I'm impressed."

"It was a pleasure," he demurred. "Once an academic, always an academic." He opened the envelope and fanned the stack of résumés and pictures upon the table.

Just then the waiter arrived with our pasta and Caesar salads. We tried to keep our fingers from leaving greasy spots on the photos as we passed them back and forth.

Simon introduced each one in turn. "This is Tony. His motorcycle is named Killer."

He passed the picture of the black leather clad youth straddling his hog, a vintage Harley-Davidson. The muscles on his thighs and calves bulged large and the cutoff vest showed his biceps to great advantage; one arm bore a tattoo of a dragon, the other a snarling tiger. "Looks like a hard-driving man." Coralee smiled, reaching for the next photo.

"This is Billy Bob and his horse, Old Paint," Simon provided. A mellow, sandy-haired, lanky guy, ten-gallon hat in one hand, the other resting on the mane of his equally mellow horse.

"A nom de plume?" I asked.

"Not at all," he said. "You'd be surprised how closely life imitates art."

I lifted the next picture. A tall slender man with a graying goatee, he was dressed head to heels in black, the smoke of a smoldering Gitane curling around his chiseled face. I read the name at the bottom and shook my head in disbelief. "Jean-Pierre. Well, at least you left out the beret."

"Prototypes...not stereotypes is what we're after. And now, the piece de resistance, Sensei Jonathan Goodman."

"A classic Jew-Bu," I said.

"What?" Simon asked.

"The Zen monasteries are filled with them," I said. "Nice Jewish boys who got bar mitzvahed, studied law and then became Buddhists."

"Jewish Buddhists," Coralee explained. "You know, as in *That's Funny, You Don't Look Buddhist*. It was a bestseller."

"I guess I don't know California as well as I thought," Simon said. "I figured he was exotic."

"He is," I said, appraising the dark robes, the close-cropped hair, the rosary wrapped wrist and mostly, the clear peaceful expression. "It's a great lineup. The bad boy. The cowboy. The Frenchman. And the Zennie. You did good, kid."

Coralee sopped up the last of the salad dressing with a heel of bread. "When do we get to meet them?"

The waiter came round with the dessert menu, but we waved it away. The pictures were treat enough. Simon insisted on paying the check and, I couldn't help noticing, added a twenty percent tip. He caught my eye. "Once a waiter, always a waiter." As he pulled out my chair and then Coralee's, he said, "I'll set up the interviews. What night is good for you, Sara?"

"Thursday," I suggested.

"Next Thursday it is," he said, waving his long fingers through the air like an alchemist transforming lead into gold. "Eight o'clock at Slow Hands."

CHAPTER 9

Thursday night was Harry's night to play bridge with the boys, and Wendy had rehearsals all that week. Her high school was doing *South Pacific,* and she was playing Nellie Forbush. She was going to be "washing that man right out of her hair" just as Coralee and I were washing them in. So the plan was for the family to eat dinner together and then go our separate ways. And as long as I was home by eleven, no explanations were necessary, which was just as well, because I was beginning to feel somewhat uneasy about this new enterprise. It had been a lark up until this point, Coralee and I playing our old game of "What If?", but now there were four real-live men arriving on our doorstep hoping to be hired. And there was Simon, who very quickly had become part of our management team. Also, the month's hiatus of my women's therapy group was coming to an end, and my focus needed to go back to where it belonged.

And yet I could barely contain my excitement. I didn't

try cooking that night, but instead stocked up on the best dim sum Clement Street had to offer, topping it off with a whole Peking duck. We sat around the dining room table, enjoying the ritual of peeling apart the soft white buns, brushing on the spicy plum sauce, layering on the shredded scallions and the tender slivers of roasted duck. If the Bay Area offered such varied culinary pleasures, why not extend it to romantic dalliances? All appetites were piqued by novelty.

We chatted amiably about our day. Harry had bought some new Sonar cleaning equipment. "For the carpets, Dad?" Wendy asked.

"For the molars, darling." He helped himself to the last shreds of duck. "How's rehearsal going?" he asked. "My parents took me to see *South Pacific* when I was six," he recalled, "and I'll never forget it." He burst into a full-voiced, though tone deaf, version of "Some Enchanted Evening."

I checked Wendy's expression. She could have shown embarrassment or disdain, but instead she smiled indulgently. She loved Harry, and so did I. I vowed not to do anything that would hurt either one of them. And yet I couldn't wait to stack the dishes and drive to Berkeley.

I had some trouble deciding what to wear. What image should I project? Not a business suit. Not jeans and sweater. Not party wear. Help, Miss Manners, what is appropriate garb when interviewing studs? I opted for Bohemian black. Black for all occasions. Black cashmere sweater. Black stretch pants. Black high-heeled boots. And for pizzazz, heavy silver hoop earrings and a silver belt. And makeup. The works.

It doesn't matter how good a marriage is, no woman gets excited dressing up for her husband. "How do you like it?" you'd ask. "Nice," he'd say while trying to figure out if it were a haircut or a new dress he was supposed to notice. Despite the countless manuals on how to spice up your marriage, a long-term relationship is not about flirtation or seduction. The joys of marriage are comfort, routine and security. We should not confuse the two and spend needless money, not to mention discomfort, on thong underwear and stiletto heels. And yet to forgo forever the pleasure of being the object of male attention seemed just plain sad. The world was filled with a myriad assortment of attractive men, and yet I had taken a vow to desire only Harry for the rest of my life. Somehow it felt unnatural.

As I drove the city streets finding my own less-traveled route to the Bay Bridge, I fantasized about the rainbow colors of the men we could bring to Slow Hands. Latino and Asian and African-American. After all, the Bay Area was an ethnic wonderland. Clearly we had only tapped the surface. We would be doing our part in creating a global community. Who needed Esperanto; we had the language of love.

When I pulled up at Grove Street, the house was ablaze with a warm golden light. As I opened the door, I noticed Coralee and Simon had lit dozens of votive candles, laid luxurious throws of satin and brocade on the sofas, draped the windows and mirrors in silk swags. Lavish bouquets of freesia and jasmine scented the air, and Kenny G's molten sax was playing on the stereo. There were bottles of chilled white wine, savory breads and cheeses, and an overflowing cornucopia of lush tropical fruits. Although the furnishings were essentially the same, the added touches had imbued the room with abundance, largesse and sensuality. Everything cried "smell me," "taste me," "touch me." Life is for the senses. A bit of hedonism, please. We are not put on this earth for toil alone. The body is not just a vehicle to transport us from place to place. It is a pleasure palace. Use it or lose it. I remember reading that the clitoris has eight thousand nerve endings, more than the fingers, the lips, the tongue—and the penis—put together.

Coralee and Simon were standing by the large picture window enjoying the moonlit panorama of the bay, the bridge and the brilliant night sky. They turned to greet me, and I was struck by their beauty and how well matched they looked. Coralee was draped in a turquoise-and-gold sari that mirrored her blond curls and cerulean blue eyes. Simon was dressed in a white dinner jacket with a cummerbund and tie of the same sari material.

I felt a twinge of jealousy, but that dissipated as Coralee draped a splendid shawl of the very same cloth over my shoulders. She kissed me on both cheeks. "Good that you wore black," she said. "It goes."

I stroked the heavy satin of the shawl. "When did you whip this up?"

"Last night. I was too excited to sleep," she said. "Oh, Sarie, we are going to change women's lives forever."

Coralee's eyes were shining. I hadn't seen that look since she was a little girl. So perhaps with all her adventures, with all her travel, something had been missing in her life just as something apparently had been missing in mine.

"Are you ladies ready for the candidates?" Simon asked.

I speared a satiny piece of ripe papaya. "Absolutely."

"They've been here all day, practicing their routines."

"What routines?" I asked.

"A little song and dance," Simon explained. "A good companion needs a sense of rhythm, drama and most important, playfulness. As an extra added attraction I've asked them each to decorate a bedroom in a style that best reflects their personality."

I bit into the papaya; it was so filled with juice that I had to cup my mouth to keep it from spilling over my lips.

Simon lifted a miniature Tibetan gong and sounded it. The tone rang through the house, liquid and clear. We waited with anticipatory silence until he intoned, "Let the revels begin." He pushed a button on the CD player, and the strains of "Under the Boardwalk" came romping through. "The swimsuit competition," he announced.

Down the curving staircase came the four men. Tony the Bad Boy was in a black leather G-string. Billy Bob wore rodeo printed boxers. Jean-Pierre sported a bikini decorated like the tricolor. And Jonathan wore a vintage one-piece black wool bathing suit. Each man had considerable assets. Tony had the brooding mien of a young Marlon Brando plus the muscles; Billy Bob a lean bronzed Arizona ease; Jean-Pierre was hairy as a bear and looked just as cuddly, and Jonathan—well, Jonathan was really hung. Never mind what women say about size not mattering. That's about as true as men not caring about perky breasts.

Each man crossed the room toward us—Tony lumbered, Billy Bob loped, Jean-Pierre sauntered and Jonathan glided. They turned in unison and stood waiting for the next command. "Evening dress, please," Simon instructed. With smiles in our direction, the quartet headed up the stairs to reappear a few minutes later in black tie. All men look good in a tuxedo, but our guys looked sensational. Each costume reflected the personality of its owner. Tony's jacket was black velvet with white satin lapels. Billy Bob's had a leather fringe and chaps. Jean-Pierre wore Armani. And Jonathan's jacket was cut like a kimono. He slipped it off to reveal the exquisite hand-painted landscape that graced the lining. Jonathan had gotten this detail just right. No ostentatious outer display. The beauty was for intimate eyes only.

"Magnificent," I said, "bravo."

"Way cool." Coralee clapped her hands in delight.

"You ain't seen nothing yet," Simon said. "It's the talent show. Hit it boys."

And one by one, the *boys* showed us their tricks. Tony launched into a medley of Rat Pack songs doing a credible version of Sinatra's "My Way," Dean Martin's "Volare," and finally Sammy Davis Junior's "Mr. Bojangles," complete with tap routine. "Amazing," I said as Tony blew us a kiss and turned the stage over to Jonathan.

Jonathan bowed low to his audience. Then to the accompaniment of a koto recording, he delivered an astonishing karate routine of whirling turns, floor dives and head-high kicks that ended with the breaking of four thick boards with his forehead. With the crack of the wood still resounding, he announced the next act. An unlikely duet of Jean-Pierre and Billy Bob singing the theme from *Gigi,* "Thank heaven for little girls," with Jean-Pierre as Maurice Chevalier and Billy Bob as Leslie Caron.

The talent show ended in a roar of laughter. I was pleased to see that the men didn't take themselves too seriously. I've always thought one of the sexiest things about a man was a sense of humor. If a classic definition of sex is the most fun you can have without laughing, it's even better when you are laughing.

Like right now, the laughter was a wonderful release. After all, this was a unique situation. No rules here. No protocol. "Well," I said lightly, "what do we do now?"

"What would you like to do?" Simon's tone was provocative.

"Sample the merchandise," Coralee cried.

"We used to have something called a taster session at university, to help us choose our elective subjects," Simon offered. "Each don would give a mini version of his class, and we students would move from one to the other, and make up our minds. Would you like to do that?"

He must have been planning for this moment because as soon as I nodded, he punched up the CD of a classic oldie. And as the men repaired to their respective rooms, Coralee and I listened to the telling lyrics. "Did you say I've got a lot to learn. Well, don't think I'm trying not to learn."

The song brought back the memory of high school dances and my standing against the gym bleachers, eyeing the boys, hoping one would ask me to dance, envying the popular girls who could pick and choose. That's

what we were going to provide here at Slow Hands, I realized—a chance for every woman to pick and choose. I
recalled in one Group session Terry morosely stating,
"What's my type? I can't afford to have a type. I like anyone who likes me."

Here was an opportunity to sample four different va-
rieties. I decided to start with Jean-Pierre, then move on
to Billy Bob, then Tony, and wind up with Jonathan.
Coralee would sample them in reverse. Fifteen minutes
each; then we would compare notes. Would these be our
men? Were they the right stuff? Simon had vetted them,
true, but the final verdict was ours. I reviewed our criteria with Coralee. "Remember they need to be attractive,
intelligent, sensitive, and most important...have slow
hands."

"Maybe for you, big sister." She grinned. "But I
wouldn't mind some fast moves."

I climbed the stairs with some trepidation, not knowing what I would discover about the men, but more importantly, not knowing what I would discover about
myself. Even though the décor was just for a night, Simon
had instructed each of the men to bring the accoutrements
needed to showcase his individual personality. I had no
trouble discovering which bedroom held Jean-Pierre. On
the door there was a gleaming poster of the Hall of Mirrors from Versailles.

When I entered, I noticed the mirror motif had been
carried throughout the room, most spectacularly on the
ceiling. Jean-Pierre greeted me with a soft and lingering
kiss on my hand. He had changed into a black brocade
smoking jacket and a white silk aviator's scarf, which un-

fortunately reminded me of Snoopy in his World War One
Ace mode. Indeed, when I perched upon his red velvet
bedspread and saw myself reflected and re-reflected, instead of feeling like a prize jewel, I felt like a lamb chop
on a meat counter. His heavy floral cologne didn't help,
either. What was it covering up? But the music was perfect, Piaf's "Non, Je ne Regrette Rien," and Jean-Pierre's
accent was intriguing. He murmured something my high
school French couldn't translate. It sounded sexy, though,
with its throaty rasps and open vowels. What woman
wouldn't like being made love to in a foreign language,
all passion and no clichés?

I raked my fingers through the long fringes of Jean-
Pierre's scarf and asked the first of my prepared questions. "Why do you want the job?" Jean-Pierre gave a
Gallic shrug. "I desire the position because *tout le monde*
knows that we are the best lovers, and it is a Frenchman's
duty to hold up the reputation of his race." Just what I
don't like about Parisians, I thought. They may have the
best cuisine in the world, but they have to keep telling you
about it.

I asked my second question. "What will you provide
for the women?" Jean-Pierre drew himself up to his full
height. "I will provide the multiple orgasm." That answer
wasn't bad. But then he wrecked it by adding, "Always."
I kissed him on both cheeks and was on to Billy Bob.

The cowboy's door was covered in burlap with a horse-
shoe acting as a door knocker. I entered to the strains of
Willie Nelson's "You Were Always on My Mind" as Billy
Bob tipped his ten-gallon hat and swept me into his arms.
He smelled of clean straw and chewing tobacco as he

Tennessee-waltzed me around the room. Was that his ornamental belt buckle or was he just glad to see me? I was breathless when he led me to a saddle serving as a chair. As I perched on it, he scratched his big blond head to dredge up the answers to my questions. Sitting spread-eagled on the saddle I had to admit was a bit titillating. I thought of Wendy's discovering her love of horses at twelve like so many young girls. All that muscle and sinew ready to move anywhere you wanted it.

"Well, ma'am," Billy Bob drawled, "I'd like the job because I'm ready to quit the rodeo and live in one place. And what can I provide?" He blushed. "I got thighs like steel, and I can ride all night long."

The twang of his speech, his high healthy color, his long legs and narrow hips in those tight-fighting jeans were all appealing. He seemed as down-home as old dogs and watermelon wine.

I wondered about subtlety, though, about finesse. "What do you think women want?" I asked.

"Don't rightly know, little lady," he said, leaning down to plant a resounding kiss on my forehead, "but I imagine it ain't too different from breaking in a filly." I thanked him and left.

Next was Tony. He had hung a picture of the Pope on the outside of his door, and when I entered, the room felt like a makeshift shrine. Plastic Madonnas decorated every surface; over the bed hung a large cross flanked by a portrait of Saint Francis on one side and Saint Jude on the other. His refreshments were Budweiser and pepperoni pizza. He had stripped down to his boxer shorts. "Hope ya don't mind, I like to be comfortable." I didn't mind; he looked good. "What can I tell ya, Sara, I want the job because I need the money. I used to do construction, but my back gave out. What can I provide?" He popped open another beer. "Rides on my hog, season tickets to pro wrestling and—" he burped thoughtfully "—can I get back to ya on the rest?"

"What would you say women really want?" I ventured.

"Well, my ma used to tell me every woman likes to be grabbed, no matter what she says." He grinned, and pulled me toward him. He wrapped his arms around me like duct tape. When I could breathe again, I extricated myself, gave him a high-five, and exited. I nearly collided with Coralee on the landing. We were on our last visits, she to Jean-Pierre, I to Jonathan.

"Isn't this fun?" She beamed. "Like a great singles bar."

I leaned against the wall. "I think I'm on overload."

"Nonsense," she said, giving me a quick hug. "Shop till you drop."

Jonathan's room was the large corner bedroom down the hallway. On the outside of his door, he had hung a brushwork scroll, a scene of mountain peaks disappearing into the clouds. He must have been listening for my footsteps, for he opened the door just as I reached the threshold. The room was lit with groupings of tall white candles that cast a warm glow. Sandalwood incense burned in a teak holder; three white irises rested in a pale-green bowl; a small fountain played upon polished gray pebbles. He had placed two black silk cushions on sweet-smelling tatami mats. I sank down gratefully, relieved to be free of the rush of sensations and stimulation I had just experienced. It was like slipping into a moonlit lake on an August night.

Jonathan sat opposite me, assuming a full lotus position, each ankle resting easily on the opposite thigh. Although I couldn't come close to matching his flexibility, I decided to at least sit cross-legged. But as I attempted the stretch, my calf muscle went into spasm. A wrenching cramp shot up my leg. I grimaced and tried to stand.

Jonathan was beside me in a second. "Lie back," he said softly. "Let me take care of that." And he did, massaging slowly and strongly from my toes to ankle to calf until my muscle released. The pain stopped, but his touch blessedly didn't. His fingers kept on stroking in ever widening circles, moving to my knee, the back of my knee, my thigh...the inside of my thigh. I was melting, envisioning where that touch might move next.

When I heard Simon's Tibetan gong signaling the end of the visits, it felt as faint and faraway as a dream. Jonathan helped me to rise, taking both my hands in his. He stood that way, for a long moment, looking into my eyes. His gaze was calm; his eyes warm and kind. I felt...*seen*. Jonathan placed his palms together and bowed. I returned the bow and glided out the door. It wasn't until I was down the stairs that I realized I hadn't asked him any of the questions. And yet of the four rooms, it was the only one I wanted to return to.

Simon thanked the men and sent them home. He brewed us some green chai, reputed to help decision making, and asked for our opinions. I signaled to Coralee to go first. I was confused by my response, especially to Jonathan, and unsure how to explain it. I sipped the thick green tea and waited for Coralee to speak. She seemed as reluctant as I. Finally, she slipped a small writing pad from her pocket and consulted her notes.

"I'm sorry to have to say this, but every one of them struck out with me except one."

"Me, too," I said. It couldn't be the same one, though. Coralee and I were so different.

"They were all attractive," Coralee said, "somewhat sensitive, passingly intelligent. But in the massage test, only one had genuinely slow hands."

"What massage test?" I asked.

"I gave them each ten minutes, and let them choose whatever part of me they wanted," Coralee said.

"And?" Simon asked.

Of course, I thought, Coralee asked for what she wanted, whereas my contact with Jonathan had happened purely by accident.

"Jean-Pierre chose my hands," Coralee continued. "Billy Bob picked my neck. Tony went for my lower...and I mean...extremely lower back."

"And what about Jonathan?" I asked.

"My feet," she answered, "and he was delicate and thorough and...divinely slow. I can still feel it."

"Just your feet?" I wanted details.

She thought for a moment. "Up to the ankles."

I allowed myself a smile. Was I competing with my baby sister? Maybe a little. "He impressed me, too," I added. "Such attention, such stillness. It's like those Japanese brush paintings. The empty space is as important as the pine trees."

"Right on," Coralee said, "it's the pause that refreshes. So shall we vote?"

"That may not be necessary." Simon held out a plate of fortune cookies. We each took one and cracked it open. All three said the same thing. "First thought. Best thought," a quote from the Zen classic *Beginner's Mind.*

"Did you know we were going to choose Jonathan?" I asked.

"I admit I had a hunch," he said, "but the decision was yours."

I munched the shards of my cookie, carefully folded my fortune. I have a whole box of them at home, only the ones that augured well, of course. "It's great that we've got Jonathan, but we still need three more. So what do we do, run another ad?"

"Fortunately not," Simon said. "If you like Jonathan, there's more where he came from."

I refilled my cup, this time noting the Japanese calligraphy on the side. Simon's subliminal persuasion? "Tell me more." I settled down to listen.

"Jonathan's part of a Zen community whose residence hall has just been bought by a dot.com company. They're displaced, looking for a new home. Jonathan joined the Zendo three years ago along with a dozen other acolytes. Four men have stayed the course. They've studied Buddhist scriptures, practiced daily meditation, trained in the Zen arts of calligraphy, flower arrangement, archery and tea ceremony. They've chosen not to become ordained as priests, for that would mean taking the vows of poverty and chastity, but they do want to continue their practice full-time and together. They're lay practitioners."

"*Lay* practitioners," Coralee said with a smile, "how fitting."

"Jonathan saw our ad in the *Guardian,*" Simon continued. "Here's the letter he wrote." He read it out loud.

"Dear Slow Hands,

"I was moved by your notice in the *Guardian* and read it with great interest. You ask for men who would be able and willing to please women. You ask for attractive, intelligent, sensitive men with slow hands. I would like to present myself and my three fellow students for your consideration. We have just finished a demanding course in paying attention, in slowing down, in being present for each moment and each action in our lives. We practice right mind, right action, right thought, right speech and right livelihood. We recognize and honor the sacred and unique beauty in every living thing. Our goal is to bring peace and healing to the world by our example. We would welcome the opportunity to practice mindfulness at Slow Hands.

"Yours in Beginner's Mind,
"Jonathan Goodman."

Simon passed the letter around so we could see the exquisite stationery, handmade rice paper, the brushstoke calligraphy, each word a visual poem.

"Puts a whole new spin on nooky," Coralee sighed.

"And the timing is perfect," Simon added. "They have to leave the mother church, and we're starting a new one."

"So, now do we interview Jonathan's fellow Zennies or what?" Coralee asked.

Simon reached into his briefcase and extracted a photo. "Here are the guys at graduation."

I looked carefully at the glossy picture. There was Jonathan flanked by three other young men. They looked remarkably alike with their closely cut tonsures, their black robes, their peaceful smiles.

"I don't think it's going to be necessary to vet them," Simon said. "They're like chefs coming out of the culinary academy. They know their chops."

"But what if they're too much alike?" Coralee offered. "Don't we want variety?"

"We don't need it," I said. "Slow Hands isn't modeled on the male brothel where men come to act out their fantasies. It's a completely new concept."

"Women have fantasies, too, Sarie," Coralee protested. "What safer place to indulge them?"

"The Zennies are quite adaptable," Simon offered. "They can be in the moment and respond to whatever is needed."

"You mean like actors?" I asked.

"Better. They won't be playing a part, they'll be living it. There'll be no ego and lots of desire. Take a look at this." Simon pointed to the postscript on Jonathan's letter. " 'Even the most clear eyed monk cannot sever the red thread of passion between his legs. Zen Koan.' "

"I was reading about a brothel in Tokyo," Coralee said, "where the prostitutes dress in schoolgirl uniforms on a mock-up bullet train and strap-hang while their businessmen clients grope under their skirts." She grinned. "So how about a school mistress seduces choir boy scenario for Slow Hands?"

"Or naughty nurse and patient in traction," Simon suggested.

"Or female lifeguard gives mouth-to mouth..." Coralee began.

"Just a minute, you two," I cried. "If we're going to do this thing, we need to create something unique here. Something that has never existed before. Something that *couldn't* exist until now. A place where women's liberation has come into full flower. Where women are no longer repressed or suppressed but are allowed to be anything and everything they can be." I rose in my excitement, my voice deep and impassioned.

"Does this mean you're in, Sara? That Slow Hands isn't just a 'What If?' anymore?" Coralee gazed at me quizzically. "What changed your mind?"

What else but the Zennies, I thought. Up until now, the concept of a woman's bordello had been an imaginary lark. Billy Bob, Tony, Jean-Pierre were the makings of a grade C movie. But with the presence of the Zennies, everything changed. Authenticity, learning, healing were possible.

"Slow Hands will be a place where a woman can be paid attention to...fully," I continued. "Where for once a woman doesn't have to cater to a man. Draw him out. Amuse him. Wonder what he's thinking. For once, there will be a place where a woman can be the center of attention. And all she has to do is be herself. Be truly herself. The way she is with a child or a close woman friend."

I knew I had their rapt attention and it felt great. "Slow Hands will be an oasis where a woman can be spontaneous. Funny and raunchy. Sad and sexy. Where she can be outrageous and irrational. Brilliant and bossy. Where she can wear too much makeup or none at all. Where she can dress like a princess or a farmhand. Where she can sing off-key and dance like a klutz. Where she can be tough or tender. Where she can regale her lover with tales of her girlhood or pictures of her grandchildren."

I raised both fists into the air. "Break the mirror! Let the gray hair and the wrinkles show. Rejoice in cellulite and liver spots and varicose veins for they are the medals of a long life. Women, yes," I shouted, "ladies, no."

Coralee stared at me in silence.

"Storm the barricades," Simon said. "Quite the manifesto, Sara. How long have you been hatching that one?"

Where *had* that volcanic eruption come from? I had a sudden image of a visit to Pompeii with Harry and Wendy to celebrate her bat mitzvah. Our guide had led us to a hidden priapic statue, a battered ceramic dwarf, who cradled his enormous erection in both hands. As I leaned across the ledge to get a better look, the young Italian had lightly cupped my breasts, ostensibly to keep me from falling. My initial shock had given way to a secret rush of pleasure. I was still desirable.

In America, since turning forty, I had become invisible. The wolf whistles and the once-overs had stopped. It may have been politically correct, but it was emotionally wrong. I was a strong feminist. I had read Betty Friedan and Gloria Steinem. I had burned my bra, stopped shaving my legs and picketed for women's right to choose. And yet, I still wanted to be flirted with, courted.

"I want this place to be a refuge," I continued. "A place

where women come out feeling better about being themselves and not by designer labels or facelifts. But by being surer about themselves. Happier about themselves."

"And they get a great piece of nookie," Coralee added.

"Only if that's what they want," I said. "Sex will be optional and confidential. Slow Hands will be a spa. The advertised services will be meditation, Zen arts, and shiatsu massage."

"And..." Coralee prodded.

"And—" I downed the last of my tea "—the rest is silence."

Simon smiled. "Who better than Hamlet to comment on moral complexity?"

We parted with warm hugs. It had been a good night's work. Coralee and Simon retired to their respective bedrooms, and I headed out the door. I glanced at my watch, the witching hour. Although my trusty Honda had not turned into a pumpkin, I had a hard time believing this was really happening to me.

By the time I got home the house was dark. Wendy was fast asleep. As I tiptoed into our bedroom, I could hear the soft drone of the TV. Harry was snoring gently as a manic comedian held court to a wildly guffawing audience. As I climbed beneath the covers, he shifted towards me, nuzzled my neck. "You're late," he murmured sleepily, "I was worried about you." I pressed my belly against his rump, a warm and familiar fit.

"Sorry," I said planting a kiss on his bald spot. I knew that place when it was covered with thick brown curls. "I'll tell you all about it in the morning."

"Sure," he said, "whatever..." but the rest of the sentence was buried in his pillow.

The next morning after cooking breakfast for Wendy and driving her to school, I returned home to Harry.

"So how was your meeting last night?" he asked as he reached for his third slice of toast.

I watched him butter it thickly, add a layer of marmalade. He paused with it halfway to his mouth.

"Aren't you going to say something?" he asked.

"About the meeting?"

"About the toast," he said. He was used to my monitoring his diet at least with a disapproving look.

I shrugged. "You're a big boy, Harry. Eat what you want."

He put the toast down. "Hey, what's wrong?"

Nothing, I thought. Nothing except that this was going to be the first real lie I ever told him. Evasions don't count, do they? I did a rapid replay of Adam and Eve in the Garden. Didn't they try to evade when The Big Guy wanted to know who took a bite of that rosy red apple? *I gave you permission to partake of all the fruits in the garden but one...the tree of knowledge.* That was the original sin. And for me, in Slow Hands, that knowledge was the knowledge of other men. Perhaps in the true Biblical sense of *knowing.*

Up until that moment I hadn't given it any thought. Would Slow Hands be available to married women? Would it be available to me...in the full service sense? Harry was looking at me strangely. I must have been silent for a long time. I made up for it with a rush of words.

"We've got a full house, rented all five bedrooms. And there's an efficiency apartment in the back for Coralee with a redwood deck that overlooks the Bay. I was going to give it to her rent free, but she wants a fair partnership, so taking in all the rents, deducting mortgage and maintenance, we stand to make a before tax profit of five thousand a month." And we would, I thought, when we were running at full capacity.

"Five thousand a month," Harry exclaimed. "What are you charging a night?"

"We decided not to go with the bed-and-breakfast. Something better came up," I improvised quickly. "Long-term renters."

"Computer nerds?" Harry asked. "They've got the dough these days."

"Not exactly," I said.

"Then who?" My uncustomary reticence had piqued his interest.

"Well, actually, they're Zen students."

"Not exactly big spenders."

"They supplement their income," I said.

"With what?" He crunched the last of the toast, licked the marmalade from his fingers.

I longed to tell him the truth. Harry was my best friend. More sensible than Coralee. Probably had a better business head than Simon, whom I barely knew. And anyway, Simon and Coralee would be living in Slow Hands together. All those opportunities for tête-a-têtes *sans moi*. Didn't I need an ally? Someone I could depend on? Why not tell Harry now before things got more complicated? Harry was a good feminist; he'd probably understand.

Understand about other women maybe, but not about me. It was one thing to run a bordello; it was another to partake of its services. And I wasn't ready to relinquish that possibility. Not yet.

"They teach," I said. "They practice Zen and they teach."

"Teach what?" he asked.

"Mmm..." I almost said massage. "Meditation."

"Meditation, eh." He reflected on that for a bit. "That seems useful. We could all benefit from slowing down." He checked his watch. "But right now, I'm late for a tooth extraction." He kissed me, gave my ass a little grab and was out the door.

I watched his car pull out of the driveway. Might as well chomp that apple, I thought. It was too late to hang it back on the tree.

CHAPTER 10

Jonathan and the boys moved in the next week; Simon, Coralee and I were there to greet them. It was amazing how simply these Zennies lived. They carried their worldly possessions in one black duffel bag. Inside were their futons, their zafus or meditation cushions, their robes, a few soft cotton pants and white T-shirts, sandals and the ubiquitous Nikes. After all, they were still American males. They moved in effortlessly, pleased with the well-stocked kitchen, the wide-screen TV, the excellent stereo, but as Jonathan explained, not attached to them.

Jonathan related the story of their teacher, Roshi Somato. One day the Roshi was on the lunch line and saw that pickles were on the menu. The Roshi smiled, "Ah, pickles, my favorite food." But when he got to the head of the line, all the pickles were gone. "Ah," he observed, "no pickles." And he smiled. The point, Jonathan explained, was not to eschew preferences but to forgo being attached to them.

At which point, Jonathan introduced his three fellow students to Coralee, Simon, and me. "This is Alberto, Barney and Charles." The three men were all clean shaven, young and fit. Although they had looked similar in the photo, up close they were quite individual. Alberto had honey-colored skin, a full curved mouth and a Latin lilt; Barney was tall and rangy with a slow Texas drawl, and Charles was blond with deep dimples and a sweet little stutter. No doubt they each had different skills and aspirations, but that would come later.

"Have you discussed Slow Hands with your Roshi?" I asked the men.

"There was no need," Jonathan said. "Our mission is to provide loving and compassionate service to the world."

"But what does the dharma say about sex?" I persisted.

"Sex is like any other interaction—it must be respectful of both parties, and its intention must be to do good and not harm. Beyond that, sex is a private matter."

That seemed pretty enlightened to me. So it looked as if we had our staff, at least for the time being. I had persuaded Coralee and Simon to start small, to begin with just the four practitioners. And these four were perfect for our experiment as they knew each other, got along well, and had modest needs. After we'd worked out the kinks, so to speak, we could easily expand our enterprise and vary the types. But for right now, all we had to do was recruit the customers.

Jonathan announced they were going upstairs to meditate. As they turned to leave, I asked, "Is it okay if we call you the Zennies? It's not demeaning, is it?"

Alberto grinned. I noticed he had an adorable spitting space between his two front teeth. "Call us anything you want. As long as you keep calling," and the Zennies trooped up the long curving staircase.

"So what do we do now?" Coralee stretched out on the Persian rug like a long-legged cat. "Put another ad in the *Bay Guardian,* this time advertising for women who want to be pleased?"

"We'd have a stampede," Simon said.

"Or they wouldn't believe it," I amended. "It would be like advertising panty hose that won't run. Or lipstick that won't fade. At any rate, I don't think we want to go that public. Not yet."

"Then how are we going to get the women?" Coralee reached down and casually grasped her toes, her spine flattening obediently. She'd been doing yoga forever. I'd break if I tried that. I noticed that Simon was also impressed.

"What about the proverbial word of mouth?" Simon suggested.

"But we need to control it," I said, "find some sort of an 'in' group who could be trusted."

"Eureka!" Coralee slid out of her sun salute position. "Your therapy group, Sara. Who could be better?"

"My Group?" I gasped. "No, I don't think so."

"Why not? They're touch deprived. You said so yourself. They requested meds or a man. And you can't prescribe the meds," she said pointedly.

"It wouldn't be ethical," I protested.

"Prescribing Slow Hands wouldn't be," Simon agreed, "but just having them visit doesn't seem to be a therapeutic infraction. Then it's up to them, right?"

"You'd be doing them a service," Coralee added. "You'd be giving them a choice. Isn't that what therapy is all about? Having more choices?"

She had me there. My little sister had listened to many hours of my explaining and defending my profession, and she had listened well.

"Your Group is the reason we thought of Slow Hands in the first place," she said.

"Well, yes," I said, "eventually, maybe. But I hadn't thought of them as being the guinea pigs. We just don't know enough. What if there's a down side? What if Slow Hands is detrimental?"

"How could loving attention hurt? Nobody is going to do anything to them that they don't want. The women will be totally in control," Simon reasoned. And then he added the final convincing argument. "You wouldn't want to deprive them of a chance to be in on the beginning of a new boon to womankind, Sara. They'd never forgive you."

The memory of my last session with The Group came flooding back. Grace's attempted suicide, their abandoning therapy. Despite my trepidation, I owed them this opportunity. And, ignominious though it was, I very much wanted to win them back.

"All right," I said. "I'll give them a call. But remember it's just an on-site inspection."

"Sure, sure," Coralee chortled. "Once they see this little vacation retreat, they're going to want to buy in. At least for a time share."

To celebrate, Simon brought out a bottle of champagne and a platter of thinly sliced smoked salmon.

"Eat it like the French," he coaxed. "Don't chew. Just

press it against your palate, and extract the juices. Savor the moment."

Savor the moment, a good metaphor for the invitation I would be proffering to The Group. It would be for one evening. It would be fun. And the time was right. It was exactly one month since our last session, and since I had promised to reconvene The Group, what better place for a reunion than the beautiful surroundings of Slow Hands? A new venue. A new perspective. A new therapeutic possibility.

I made the phone calls from my office the next morning. I spoke to Mary Ann's secretary and left messages for Terry and Laura on their answering machines. Grace was the only one in when I called.

"Sara," she fluted, her voice warm and modulated in her best Bryn Mayr greeting, "how lovely to hear your voice. How are you?"

"Fine," I said, "but never mind me. What about you?"

"Never been better," came the quick, automatic reply.

"Grace," I admonished, "I'm your therapist. What about that jump?"

"Actually it was more like a fall," she said. "I guess I'm just not the impulsive type."

"What happened?"

"I climbed over the railing, and when I looked at the water close up, I couldn't do it. I just froze. Someone spotted me from the tollbooth and sent out the police. When I heard the sirens, I tried to run. That's when I fell and broke my ankle. I'm still in a cast."

"Why did you try to run?"

"Because if I were caught, it would have been humiliating," she whispered. Of course, I thought. To be so needy, so desperate that you attempted suicide. What could be more embarrassing?

"Never mind," she said. "I miss you and The Group. When do we get together again?"

"Next Thursday, our regular night. But at a different place. My sister and I have bought a beautiful old Victorian in the Berkeley hills. We'll meet there."

"A house warming?" Grace said with delight.

"Yes, a party. Dress up and wear something sexy."

"Sexy?" she said. "Oh, it's going to be co-ed?"

Dear Grace. I hadn't heard that phrase in years. Shades of prom night. "Eight o'clock, 69 Grove. Easy street parking," I said and rung off.

Laura left a message, saying, "Great time for a party! I lost twenty pounds." And Terry's smoky voice mail drawled, "They put me on testosterone—I'm ready to rock and roll."

When I got home from the office, I drew a hot lavender-scented bath, the better to think. How much should I tell The Group before Thursday? Maybe nothing more? I didn't want to spoil the surprise or the impact. Slow Hands had the potential to be something important. Perhaps revolutionary? Freud had discovered the unconscious, Jung the higher self. What if the Russack sisters revealed women's true sexual nature? Would women pay for sex? If so, what would they want? Slow Hands would challenge the belief that women could only enjoy sex in committed relationships. I could see the text now, *Zen and the Art of Sexual Satisfaction.* It should sell better than the *Zen of Archery* or *Zen and the Art of Motorcycle Maintenance.* At least to women.

It took forever until Thursday rolled around. Harry was getting ready for his regular bridge game. He marched into the kitchen holding his favorite khakis. "Did the cleaner shrink these?"

I took them from him, and put my arms around his waist. "I'll move the top button tomorrow. And lay off the cookies tonight."

"Give up cookies! Never!" He headed out the door. "Give up the cleaner."

A little plump, a little bald, Harry still looked fine to me. But I couldn't help remembering Jonathan when he slipped off that kimono, shades of Michelangelo's *David.* All those ancient marble torsos had been inspired by real bodies; men had actually looked like that, and some of them still did. All those muscles—abs, pecs, thighs—taut and gleaming. Indeed there was a wide band of muscle directly above the hipbone that I thought was artistic invention until I saw it on Jonathan.

As I was getting dressed, Wendy wandered into the bedroom, her face papered with wings of drying tissue. Together we were like the Middle East; my skin was the desert and hers produced the oil. We women are slaves to the pharmaceutical industry, only the faintest reprieve between acne and wrinkles. I looked at my daughter, slender limbed in jeans and tank top, the firm flesh, the glossy dark hair, the sweet plump mouth. Such a beauty, I thought, so young and healthy and yet, she would not agree. She would compare herself to the golden girls of her school and come up wanting. But then again, I would often appraise myself in the mirror harshly, bemoan each new wrinkle, each new droop. "You know how to handle aging," Mom used to say. "Just realize you'll never look this good again."

"Don't you have a rehearsal?" I asked.

"It's called off," she said. "The director ran out of Prozac, and he can't face 'Happy, Happy Talk' without it." She eyed my low-cut black dress suspiciously. "Why are you getting so dressed up?"

"I told you. Aunt Coralee and I bought a bed-and-breakfast in Berkeley. It's opening night."

"Opening night for a bed-and-breakfast?" She tried on my large rhinestone hoops. "Can I go?"

"It's just for the tenants," I said.

"Then why did you invite your Group?"

"How do you know that?"

"Mary Ann called. She said, 'Tell your Mom it's about time. I was getting ready to sue her for negligence.'"

"Thanks for the message," I said retrieving my rhinestone hoops.

"What time are you coming home?" Wendy slipped her feet into my one pair of Manolo Blahnik pumps.

"Hey, who's the mom here, and who's the kid? And hand over the shoes." A quick kiss goodbye, and I was out of there. Enough with the questions. What was it with kids? Wendy developed this unfailing ESP if I even thought about sex. I got into the car, popped a Springsteen tape into the player, and roared out to "Baby we were born to run."

When I arrived in Berkeley, the street was crowded with cars. I recognized The Group's immediately. They say we come to resemble our spouses. I would add our dogs and our cars. And there they were, the vehicles of my four women; I could read their personality in each one.

Laura drove a vintage Volkswagen Bug that must have belonged to her parents. I could just imagine her embarrassment when, in her fat phase, she had to squeeze behind the cramped steering wheel. The car was doubly protected with a blinking alarm and a red iron bar; Laura overdid everything. Grace drove a BMW befitting her economic station, but it was a modest town car model in a soft gray, unobtrusive but spotless. Mary Ann's red Porsche was parked half way up the sidewalk, even though there were lots of empty spaces, defying the police to ticket her.

Finally there was Terry in her SUV, the epitome of suburban safety, but she had left all the windows and the sunroof open. Clearly she was still in the throes of hot flashes. All four of my clients had arrived before me. Were they eager or what? Perhaps I had finally hit upon a remedy for simple human unhappiness. Give people a modicum of erotic hope, and they're likely to be forgiving about everything else.

But was this evening appropriate? After all I was their therapist, and even though I wasn't prescribing Slow Hands, I was introducing it. Was this responsible behavior? If Slow Hands were a drug, would it not bear the warning, Can impair judgment, cause drowsiness or insomnia, raise heart rate, and can be habit forming. It did lack the one dastardly side effect of other antidepressants, though. Slow Hands would never lower libido. On the contrary, it would raise it to new heights. And the Greeks who knew a thing or two about human behavior equated erotic love with creativity and happiness. Eros was an essential part of life. Bad things could happen to women who didn't get their share. They could dry up, become brittle, bitter, unloving. They could substitute animals or, worse, fur coats for their heart's affections.

I rang the doorbell; Simon answered it, looking splendid in his dinner jacket. He swept me up in an embrace, then planted a light kiss on each cheek. He held out a gardenia. "Where do you want to wear it?" he asked. I reached for the white flower, inhaled its sultry scent, recalling the exhilaration of school dances. Afterward we used to float our corsages in cereal bowls until the petals browned and fell apart. I'd come into my bedroom, and the smell of the gardenia would recreate the dance, the feel of my date's hand on my waist, his rough cheek against mine, his breath stirring the small hairs on my neck. It brought back my youth when love was always just about to happen.

Simon touched my shoulder. "Sara?" he said gently. "Where?"

"Here," I said, holding out my hand. He attached the flower to my wrist with a black velvet band and ushered me into the living room. The spicy scent of gardenias filled the air. There were my women. Laura wore the flower in her hair, Terry at her waist, Grace on her shoulder, and Mary Ann had placed it in her V-necked cleavage. Coralee smiled at me from across the room. As she walked toward me, her lei of gardenias interspersed with frangipani released the fragrance of a balmy tropical night. The Zennies all wore gardenias in the buttonholes of their sleek black kimonos, and there were gardenias in the floating crystal bowls that rested upon each table next to the soft glow of the gardenia scented candles.

You could call it overkill or very coordinated. Whichever it was, my Group had never looked lovelier or happier than in that gardenia-drenched living room, illuminated by the shamelessly flattering candlelight, basking in male attention. There was soft laughter and slow gestures, the arching of a wrist, the bending of a neck, the flirtatious, surreptitious touches to emphasize a point, a playful tap on the hand, a lingering brush of the shoulder, a holding of the gaze, an open, teasing smile. The women swayed gently; the men mirrored their movements, in synch, like good dancers. But here the women were leading, the men following so subtly, so smoothly it almost seemed simultaneous. Like great sex.

Coralee appeared with a tray of canapés, shaped like fish and flowers, miniature works of art ready to be consumed. Simon passed the golden flutes of champagne. The theme was pleasure. Sensation. Delicacy. Passion. No fast food here. It was deliberate, extravagant. It said this is special. And so are you. You deserve this.

On the stereo was the music of the koto, the notes drifting like a slow-motion waterfall amid the room's new party décor, the rosewood screens, the calligraphic scrolls, the pleated paper lanterns.

We were transported to Old Japan. But there had been a gender shift. These geishas were men, and I wondered how and when that would be announced.

Simon and Coralee must have been wondering about

that, too, for the cocktail hour spun on until the sushi was gone and the champagne running low. It was an awkward moment. We hadn't thought this one through, just assumed we'd know when the time was right or that couples would just slip upstairs without our having to say anything. But the proceedings ground to a halt in that strange quiet time at parties when no one is sure whether to start a new conversation or reach for their coats.

It was clearly up to me. The Group were my clients, and even though this was not an official therapy evening, I was the one who needed to explain the rules. Coralee and Simon discreetly retired to the gazebo as did the Zennies, the better to give me a clear field.

I waited until the women were comfortably seated before I began. I took my time setting it up, recalling the last therapy session, and Mary Ann's throwing down the gauntlet of meds or men. I explained Mom's legacy and the conditions it came with, then finally described the multipurpose presence of the Zennies.

I concluded with a disclaimer, "So it's completely up to you. Slow Hands is a full-service spa. You can avail yourself of a meditation session, a massage, or a full-blown...whatever." I smiled, attempting lightness. "They're here to serve you." I paused and there was a thundering silence.

Laura gasped. "You mean those guys aren't really Zen students?"

"They are," I explained, "and they're also really..."

"Fabulous," Mary Ann chortled. "I can't wait to see what they wear under those robes. Count me in."

Grace primly smoothed her skirt. "Paying for love!

No, thank you, Sara. That's not for me." She stood up to leave.

Terry took her hand. "It's not love we're paying for, Grace. It's attention, complete attention, from mindfulness experts. We need it for personal growth, for physical and mental health. So what's your major objection?"

Grace thought hard before she ventured an answer. "The humiliation factor. To think that some beautiful young man was doing it...doing me...just for the money, that actually he was repulsed."

"Are doctors repulsed? Nurses? Therapists?" Terry asked. "It's the state of mind. If they know they're doing good, if their touch is a healing act, then it's something they do with an open heart."

"Haven't any of you read Tennessee Williams?" Grace objected. *"The Roman Spring of Mrs. Stone?"*

"Yes, I've read it," I said. It was a cautionary tale of an aging American actress who is degraded by her affair with a young and unscrupulous Italian gigolo. "But, Grace, Mrs. Stone was deluding herself," I said. "She wanted to believe that boy was in love with her."

"The difference is at Slow Hands it's a professional arrangement," Terry said. "And it's all up front."

"With no illusions," I added. "The parameters are clear, you want sensitive, loving touch, you pay for it, and you get it safely and with respect."

"Sexuality is our goddamn birthright," Mary Ann said. "Come on Grace, you're too juicy to just be someone's Granny."

"And we're the one's in control here," Terry added. "It's empowering."

Grace's expression was still skeptical, but she slowly resumed her seat.

"I've got a practical question," Terry said. "I'm on a limited budget, Sara. How much is this going to cost?"

"The first time is on the house," I said.

Mary Ann looked thoughtful. "And it is a spiritual practice. Maybe it's deductible? I'll look into it."

That left just Laura, who sat glued to her chair, quivering like a rabbit. She beckoned to Terry, who knelt by her chair as Laura whispered her secret. "Laura wants you to know it's her first time," Terry said, "and she's scared...."

"And very grateful," Laura quietly added.

"All right." I sighed with relief. "Then it's settled. Just remember it's all up to you. You can do as little or as much as you like."

"We know," Mary Ann cried, "get those guys in here."

At Mary Ann's summons, Simon and Coralee returned, followed by the Zennies. With a flourish, Simon held up a red satin pouch embroidered with interlocking golden dragons, the tail of one dragon held in the mouth of the other, like circus elephants, but sinuous and sexy. "In here are the names of our gentleman hosts," he said, shaking the bag so the papers rattled. Each of the Zennies stepped forward, swept the room in an engaging glance, and humbly bowed.

"So, ladies," Coralee said, "we suggest you close your eyes, slip your hand into the pouch, and select your company for this evening." As the women murmured their approval, and subtly elbowed each other out of the way to be first at the purse, I saw Simon and Coralee exchange a satisfied glance. They had planned this device, cooked it up together. Some time this afternoon, I supposed, between filleting the fish, and arranging the flowers, I could imagine them concocting a method to match the pairs. Musical chairs? Fortune cookies? Blind man's buff? I had to admit it was a good choice, this silken dragon purse with its tasseled drawstrings. Mysterious. Exotic. Sensual. The thing that disturbed me was that I wasn't part of the scheme. After all, wasn't I the mastermind, the planner? How did I get out of the loop?

I watched Simon and Coralee as they stood close together, shoulders almost touching. I was an expert at detecting the pulse of feeling between two people; it was as palpably visible to me as a dotted line on a package of frozen peas. Were they an item? Had I lost my chance with Simon? Did I want him? And if so, as what? Although I had decided not to avail myself of Slow Hands' services and Simon was not a provider, I still felt an undercurrent of intrigue and attraction. Damn it. I had to admit it, I had the hots for Simon. I hadn't intended to act on it, but I did, at least, want the titillation, the flirtation, the fun of wanting, and being wanted by a new man.

Now it looked as if Coralee had gotten there ahead of me. I was used to Coralee's love affairs; they changed with the seasons. Even the one with Bruce had been more of a convenience than a passion. But this one felt different. If she and Simon became a couple, I could lose both of them. I suddenly felt bereft, and found myself walking toward them. As I approached, Simon slipped one arm around my waist, and the other around Coralee's. And as we stood there fused, a unit, a team, my breathing slowed, and my spirits lifted. I was being foolish. We were a triumvirate not a triangle.

In turn each of my women came forward and fished into the purse for her evening's escort. Mary Ann was first. She selected her paper quickly, opened it with the flourish of an Oscar presenter, crooked her finger at Barney, and sauntered off. Barney, the tall Texan, loped after her like a well-trained stallion. Next came Terry, who riffled the papers carefully. Finally, she held up her slip: "Bonnie Prince Charlie." Charles flashed his dimples and took her hand. Grace and Laura vied for who would be last. Indeed, I feared they might both flee. Simon approached them and held out the two remaining slips, one paper folded in each closed hand. Laura blushed scarlet but tapped Simon's right wrist. His hand opened to reveal Alberto's name, and the dark-eyed young man came forward. *"Ciao bella. Cosita rica."*

"What does that mean?" Laura whispered.

"Hello, my beauty, you precious little thing," he said, slipping his arm around her shoulders and leading her away.

"I'm afraid you've got me by default." Jonathan appeared at Grace's side. "I hope you're not disappointed."

Grace ran her fingertips along the young man's face, his smooth skin, his firm jaw and rosy lips. "Hardly," she murmured, "but what about you?"

He touched her face in the same appreciative manner. "I am honored," he said.

I felt my eyes grow moist. You go girl, I thought, as I watched Grace ascend the stairs. A damn sight better than climbing over a guard rail on a bridge. The opening night of our grand scheme had begun. I thought of my four women with their unique histories and personalities and their shared unhappiness. Would this temporary liaison help? Or would it frustrate? Would it conjure longing, discontent and suffering? Or would it provide pleasure and satisfaction? It seemed to me that the spirit of the encounter is what mattered, the full-hearted presence of both people. Not its longevity. For tonight the only moment was the present one; the only certainty was desire.

So there we were, our charges retired to their respective rooms to begin their night's adventure. Simon opened the last bottle of champagne, and we toasted each other.

"Did they ask about money?" Coralee wondered.

"I told them tonight was complimentary, but we ought to decide what we're going to charge."

"We had a staff meeting this morning," Simon said, "and I think we've come up with some workable guidelines."

"We don't want to run Slow Hands like a conventional brothel," Coralee said. "Women aren't as interested in the mechanics of sex as they are with the feeling and flow."

"And they love to be kissed," Simon said, "and of course in male bordellos the girls refuse to do that. Too intimate."

"But at Slow Hands we think intimacy is the key," Coralee said.

There was that ubiquitous *we* again. When did Coralee and Simon become a *we?* Simon, perceptive as always, read my expression. "Sara, that's as far as we've gotten. You're the expert on relationships. We really need your help."

Coralee slipped to my side, placed her cheek against mine. "We didn't know where to reach you this morning."

"At home." My tone was cool.

"But you haven't told Harry yet, have you?" she continued.

"Not yet," I said, pushing that troubling thought away. "Just leave a message for me next time. I want to be involved. As a full partner." My voice was whiny, accusative. I didn't like the sound of it. Clearly I was more invested in this project than I realized. And it wasn't just my concern for The Group.

"So we'll charge an overall membership fee which grants admission and complete services one day a week," Simon said.

"And what do *complete services* comprise?" I asked.

"The use of a hot tub and Jacuzzi, a full-body massage, and a choice of aromatherapy or herbal wrap. They can also avail themselves of complimentary sessions in ikebana flower arrangement, tea ceremony, koto playing and meditation," Simon enumerated.

"And the pièce de résistance or more accurately non-resistance...an extended session of one-on-one loving kindness," Coralee added.

"You mean, sex?" I asked.

"I mean whatever they want," Coralee answered. "Anything goes from conversation, to holding hands, to cuddles and kisses to..."

"To the full range of the Kama Sutra," Simon said. "From the 'Song of the golden flute' to 'Peony blossom unfolding.'"

"And how is this continuum determined?" I asked.

"We're not sure," Simon said. "That's why we need your advice. You're the expert on female psychology."

"You're no slouch, yourself." I knew when I was being buttered up even though the emollient was not unappreciated. "The important thing is choice. Some women need to feel desired, seduced. Others are comfortable being the seducer, some overtly, others covertly."

"Okay, seduction," Coralee said. "What else?"

"The second most important thing is surprise. That's what an affair has over a marriage, the unexpected."

"You mean the guys can refuse?" Simon said.

"Not entirely. We don't want the women to feel rejected. If they want touch, they have to get it. In one way or another. That's why they're here. But, this is the important part—they have to find a way that's mutually desirable. I think our women will enjoy the directness, the honesty of finally asking for what they want. They'll experience power without coercion. And since the Zennies are autonomous as well, the nature and the extent of the contact are open-ended. That's what makes it exciting."

"And human," Simon added.

"Exactly. I want my women to feel safe and honored. I want them to proceed at their own pace."

"Not to worry, Sara. We've given the Zennies extensive training. They know how to read body language, how to wait for an invitation."

"I hope so. It still makes me nervous. I feel responsible for these women."

"Would you like to see for yourself?" Simon offered.

"What do you mean?" I asked.

"All will be revealed." He led us into his office and

lowered the lights. As we watched, the dark television screen dissolved into a long shot of a partially dressed couple sitting on a futon.

Simon pushed a button to provide a zoom shot.

I recognized them. "Grace and Jonathan."

"Never looking better," Coralee added.

"You're spying on them!" I cried.

"We're monitoring them for quality control," Simon explained. "Just this once. And we are not invading their privacy, Sara. The Zennies informed each woman that she can turn off the camera any time she likes. No one has."

"Mary Ann even asked us to tape it," Coralee said. "Then they all thought that sounded good. So we're going to give it to them as birthday presents. Beats mango moisturizer, don't you think?"

I leaned my head back against the chair. It was not surprising that the women might want to preserve this session. Often in psychotherapy a client would ask to tape-record our conversation, the better to reflect upon it in private, especially when the immediate experience was too intense to take in fully.

I realized that there was a new picture on the screen. Simon must have changed it while I was ruminating. I tried to recover. "Is there any sound?" I asked. He turned the volume up, and I heard Laura and Alberto.

His hand was beneath her chin, lifting her face into the light. *"Chiquita de mis suenos. Tu ojos. Maravilloso. Mi querida."* Laura smiled, and so did I. Ah, to be courted in a Romance language!

Laura stretched voluptuously, sighed with pleasure, and for the first time I saw the deep furrow between her eyes relax. Her flushed cheeks were a velvet frame for her sparkling eyes.

" 'The talented lover will always find some noteworthy part to praise in his beloved, and that part expands to become an admirable whole,'" Simon said. "Andreas Capellanus, *The Anatomy of Love*."

"There are two types of lovers," he continued. "The first seeks perfection in each woman he meets and is always disappointed. The second finds something perfect in each woman and is never disappointed."

As if to illustrate the doctrine, Simon moved quickly from one room to the next, a rapid montage of images of seduction and delight. We saw Barney unwrapping Mary Ann's breasts as if they were Lalique crystal and might break. He knelt before her, enraptured. "They're perfect," he said, "classic." He sighed with admiration. "You can't see their shape in what you wear. You mustn't hide them. They're so beautiful." I knew what pain Mary Ann's small breasts had caused her. She had bemoaned being flat chested in The Group once, recalling how she had been called Pancake in high school and been ashamed to wear a bathing suit.

Simon flicked the button. Another scene popped into view; clouds of vapor filled the screen. Slowly they cleared to reveal a marble bathroom. A man knelt at the side of the tub, while inside, her head resting upon an inflatable cushion, lay Terry. Charles was stripped to the waist, his lean swimmer's muscles rippling as he bent to his task. He dipped a large natural sponge into the bath water and then, holding it aloft, sent a small waterfall of warm water onto Terry's chest and belly.

Charles was murmuring something we couldn't quite make out. Simon raised the volume, but all we heard was Terry's voluptuous sighs. We watched a long time, lost in the ritual of the bath as Charles slowly raised each of Terry's limbs, in turn, soaped them with a soft cloth, and rinsed them with flowing water. Terry lay back, eyes closed, a beatific smile wreathing her lips. Every now and then, she slid a finger slowly over Charles's muscled forearm, as if she were reading a Shakespearean sonnet in braille. I was just about to ask Simon to switch the channel and check in on Grace when Charles shed his loose cotton trousers. He stood naked, glorious. The steam made his skin shine, and his downy buttocks, it must be said, were works of wonder, round and firm as a peach. I couldn't help noticing that his dangly bits, as the Brits call them, were quite fine as well. A healthy pink, good-size and friendly looking.

Some men's penises were purple, inflamed or straggly as the neck of a turkey; some virtually disappeared when they were flaccid, and their testicles could look swollen, uneven or just plain homely. Charles's privates, however, were state-of-the-art, and under the soft track lighting exquisitely displayed.

As Terry opened her eyes to see him standing there in all his natural glory, her expression was like Leda's when Zeus revealed himself not to be a swan but a God.

Charles whispered to Terry that she move forward in the tub. I noticed he had lost his stutter. He slipped in behind her, his legs enclosing hers. She leaned back until she was resting gingerly against him. His arms folded firmly about her waist, and she let go, sinking into his cushioned supporting embrace. They rested that way for a long time, and we three viewers were silent, lost in the same still waters.

Time passed, and I thought Terry might have fallen asleep except for the occasional resettling of her head against Charles's strong shoulder. He whispered something, and she nodded eagerly. Terry wore her graying curls swept into a French knot. Charles released the pins, placing them one by one in his mouth, until her hair hung loose about her shoulders. There was something so intimate, so relaxed, and playful about the way he held the pins. He placed them carefully on the side of the marble sink, reached behind him, and opened a glass vial; he poured some clear liquid into his palm, and gently anointed her head. What exotic unguent? I wondered. But then it foamed. It was shampoo. Lowly shampoo. But the way he moved his hands through her hair was anything but ordinary. Slowly, reverently, he massaged her neck and temples, scooping up the tendrils of her hair and piling them on the top of her head, oozing the suds through his fingers. Pausing with his hands wrapped in her hair, he brought his face close to hers. I felt a rush of feeling, everywhere at once.

Simon turned to me and smiled. "Do you fancy that?"

"What?" I could barely speak.

"A tub."

"Oh, well," I stammered, "I don't know. I usually bathe alone."

"Many hands make light work." He shot me a teasing grin.

I struggled to regain my professional demeanor. "It

does look like good clean fun. Maybe we can add it to the general services." Then, "It's getting late, I ought to be going."

"But we haven't seen Grace yet," Coralee protested.

"I've seen enough." I reached for my coat, still unsettled by the intimacy I had witnessed and by my own arousal.

"We ought to get together to finalize fees and guidelines," Simon said.

"Sure. Anytime," I said.

"Tomorrow?" he suggested.

"I've got a dental appointment tomorrow," Coralee said. A childhood love affair with chocolate kept her dentist flush. "But you two can meet."

"That would be great," I said quickly. "It'll mostly be financial, anyway, and we can make a first stab at things, sort of a blueprint. It could save time all around, and..." I was babbling.

Coralee threw me an amused I'm-wise-to-you-sister look but nodded amiably, and I hurried home to Harry.

When I got there he was asleep, with the TV droning. I climbed into bed naked, untied the string of his pajama bottoms, and rolled on top of him. He never opened his eyes but smiled broadly. Our union was sweet, companionable and familiar. Like low-fat yogurt. Healthy. Sensible. Nourishing. But afterward I still lusted for that hot fudge sundae.

CHAPTER 11

The next morning I dressed with extra care or more precisely with a different purpose. Sure, my neck was a bit
crepey, a small wattle appeared when I turned sideways,
but in the proper bra, my cleavage made itself known.
Once I had asked a male colleague, who was diligently
tracking a young waitress's breasts, what he was drawn
to. The bounce, he said. So I let them bounce.

I chose a silky white sweater and added a pencil-thin
red skirt. Yes, there was a belly bulge, but my rear was
round and high, and although my thighs had their requi-
site cellulite—why do women's fat cells have a clinical
name as if they were some heinous disease?—my calves
and ankles were still trim.

I decided to wear a pair of strappy red sandals, a hot
color, but low heeled. Suffering for beauty wasn't necessary; in fact, sore feet or a pinched waist made me
cranky. The key was to wear fabrics that slid across my

skin and felt good. Nothing too fragile or too ornate. Nothing that wore me. The point was to feel natural, at ease, and I would draw good things toward me. Tension attracts the obstacle and relaxation the open door.

I was feeling more excited than relaxed, though, as I drove up to Slow Hands in my trusty Honda. I decided to use my key rather than ring the doorbell. Jonathan had presented us all with yin-yang key chains, a half circle of white containing a black dot, a half circle of black containing a white dot. "So all things," he had said, "pass onto their opposites, and all things contain their opposites." And then he had grinned. "It also lights up in the dark."

I turned the key chain over in my hand like worry beads. Somehow this so-called innocent business meeting had a resonance, an aura that was making my palms sweat. There was something here in this place, and with Simon, that I wanted...that perhaps I even needed. I wasn't exactly sure what it was, and even if I were, I didn't know if I'd have the courage to go for it.

Instead I walked purposefully to the gazebo where Simon had set up his office. He was seated at his desk as I entered. The sun lit the fine bones of his face; his moss-green shirt matched his eyes. "Sara." He covered the distance between us in two long strides and took me in his arms. Like my sister, Simon hugged with his entire body. I felt the length of him; we were aligned from top to bottom and particularly in the middle. It was as if he'd put his hand there and stroked. I realized I was as moist and pulsating as a Danielle Steel heroine. She was right, maybe not original or deep, but hell, she was right. A certain man came along and everything melted.

Simon leaned back, his arms still around me. "You look wonderful," he said, appraising me closely.

His scrutiny was unnerving. "Last night was great," I said. "Everything went beautifully."

"A home as well?"

" hat?"

" hope you got turned on, Sara, and had a good time at home. After all, this venture is for you, too."

"In more ways than one."

"Oh?" he queried.

"I mean it's a business and..." I added quickly, "a therapeutic experiment as well."

"Right. How about a coffee? The cappuccino machine just arrived."

I followed him into the kitchen; we were the only ones in the house. The Zennies had gone to their temple for early meditation. I watched as Simon ground a handful of dark espresso beans. "Jamaican Blue Mountain," he pronounced. The aroma was rich and heady as the beans released their oil. "Collected on one mountaintop at the hour before dawn. Very rare. Very expensive. But some things are worth it," he said. He steamed the milk, and we were silent as the pleasant hissing filled the kitchen. He removed two Italian ceramic cups from the cupboard. They were mustard gold, the color of summer sunshine and painted round with twining leaves and violet flowers; the bowl so large and deep you had to hold it in both hands.

Simon poured in the dark shot of espresso and then filled the cup with the frothy milk. "Chocolate or cinnamon?" he asked.

"Both," I said.

"That's my girl," he said. "*Yes and*...my philosophy exactly."

"Yes and...what?" I asked.

"The credo of my old drama school teacher," he explained.

"You went to drama school?"

"For my sins." He lifted the back of his wrist to his forehead. "Royal Academy of Dramatic Arts, but I never graduated. Never mind, I learned the most valuable lesson in the first week. It was during a class in improvisation. The essence was this. When someone presents you with a new idea, or a new situation, you can have one of two major responses. You can say 'no, but'...reject it and show how it can't work. Or you can say 'yes, and'...acknowledge their contribution and build upon it." He paused. "Guess which produces the better results?"

I sipped the excellent cappuccino. "Undoubtedly the latter."

"Indeed." He added a cube of sugar to his own cup, stirred it thoughtfully. "Applies in all sorts of situations, even with us."

I busied myself with the coffee.

"Well, we're here ostensibly to discuss the budget of Slow Hands, but there's another agenda. Isn't there?"

"Like what?" I kept my tone neutral.

"Why, your own sexuality, your own pleasure. Surely you're not immune to desire?" He paused, eyeing me mischievously. "So which of the Zennies do you fancy, Sara?"

"They all seem like fine young men."

"Which means all of them?"

"Or none of them. At least, not for me."

"Are you saying you'll abstain? We've arranged a banquet, and you've decided to go hungry."

"I'm hardly hungry." I stood up, setting my cup on the counter harder than I intended. "I'm a married woman."

"All the more reason. Slow Hands isn't just about needing...it's about wanting. It's about curiosity. Variety. Isn't it?" He folded my hand in his.

And I did not move away. I did not want that touch to end, that contact to be broken.

"Sara, there are many ways to partake of Slow Hands. If you're going to be a full partner, you need to feel comfortable here." He smiled. "The least you can do is have a massage."

"I've never had a massage from a man before."

"You haven't?"

"Not from a man."

"Well, then it's time you did," he said. "I'm a little rusty, but I am certified."

I flashed back to the video clips from last night, the sensual bath, the lingering touch. "Do we have time?" I asked weakly.

"There's always time for what we really want to do. I've got a massage table in my room. I'll set it up and meet you upstairs."

He was gone before I could answer. I climbed the stairs as if I were summitting Everest, short of breath and weak kneed. As I entered his sun-drenched room, I was relieved to find it decorated in Southwestern motifs, something to talk about. A vintage Navajo chief's blanket lay upon the bed and a copy of O'Keeffe's Taos pueblo church dominated one wall. "I just love her work," I said.

Simon nodded. "Especially how she did dozens of versions of a subject eliminating everything until she was down to a single defining aspect. Do you know what she said about her mountain?"

" 'God told me if I painted it often enough he would let me come back to walk on it after I was dead,' " I said. Not only did Simon and I love the same books and paintings and ideas, but we were gluttons for literary quotations.

He pointed me toward the large maroon leather massage table in the corner. He produced two dusky pink sheets. He lay one upon the table and handed me the other. Dimming the lights, he lit a handful of lilac-scented candles and slid in a tape cassette of Chopin. He turned on a space heater, dispensing the ever present morning chill, and the room became warm and cozy.

"Should I take off everything?" I asked.

"But of course. Clothing is a barrier to the senses. I'll be back in a moment." He slipped out of the room.

I stripped quickly, trembling despite the warmth of the room; unattractive goose bumps covered my arms and legs. I slid quickly beneath the top sheet, first lying on my back, then feeling too exposed, turned over on my stomach, listening for the sound of Simon's footsteps. What was going to happen? What did I want to happen? What would I allow? Encourage? I felt my nipples stiffen. I hadn't been this excited in years. There was a part of me that was coming alive again. I remembered a time when every love song seemed to be written for me and the boy I was yet to meet.

I thought of Wendy. When she sang "Some Enchanted Evening" what stranger did she dream of?

The Greeks believed that erotic love was madness, that it swept like a fever through your body burning reason away. I was dangerously close to feeling that now.

I turned to see Simon reenter the room. He was naked except for a pair of gym shorts. His body was long and lean, burnished with golden hair; his arms and chest strong and muscular.

I smelled the musky perfume of lavender, the crisp green of eucalyptus.

Simon held up two vials. "Which do you prefer?"

I pointed to the lavender, not trusting myself to speak.

I heard the soft exhale of the bottle as he poured the fragrant oil onto his palms, carefully warming it. I felt his gentle touch first on the back of my neck. He let his hands rest there until my breathing quieted, and then in a long slow caress they moved down my spine. He spread the unguent in seamless strokes, kneading the muscles of my neck and shoulders and back. My tension evaporated into the warm steamy air. I felt liquid and loose as his hands skillfully massaged my hips and thighs. I sighed deeply. "Yes," Simon murmured, "a good release."

I whispered something about it being marvelous, about him being a wonder. He proceeded to massage my hands, cupping each finger, kneading the spaces between. He stroked the backs of my knees, the insides of my elbows, the coils of my ears...all those hidden places. He moved to my feet, massaged my heels and soles, and each toe in turn. He held my feet in his hands for a long blissful time. I had never been cared for so thoroughly, so selflessly.

The mounting sexual excitement I had first felt melted into a series of concentric circles, growing softer and wider. "Ready to turn over?" he whispered. I moved slowly onto my back, and he gave his attentions to my chest and belly. Finally I just gave up my body to him, experiencing everything, monitoring nothing. Intellectual nattering had evaporated. Judgment and comparison were gone. So this is what was meant to be inside my body. To inhabit my own skin. To be open to my own instincts. This is what animals feel. This is what children feel. This is what lovers feel.

And in the midst of that joy, I felt my tears start. Tears of loss. I had been without that feeling for so long. And, oh God, how I had missed it. The ecstasy of the body, of wanting to be nowhere else but here.

Tenderly, Simon brushed my tears away. "I'll get you some water," he said. He returned a moment later, and as I sat up shakily to reach for the glass, the sheet fell away from my breasts. I sat there for a moment, wishing my breasts were higher, firmer. He tilted his head in pleasure, eyes smiling into mine. "You look sixteen," he said.

And I leaned forward, my breasts against his naked chest, and said softly, "Would you kiss me, please?"

I felt his warm lips upon my forehead, my eyelids, and then ever so gently on my mouth. Like a benediction.

Gradually we drew apart, still holding each other's gaze. The space between us was charged. I gulped hard. "What...what do we do now?"

"Whatever you like," he answered.

What did that mean? Was he leaving the next move up to me? I hesitated, beset by two conflicting images:

Harry's familiar, trusting face in my mind's eye and just inches away Simon's alluring, mysterious body. All I had to do was lift my hand. But despite my curiosity, despite my desire, I couldn't; it felt too heavy, tethered to my side by the weight of my wedding band. I wasn't ready. For now, this was enough, maybe more than enough.

I drew the sheet tightly around me, took a sip of the now tepid water. "I guess we should have that business meeting now. If I can think straight."

"You'll be thinking even better now," he assured me. "From both sides of the brain."

He left the room, and I took a light and leisurely shower, reluctant to wash away the scent of lavender. I thought it might feel strange segueing into a business meeting, but when I entered the kitchen Simon was fully dressed and his usual professional self. He poured us cups of fresh coffee, and just as he had predicted, what had passed between us seemed to smooth the way. We made short order of the ledgers and quickly established a fee scale. There was only one troublesome detail to deal with: a neighbor had filed a complaint with the police, Simon said.

"Who was it?" I asked.

"A certain Ralph Rater," Simon said. "He lives directly across the street. Says he couldn't find a place to park."

"What's wrong with his garage?" I asked.

"He uses it for his business."

"Which is?"

"A video rental service—Moral Majority Movies." Simon held up a slick black and white brochure that read, "A family film enterprise. All movies selected and pre-screened for ethical elucidation."

"Elucidation," I said. "I'm impressed. Let's mark that guy's parking space not just reserved but sacrosanct."

"A small price to pay to preserve the peace," he said. "And, by the way, have you heard anything from the ladies?"

"Not yet. We'll be meeting back in Group next week. What did the Zennies have to say?"

He handed me an origami swan.

I unfolded its paper wings to find a picture of a smiling Buddha and the caption, "What is the sound of four hands clapping?"

CHAPTER 12

It was precisely one week after the great success of opening night. The Group was meeting in session for the first time since our hiatus, and I was nervous. As I waited for the women to arrive, I kept moving the chairs around and readjusting the blinds. I even went to the corner deli and bought pretzels and red licorice as low-cal snacks, although I ate half of them myself before the doorbell rang.

As usual it was Laura who arrived first. "I know I'm early," she said, "but I just couldn't wait to get here." She threw off her heavy cape, revealing a full but shapely body encased in a black spandex mini dress. I gestured for her to sit down, deliberately not commenting on her new garb. Previously, even in her svelte phases, Laura would never wear revealing clothing.

But she stood at the door stubbornly refusing to move. "Well," she prodded, then pirouetting for emphasis, "what do you think of the outfit?"

In my best shrink fashion I batted back the question. "The point is...what do *you* think? What do *you* feel?"

"I feel terrific. Mah-valous." She grinned.

"That's what counts," I said.

"How I *look* counts, too," she said. "Big time." It was the most authoritative, assertive statement I'd ever heard from Laura. She waited for my response.

"Sure, it matters," I conceded.

She reached for a diet soda, and lifted it high in a toast. "To the healing power of touch, Dr. Russack. And thanks for providing it."

"I hope you don't think I'm professionally advocating Slow Hands," I said quickly. "It was just that it was opening night, and I wanted to let you know it was available."

"I don't need a prescription, Dr. Russack." Laura drank deeply. "Where do I sign?"

"Coralee and Simon are handling all the arrangements. I can give you their number...." My voice trailed off as the doorbell rang.

It was Mary Ann. As she sauntered into the room, I barely recognized her. Gone were the pinstriped business suit, the severe bob, the brimming alligator briefcase; instead she wore jeans, a loose sweatshirt, and tennis shoes. Her face was clear of makeup, her hair tousled and sun-streaked; she looked ten years younger. She thrust a bouquet of yellow daisies in my hand. "Thank you for one of the best evenings of my life." She sashayed to her chair. She reached for a handful of red licorice and ogled Laura's outfit. "That girl's got legs that will not end," she pronounced.

Grace and Terry arrived arm in arm, toting a magnum of champagne. Grace popped the cork.

"No alcohol during group," I cautioned.

"Just this once," Terry begged, "to celebrate Grace's return from the dead."

"How about the rest of us?" Laura said.

"It's the resurrection," Mary Ann chortled, "and we're the first ones up."

Grace held the bottle poised, plastic flutes at the ready. "Mother, may we?"

"Why the heck not?" I relented. "This has been an unorthodox couple of sessions." I held out my glass. "And who's going to say no to Dom Pérignon?" As I watched the golden bubbles rise in my glass, I wondered what the American Psychological Association would make of our venture. Was there a conflict of interests? Was I an irresponsible therapist or a prescient pioneer? At any rate, I was happy to return to more familiar ground. I leaned back in my chair and tossed out my traditional opening question, "Well, what kind of a week has it been for you?"

There was the familiar silence, the usual shuffling about as the group glanced at each other, jockeying for position as to who would speak first. There were strategic advantages and disadvantages in each choice: opening (you set the tone), rebuttal (you balanced the argument), bringing up the rear (you capitalized on the suspense).

"I don't know about you guys," Mary Ann said with a grin, "but I'm still rocking from the aftershocks."

"Me, too," Terry chimed in. "I thought it was so weird. All of a sudden, after being asleep 'down there' for years, I'm like...wired."

"It's all I think about," Laura sighed. "That sweet man. I know this is corny. I read it in *Ladies' Home Journal* but still...they defined intimacy as...in-to—me-see...and Alberto did. He was so...attentive."

I turned to Grace, who was noticeably quiet. "And what about you, ma'am? How was it for you?"

"I don't want to throw cold water on this heat wave," she said, "but..."

"But what?" the others said in unison.

"It really rattled me."

"Isn't that what it's supposed to do?" Terry said.

"Not in a good way." Grace spoke slowly, choosing her words carefully. "It felt wrong. Not morally wrong. Although I must admit I wouldn't want my kids to find out about it, but it felt...inappropriate. Like I was reading *Seventeen* instead of *Vogue.* Even if I could fit into one of those outfits, it wouldn't fit into my lifestyle. I'm sorry, but I can't do it."

"Do it again, you mean," Mary Ann gibed.

Grace looked down at her hands. She rubbed the faint red mark where her wedding ring had been. "I couldn't."

"Nothing at all?" Terry asked.

"Well, we did fool around a little," Grace admitted.

Mary Ann, ever the lawyer, wanted a full deposition. "Hugging?"

Grace nodded.

"Kissing?"

"Some," Grace said.

"Petting?" Laura asked.

So they still called it petting, I thought.

"He mostly. And then..." Grace blushed violently.

"Then what?" Mary Ann demanded. We all leaned forward.

"He...um...offered to..." Grace's hands churned wildly in her lap.

The Group provided the language her stammering tongue refused.

"Oral sex?" Laura whispered.

"Cunnilingus," Terry clarified.

"Box lunch at the Y," Mary Ann chortled.

Grace turned to me, shocked. "And he said it was delicious."

"Absolutely," Mary Ann said. "What's not to like?"

"My husband didn't. He wouldn't. Ever."

"Maurice was perverted," Terry said vehemently. She crossed the room and put her arm around Grace. "Aren't you glad you didn't kill yourself before Jonathan and Slow Hands?"

Grace fingered her ever present two-strand pearl necklace and smiled at the memory.

"So what's the problem?" Terry persisted. "You don't want that feeling again?"

"I *do* want that feeling again," Grace said. "Definitely. But I don't think I could 'go all the way'..."

Our euphemisms for sex, I thought, date us as surely as our taste in music.

"...unless I was in love," Grace continued.

There was a silence in the room as we took in the truth and gravity of Grace's statement.

"Well, sure," Mary Ann said. "Who doesn't want love and marriage and enduring passion? But really ladies, how often do you get the whole package...in one place? So in the meantime, what's wrong with paying for a bit of it? Retail therapy works with clothing, why not with sex? You don't have to go for the full makeover, you can just buy a new accessory." She grinned, looking around the room. "I thought there might be a touch of buyer's remorse at this session, so I brought in something for Show and Tell. To keep that lust alive." She opened her purse, extracted a stack of pink brochures and passed them out. "This, ladies, is the latest catalogue from Deep Sensations."

Laura scrutinized the line drawing on the cover. "That's a Picasso," she said. "A drawing of his lover Marie-Therese."

I studied the picture of the young woman, her eyes closed, head thrown back in rapture; hands nestled suggestively in her lap.

"It's called *The Dream,*" Laura explained. "He spotted Marie-Therese at a Paris metro station. 'I am Picasso,' he said, 'come with me. We can do great things together.'" She sighed. "He was forty, married with children and she was seventeen. She was his lover and his model for the rest of his life."

"Along with plenty of others," Terry scoffed. "Another woman, another style."

"And he always had at least two at a time, just like Maurice." Grace tossed the brochure angrily into the wastebasket. "Men!"

"Hey, just a minute," Mary Ann retrieved the brochure, "this is a veritable cornucopia of mother's little helpers. For your information, Deep Sensations is a play shop for women filled with erotica, and the largest selection of sex toys in the country. A place where you can shop till you drop in comfort and privacy. It's well lit, offers free parking, helpful saleswomen and get this...a trying on booth where you can sample the equipment from tiny hand buzzers to a mega Hitachi magic wand."

What Pandora's box had I opened? I wondered.

"I was always curious about vibrators," Terry admitted, "but I worried about getting addicted."

"No one's suggesting them *instead* of a man," Mary Ann continued. "You can use them for that added pleasure or for those in between times. But listen to this...the history of vibrators. We are not alone in our frustration." And she proceeded to read, "'As long ago as Ancient Greece and Egypt, female troubles were called 'hysteria' and were thought to be the revolt of the uterus against sexual deprivation.'"

She passed the pamphlet to Terry. "'In the Middle Ages, the symptoms of hysteria were chronic arousal, sleeplessness, irritability, erotic fantasy and excessive vaginal lubrication,'" Terry read. "Yep, all present and accounted for." She grinned. "'To relieve these symptoms, midwives were asked to lubricate one or more of their fingers with oil of musk and place them inside the patient's vagina until a hysterical paroxysm was affected.'"

Grace finished the section. "'This procedure was recommended for single women, widows, nuns or unhappily married women.' Who's left?"

Mary Ann retrieved the pamphlet and quickly summarized the rest, "By 1600, doctors took over the act of pelvic massage. It was recommended to those who had clean hands and a pure heart."

"Like the Zennies," Laura added.

"Later therapies," Mary Ann went on, "included massage with a jet of water."

"I figured that one out myself in the shower," Terry said. She held up an ad from *Woman's Home Companion* circa 1900; it was a picture of a large black vibrator captioned Rub-a-dub-dub. "'Buy this handy home appliance, use daily and feel all the lost pleasures of youth throb within you.'"

"What are we waiting for? Let's take a look at the catalogue," Grace said.

"No need to look at pictures." Mary Ann opened a large brown shopping bag and began tossing out an assortment of dildos and vibrators, ben wa balls, harnesses, silk restraints, and edible massage oils.

I caught a vibrator in the shape of a pink bunny, whose ears were bent at a most suggestive angle. This was getting very strange, indeed.

Grace waggled a huge gelatinous penis in a fetching shade of puce.

Laura examined a jar of chocolate-mint body paint. "It also comes in banana daiquiri and burgundy cherry," she said gleefully.

Mary Ann held a fur mitt in one hand and waved a peacock feather in the other. "Lead me to your hot tub," she cried. "Now all of these toys, ladies, sad to say, are samples and for perusal only. You can, of course, order your own. But I do have a free gift for each of us." She held aloft a tiny battery operated flower. "The Venus Flytrap," she said proudly. "A look Ma, no hands, vibrator. Convenient. Discreet. Fits into your purse. Glove compartment. Bedside table. No need to ever be found wanting. Okay ladies, one two three...buzz."

The Group turned their switches on, and the air was

filled with the soft sibilance of small whirring motors. "Come on ladies," Mary Ann exhorted, "be creative. Boogie with those blossoms."

I looked around the room at my clients. Terry was flicking her Flytrap on and off in a samba beat. Laura was holding hers up to her cheek like a kitten. Mary Ann had boldly placed hers on her crotch, while Grace was holding hers out at arm's length, studying it bemusedly. The room was filled with smiles.

I waited until the activity died down and let the quiet prevail. It was the kind of soft, easy silence which could have ended in a leave taking, but instead Mary Ann proffered a question. "So, while we're on the subject, is there really a G spot?"

I had recently taken a course on sexual dysfunction to fulfill my credential renewal, and I was up on the latest findings. "Yes, I am happy to say, there is a G spot. It's an area of spongy tissue surrounding the urethra. When a woman is aroused it swells to about the size of a quarter, and can be felt through the front wall of the vagina about two inches in."

"What does it do?" Laura asked.

"Some women can have powerful orgasms when it's stimulated," I said.

"And sometimes," Terry added, "you can even ejaculate fluid."

"Wow! Just like a guy," Mary Ann said. "I want to try that."

"Some women like G spot stimulation, but some can find it irritating," I added. "There's no general rule."

Grace patted her Venus Flytrap. "It's just like what

Jonathan said, if you want to know what women want, you have to ask them. One at a time."

We ended the session on that note. The women reluctantly returned the array of sex toys to Mary Ann's shopping bag after recording the item number of their favorites. Laura chose the edible massage oil, all three flavors, Mary Ann the black silk restraints, Grace and Terry the Oriental ben wa balls, little metal spheres that when properly inserted were said to produce deep and long-lasting sensations. I reflected that Mom might have chosen those, as well, another happy bit of Chinoiserie. Ah Mom, I thought, here's your legacy at work. Would you be pleased? I hope so. The women tucked their Flytraps into their pockets and prepared to leave.

"Before you go," I said, "we still have to make two decisions. Do we continue to meet in session? And what do you want to do about participation in Slow Hands?"

Mary Ann, as usual, was the quickest and most vociferous. "Yes, to both. I support the Greek ideal. A sound mind in a sound body."

"And everything in moderation," Grace added quietly.

"Does that mean you're in?" Terry asked.

In answer, Grace lifted her vibrator high above her head. She turned the motor on to its lowest marking. "But at my own speed."

Terry gave Grace a high-five. "How about alternating? One week of Group and..."

"One week of grope." Laura raised her hand. "I vote yes."

Soon there were four hands waving in the air.

"All right then, we'll meet here in two weeks. And you

can call Coralee to enroll in the charter membership of Slow Hands," I said.

"What about you, Sara, aren't you going to be a player?" Mary Ann asked. "No professional taboos there. You're not a therapist at Slow Hands."

"I'm still management, though," I demurred. "And I'm still married."

"So does that mean you don't have a G spot?" Mary Ann jibed and the women exited laughing.

Mary Ann's question reverberated as I sat at my desk to write my notes about the evening's session. Does married management have a G spot? And when was the last time I visited it? I leaned back in my black leather chair, closed my eyes and remembered Thomas and Big Sur. It was over a decade ago. For my thirty-fifth birthday, Coralee had given me a yoga weekend at Tenemos, a coast side health spa. Thomas was my teacher, a calm, patient presence, urging me and my fellow students to greater flexibility and deeper relaxation. I guess all the women had a crush on Thomas, his boyish smile, his liquid grace. He smelled like fresh bread, and he was the only man in the room. I thought I was no different to him than anyone else, until that last night when I came to his cabin to return a Krishnamurti book I had borrowed. We sat near each other beneath the one lamp and read our favorite passages out loud. As we turned the pages, our shoulders touched. I thought it was an accident, until his fingers brushed the underside of my wrist and traveled slowly up my bare arm and shoulder. I had never been unfaithful to Harry. I had never wanted to be...until Thomas. Although I had quickly closed the book and returned to my room, I couldn't sleep that night.

I shivered and came back into the room, into the present moment. Hadn't I felt some of that same stirring with Simon during the massage? Was it equally as dangerous? Couldn't those erotic feelings threaten my world again? And yet, if at Slow Hands those feelings could be contained, if they could belong only to that place and be left there, then we would have created an erotic haven. Indeed, an erotic Heaven! A ritual space, safe and sacred.

And the Group seemed so happy, even Grace. Was Slow Hands any worse than Prozac? At least I could prescribe it, and it was human chemistry not synthetic. But what about the dosage? And how would I monitor the results? And what about me? Would I partake? I needed help; I needed to talk this over with someone. Coralee and Simon didn't see it as a problem. And, of course, I hadn't told Harry. My colleagues? I didn't trust them to understand. Who could advise me but Mom? I envisioned her, sitting across from me, that night I was leaving home for college, her smile bright as a halogen lamp.

I was trembling with fear of the unknown. She had taken my hand. "Any time you want me, sweetheart, just whistle." We both loved Bogie and Bacall.

I laid my head back against the chair and very softly whistled.

And I heard her voice. *Our loved ones don't ever leave us. They just talk from to us from farther away.*

"Life is simple, baby bear. There's only one thing to remember," she had said.

"What's that?"

"Be kind."

"Says who?" I countered.

"Me and the Dali Lama."

Now who's going to argue with that? I closed my note-book and headed home.

CHAPTER 13

I always tried to sleep on important decisions in an attempt to avoid the twin polarities of impulse and procrastination. Sometimes, though, it was easier to cross a rocky stream by striding confidently across. Too much caution and you teeter; balance comes through momentum.

I surprised Harry and Wendy by rising early and preparing buttermilk pancakes from scratch. When my family arrived at breakfast they looked particularly endearing. Harry was wearing a yellow shirt that made his eyes look as shiny as coffee beans and Wendy's just washed hair fell in ringlets. Despite the breasts and her new gangly height, she was still my little girl. And Harry's. He beamed at her as he forked the last pancake on to her plate. *"Ess, ess mein kindt,"* he crooned. It was the same benediction we had heard as children. Food is a gift from the heart. It feeds the soul. Like love itself.

So why wasn't my wonderful family enough for me?

I kissed Harry goodbye full on the mouth, surprising him with my ardor. Wendy gave me a quick hug and danced away before I could embarrass her with more. I waved to them through the window and watched them drive away. They had both seemed a bit puzzled by the attention, but pleased. What's gotten into Mom? Intention, that's what. Psychological research has shown that if you wanted to feel more cheerful, hold your head up high, and if you wanted to feel more loving, hug and kiss. And the feeling will follow.

I needed all the help I could get. I did not want to be seduced by Slow Hands. Dalliance was fine for Coralee and The Group; they weren't married. It wasn't fine for me; yet here I was, severely tempted. Yes, I loved Harry, but I also remembered desire. The memory of Simon's lips on mine still burned. It brought me back again to that other time...the time of Thomas.

I left the dishes in the sink, the beds unmade and went down to the basement to unearth the diary. I had hidden it at the bottom of a camp trunk, beneath a pile of old blankets. I had the only key to the trunk. The lock had rusted, and I had to force the trunk open. When I found the diary, its blue satin binding was covered with mold. I brushed away the cobwebs and opened it. The last entry was dated ten years ago; the first, three months before that. I had gone back to Big Sur twice since that first weekend. Ostensibly for yoga.

I turned the pages slowly, recalling that time.

January 18
   So this is what it's like to be besotted. Over the moon. I spend each day in class gazing at Thomas.

No matter where he is in the room, I sense him. When he stops to adjust my position, the hair on the back of my neck rises. We spend each evening in deep conversation, in the dining hall, sitting close, knees touching. Sometimes I see him in the garden, framed by golden sunflowers or purple irises, and he takes my breath away.

January 25

It is the last morning of the yoga retreat. Thomas helps me stow my gear in my car. He holds me close in a warm embrace. "I hate to leave," I murmur.

"Then don't," he says.

"I have to."

"Come back," he urges.

"It's a long way and it's expensive," I demur.

He steps back, looks into my eyes. "You can always stay with me. There's room."

February 12

Friday night and the weather forecast is for heavy rain and thunderstorms. Highway 1 to Big Sur is notorious for its washouts and closures. "Sure you want to go, hon?" Harry asks.

"They're expecting me," I say. Then add, "I'm helping the instructor."

Harry carries my suitcase out to the car. "Drive carefully." He kisses me and checks my seat belt.

The rain is torrential and the drive takes twice as long. The car skids along the dark mountain roads, and I am terrified of plunging off into the Pacific.

I arrive at Temenos, park the car and run down the path to Thomas's cabin. He meets me at the door. "Get out of those wet clothes," he says, and hands me his bathrobe. When I emerge from a hot shower, he has built a fire and poured two snifters of brandy. Bob Dylan is on the tape deck; Thomas sings along softly "Lay, lady, lay. Lay upon my big brass bed."

"You've...you've got a nice voice," I stammer.

"Thank you, ma'am." He taps my glass with his. "Drink up."

I sip the potent liquor slowly. Thomas sits next to me on the couch. He lifts the hem of the bathrobe, "Cold feet, Sara. Come on, put them here." He lays my freezing feet onto his lap and envelops them in his warm hands. His hands are strong and smooth. And large. My breathing slows. The pine scent of wood smoke, Dylan's throaty rasp, the heat of the brandy, I am melting into his hands.

From far away I hear a faint ringing. Thomas doesn't answer it. It goes on and on. I realize it's mine, my cell phone. I reach for my purse.

"Let it ring," Thomas says.

I can't. Somebody might need me. "Hello."

It's Harry. "Did you get there okay? I was worried."

"I'm fine."

"Good, now I can go to bed. Good night, hon."

I hold the phone for a long time. Thomas watches me in silence. Then says softly, "This is not about him, Sara."

But it is. It is now. I retreat to the bathroom, slip

off the robe, dress hurriedly. "I'm sorry. I feel like such a jerk."

I run out into the rain, make it to the car before the tears start. My hands are shaking so hard I can't put the key into the ignition. Just as well. I'd probably crash into a tree. I put my head down and sob. In shame. In gratitude. In loss.

When I get home, I tell Harry the workshop was called off because of bad weather.

I closed the journal. The sun slanted through the basement's dusty windows. It was nearly noon; I had been wandering through my memories for hours. I thought about throwing the journal into the trash, but I couldn't. It was evidence of something important. I placed it back into the trunk, burying it beneath the blankets. It was a testament to a time spent with a man who had awakened a passion in me that had lain dormant until his touch.

I had returned home that night like a grateful convalescent, valuing the everyday, blessed by the presence of Harry and Wendy. My primary values were peace and calm. An affair was not a substitute for a marriage, and Harry's was the only marriage I wanted.

And yet something was missing. Some excitement, some risk, some frisson that would make my pulse race and my heart leap, make me want to wear scarlet lipstick and lace teddies. And now it was back...with the opening of Slow Hands. With the presence of Simon.

Dare I go down that road again? It had almost brought disaster. I could have lost what I valued most for a trivial adventure. And what if it hadn't been trivial? What if I had fallen in love with Thomas? That would have been even worse. And yet I had so wanted what he had brought me that I had been willing to endanger my marriage and my family. But now I could have that excitement as an adjunct to my life, not a replacement. Slow Hands could change all of that. It was a theme park of romance. An in-flight movie. An educational tactile dome where I could live out my fantasies. Explore my sexuality. What woman, if she were truly honest, would never want to experience being with another man? It was the consequences we worried about.

I felt a surge of joy. I had agreed to build Slow Hands at Coralee's insistence, as a memorial to Mom, as a psychological aid to my patients, but now I saw it as something more. It could provide a safe, sexual haven not only for single women but for married women as well. And more...even more...it would provide me with an opportunity to partake of a romance with Simon. A no-holds-barred fling. I could join The Flying Wallendas, but with a net.

A sanctioned, ritualistic meeting at Slow Hands would not impinge on my marriage or the rest of my life. It would be my occasional afternoon exercise. While Harry was playing doubles with his cronies, I could be playing singles with Simon. It would be a game, with rules and a scoreboard. And within those parameters, I would be safe. It would be loving without the danger of falling in love.

I decided to act on my impulse before I lost my nerve. Simon answered the phone on the first ring. "Are you free this afternoon?" I blurted. "There's something important I need to discuss with you."

"I was just about to call you," he said. "I could barely sleep last night."

"Really?" My heart skipped a beat.

"Let's talk about it at lunch," he said. "I'll cook. What would you like?"

"Anything at all. Don't fuss," I admonished and hung up the phone. I raced into the bedroom, tore into my closet, and with trembling hands tried to take my own advice. What did it matter what I wore when I might be taking it off at the first opportunity?

CHAPTER 14

Simon was waiting for me as I pulled up in front of Slow Hands. He rushed out the front door and took both my hands in his. "I'm so glad you're here, Sara. I'm almost at my wit's end."

He drew me into the house and looked both ways before hurriedly closing the door. "New lipstick," he said.

"I don't usually wear red," I babbled, "but this is more a purple-red than an orange-red. So I thought..."

But it was a perfunctory comment; he wasn't looking at me at all but at a large manila envelope in his hand.

"We're in trouble, Sara. We've been found out."

"Found out? But we haven't done anything. Not really. Not yet."

"We've provided all the services we said we would," he said.

"Services?" I asked in confusion. "You and I?"

"Are we talking about the same thing?" he asked.

"Maybe not," I admitted. Too bad, I thought. My personal agenda would have to wait.

He opened the envelope and handed me a letter. "This is from our neighbors."

"From that Rater guy?"

"No, this is from our next-door neighbors. Sandy and Les."

"That married couple?" I asked.

"They're on the other side. These are both women," he said.

"Oh, the lesbians," I said.

"How can you tell?" he asked.

"No makeup and no nonsense." I glanced at the letter. It was single-spaced and three pages long. "So what's the problem?"

"What isn't the problem?" Simon led me into the kitchen where he made us tall Campari and sodas.

As he turned to slice the lemon, I stared at his broad shoulders and back, his narrow hips. Why was I dealing with complaint letters when all I wanted to do was jump his bones? No wonder every civilization has placed taboos on sex; when lust is on your mind, there's no space for anything else.

"They are complaining about the noise. The foot traffic. The hours we keep. The excess garbage. And the document is in serious language, party of the first part, whereby, whereafters..."

"Which one's the lawyer?" I asked.

"Sandy," he said, garnishing my drink with mint. "Les is a radiologist."

"DINKs," I said.

"What?"

"Double Income No Kids. They rule the world."

"They're the only ones who can afford to buy a house." Simon took a healthy slug of his drink.

"Which one is Sandy?" I asked.

"Sandy's taller, more buffed."

"Oh, yes," I said, "I remember seeing them get into their twin Volvos."

"And they keep those cars so clean," Simon added.

"It must be nice to live with someone who picks up after themselves," I mused.

"They're calling back in half an hour, but first, lunch."

Simon placed a plate of pumpernickel and smoked salmon sandwiches in front of us; the brown bread and pink slivers of fish forming a star on the cobalt blue plate. "Well, I don't lean toward the same sex attraction myself, but vive la différence."

I helped myself to a corner of the star. "Sexual attraction is the great mystery. Freud said we marry our parents."

"Jung said we marry the qualities we lack."

"Gloria Steinem said we become the man we want to marry."

Simon popped a sandwich into his mouth. As he chewed, I watched the muscles in his jaw ripple and momentarily lost track of the conversation.

He smiled at me and continued, "So often we love someone for a particular trait, and then we live with them, and it drives us crazy. I once had a girlfriend who was wonderfully efficient. I loved that until she cooked a pot of stew on Mondays and expected us to eat it all week."

"Every trait's got its flip side, and you rarely get one without the other. So you may like the spontaneity, but you also get the irresponsibility. You like the passion, but you get the irrationality. You like the neatness, and you get the nagging. You like the social charm, but then they never want to leave the party."

We finished the salmon, and Simon brought out a bowl of fresh figs and two chilled glasses of vino santo.

"What about you, Sara? What's the flip side of you and Harry?"

"Well, I can't speak for Harry." I sipped the fruity wine. I loved the ceremony of this lunch, how the wine prolonged the pleasure of the food. "But you know what Tolstoy said?"

"All happy families are the same, but each unhappy one is unhappy in its own way," Simon supplied. "So which are you?" His hand covered mine, long, graceful fingers warming my skin.

"I love Harry very much," I said. "And yet..."

"And yet..." he prodded.

"I think there may be something more."

"Like what?"

I thought for a moment. "Curiosity."

"About?"

"About another person. About myself with another person. About that part of me that gets to be evoked, to be discovered, to be played out."

"But surely you've had that with friends?" he said.

"Yes, but when you add physical intimacy to friendship..." I paused, searching for the right metaphor. "It's the difference between poetry and prose."

He closed his eyes, savoring the idea, his hand tightening on mine. I was suffused with warmth. Who was it who said that the largest erogenous zone was the mind?

The phone must have been ringing for some time before we heard it. "I'll get it," I said, "you stay right there."

"Hello." The voice on the phone was cool and crisp. "This is Sandra Cummings, your neighbor. To whom am I speaking?"

"This is Sara Russack," I said. "I'm one of the owners of the house."

"Oh, yes," she said, "you're the older one."

And you get a D for diplomacy, I thought. "How can I help you?"

"Les and I would like to get together. You've read our letter."

"Yes, I have. When would you like to meet?" I asked.

"At your earliest convenience," she snapped.

I matched her tone, "How about right now?"

"Right now?" she said. "Is your sister there? I didn't see her car."

Now I was taken aback. They were watching our cars? "She's out for the day. But my manager and I can see you."

I heard her shout to someone upstairs, heard the muffled consultation, then, "We'll be right over."

They were women of their word. Simon just had time to put out two more wineglasses and some triple crème boursin when there was a knock on the door. I ushered Sandy and Les into the living room, deeming the kitchen too informal. They were clad in their leisure outfits of jeans, turtleneck T-shirts and Pendleton jackets. They both wore penny loafers and matching gold charm bracelets. I marveled at the bracelets; I didn't know they sold them anymore.

Sandy gave Simon a brisk handshake, nodded to me. Les shook my hand and nodded at Simon. They each took a large armchair. Simon proffered the wine and cheese, which they refused.

"Let me come directly to the point," Sandy said. "I take it you can speak for your sister?"

"Certainly at this juncture," I said. Juncture, where had that come from? Legalese was contagious.

"By our calculations, you've owned this house several months," she continued. "The first month was renovation. We endured weeks of construction, sawing, drilling, hammering. Workmen coming and going. But you were completely in your rights." She turned to Les.

"And then Simon moved in," Les continued. "There was a nonending flurry of decorating. Paper hangers, painters, antique dealers, florists. Delivery trucks everywhere. But still you were completely in your rights." Les flashed Sandy a smile at the repeated refrain. They were building their case.

"But then," Les said, throwing the touchdown pass to Sandy.

"Instead of this house being a private residence, you've converted it into a commercial establishment," Sandy accused. "We've seen deliveries of commercial exercise equipment, whirlpool baths, a restaurant-size stove, refrigerator-freezer and dishwasher. Not to mention a laundromat-size washer-dryer."

"And we've seen several women, who do not live at this

address, come and go," Les fairly chortled. "And let me tell you, they were walking differently when they left. Like they'd had a good workout."

"Therefore it is clear to us," Sandy said, "that you are running an illegal establishment. You are serving clients, and no doubt you are charging for those services. And that constitutes a commercial enterprise that is specifically prohibited under the residential zoning law." She stood up, and Les rose with her. "We'll give you thirty days to cease and desist or we'll begin legal proceedings."

"Just a minute, please," Simon said. "We can explain all this."

We can, I thought. How?

" 'There's more in Heaven and Earth than is dreamed of in your philosophy.' " He smiled his most engaging smile.

There was a moment of charged silence as the two women gazed at each other. Then Les smiled softly. "Sandy and I met at a Bennington all-women's production. I was her Horatio. She was my Hamlet."

"I wondered where you two honed those declamatory skills," Simon said, pouring them each a glass of vino santo. He spread the fragrant cheese on slivers of walnut bread and waited until the women had sampled both offerings. "You're quite right in your observations. I'm amazed at your perspicacity. I know how demanding your professions are, law and medicine, jealous mistresses, both, and yet, you have managed to stay *au courant* of our little comings and going."

"It's not that we're nosy," Les said. "But this used to be a very quiet neighborhood."

"We're sorry for any inconvenience we've caused," Simon said quickly. "We can certainly take care of that."

"I'm afraid you don't get it," Sandy said curtly. "We want you out of here. There are plenty of other places you can open a health club."

"Health club..." I gulped. "Is that what you think we're running?"

"Well, with all that equipment," Les said, "what else?"

"And in our opinion, Berkeley does not need another women's health club," Sandy added.

"Maybe not," I blurted. "But what about its first women's bordello?"

"What?" Sandy clutched her wineglass. Les downed hers. Simon looked at me as if I had lost my mind. I was relying on intuition now, trusting in the truth.

"We're not a health club," I said, "not a conventional health club." And I proceeded to tell them about the services that Slow Hands offered. Services I was quite sure Les and Sandy had no interest in or need of. I told them about The Group and how we had selected the Zennies, how the Zennies' attentions differed from those of ordinary men, about the respect they showed the clients, about the gentleness and unrushed quality of their touch. The women listened in rapt attention. There was a long, pregnant silence when I finished.

Simon shot me a troubled glance. I had just provided a savvy lawyer with enough information to throw us in jail.

I couldn't bear the suspense any longer. "So, what do you think?" I asked.

The two women exchanged looks. Then Les reached

into her pocket, extracted a large linen handkerchief and dabbed at her eyes. "It's so sad that women have to pay for it."

Sandy placed her arm around her partner's shoulders. "That's because men don't have a clue. Most men," she qualified, with a nod to Simon.

"Not all lesbians have great sex, either," Les reminded Sandy, squeezing her partner's hand.

"That's right," Sandy said. "Ever hear of lesbian bed death?"

Simon filled our glasses. "Sounds awful."

Sandy sipped her wine, "It is. Women aren't used to initiating sex, so when there are two of them, each waits for the other to make a move."

"It's so important, that part of life," Les said fervently. "No one should be without it." She turned toward Sandy, tenderly stroked her cheek. "Honey, it was hell before I met you. I had guys who tugged my nipples like a milking machine. Couldn't find my clitoris with a Day-Glo compass." She gestured toward us. "They are doing the straight women of American a great service. What do you say, San, shall we give them a chance?"

Sandy hesitated, then meeting Les's gaze, said, "If those Zennies can provide half the satisfaction that we have, the world will be a better place. We'll talk about it and get back to you. Thanks for the refreshments."

"Any time," Simon said. *"Mi casa es su casa."*

"How about good fences do good neighbors make?" Sandy grinned.

Les whispered to me as she left, "I think you're another Mother Teresa."

"Try another Benedict Arnold," Simon crowed as he closed the door. "I couldn't believe it when you told them the truth. I thought we were done for."

"I threw us on the mercy of the court. Those women have suffered through the same indignities of male rejection for not fitting the Barbie doll stereotype, the same male fumbling and ineptitude that all women have. They could empathize."

"I think you handled the situation masterfully."

"It wasn't hard. I really believe in Slow Hands. I want it to survive."

"No more ambivalence?" he asked.

I shook my head.

"What brought about the change?"

I shrugged. "The Group's happiness. The integrity of the Zennies. And—" suddenly I felt shy "—your massage."

"I was happy to provide that."

"I was thinking..." My throat was dry; I swallowed hard. "Maybe I could return the favor."

"Sure," he said, "whenever you like."

"Now?" I said. "To celebrate our victory."

"Sounds great, but there is one more thing."

"What's that?" I ran my hands along his broad shoulders, cupped my hands around his biceps. God, I loved muscles.

Simon leaned back into my touch. "Ralph."

"Ralph who?" I asked dreamily.

"Ralph, the guy across the street."

"The one with the NRA sign," I said. "Very un-Berkeley."

"So is his cottage industry. But he does seem to have some clients, and thanks to us, they can't find a place to park when they want to drop off their films. He's been leaving us messages."

"Like what?" I asked, my hands slipping around his chest, opening his shirt button. "Is this distracting you?"

"I enjoy being distracted," he said, smiling. "Especially by you."

"So what did Mr. Rater say? Is that really his name?"

"His *nom de* film, at any rate. And every video gets the Ralph Rater Seal of Approval. No violence. No sex. No profanity."

"So what does he want from us?" There was only one more shirt button to go.

"He suspects something's going on. Just like Les and Sandy. He can smell it. Our clients look too happy. Too relaxed. Only unlike our lesbian lovelies, he's not getting any, and he doesn't like the fact that someone else is."

I was alarmed now and turned to face Simon. "He doesn't know what's really happening, though. Does he?"

"Not yet," Simon said. "But if he keeps snooping around, it won't be too long before he does."

"Then we've got to keep this guy off our trail. Best way is to give him what he wants. He wants asphalt, we'll give him asphalt to the max. From now on, no Slow Hands parking on Grove. The Zennies can park their van in the garage, and our ladies need to park somewhere else in the neighborhood. Mr. Rater can have the entire block for his video virgins."

"For his video vigilantes, you mean," Simon said. "Those people are downright scary. Why do they wear camouflage?"

"Never mind them. Why are you wearing anything?" I countered.

"I forget," he said with a grin. "Now where were we?"

"I believe we were on our way upstairs," I said. "And I was about to return the favor." I opened the last button on his shirt and gently pulled out his shirttails, exposing his broad tanned chest and firm stomach dusted with golden hair. I couldn't resist bending down to plant a kiss between his sculptured pecs and just as I did, I heard the front door click open.

I wheeled around to see Coralee standing in the doorway. I fell to my knees, speechless. It was Simon who saved the day.

"Did you find it?" he asked calmly.

"What?"

"The button," he said.

"Oh, the button. No, I don't see it."

"Well, never mind. Let it go." He quickly closed his shirt.

I took a deep breath and stood up. An explanation flew to my lips but then I thought, what the hell, I had nothing to apologize for. This is what Slow Hands was all about. I was like a baker sampling the cakes. But right then, I felt more like a kid with her hand in the cookie jar.

"It's not what you think," I said, "Simon and I were just..."

But Coralee wasn't looking at either of us. She collapsed onto the sofa, head in her hands. "Dr. Webb found a lump in my breast."

"Oh, my God, sweetie." I was beside her in a second. "I'm so sorry."

Simon hurried to her other side and took her hand. "Tell me what happened...start from the beginning."

Coralee bit her lip, gave a shuddering sigh and proceeded to describe her visit with Dr. Webb. "It was a routine annual physical. Weight, blood pressure, pap smear, breast exam. He found a lump in my left breast under my arm, about the size of a peanut. It wasn't there before. It could be a benign cyst or it could be malignant. He called down for a mammogram. And they had had a cancellation, so they could fit me in. My first mammogram." She paused, a faint smile. "I felt like a salami on a slicer. But the radiologist read the films right away."

"And..." I said. "What was it? What did he say?" In the silence, I realized I was saying a prayer. Sympathetic magic. On some level, I hoped that I could protect my baby sister; that somehow by due diligence, by bargaining, I could ward this off.

"There's good news and bad news," Coralee said. "Which do you want first?"

"The bad," I said, steeling myself for the worst.

"The good," Simon said, revealing once again his inherent optimism.

"It's cancer," Coralee said. She said the word bravely, full volume. "But it's operable. They think it's in situ, still in the duct. They think they caught it early. That it hasn't spread. That they can remove it."

"Remove it how?" Simon said.

"A lumpectomy, they call it. They'll remove the lump and some of the surrounding tissues. If everything's clean, that's it. They stitch me up, and I go home."

"And if...if...they don't get it all?" I stammered.

"Then...they lop off my breast." Her voice quavered.

"Sweetie." I attempted to draw her into my arms, but she pulled back, reached into her purse for a handful of tissues and loudly blew her nose.

"And anyway," she said, "I still have another one." She stood, squared her shoulders and announced, "I'm going to my room now." I watched her walk away with great dignity and purpose. She wouldn't allow the tears to come until her bedroom door was safely closed. I thought of all the times I had been a witness to Coralee's disappointments, on school tests, with boys, track meets; how Mom and I had learned to let her alone, let the tiger cub lick her wounds. And in her own sweet time, the bedroom door would open, and Coralee would emerge, hungry and ready to talk.

Simon and I sat waiting, listening for Coralee's door to close. When it did, it made the smallest sound, but that sound resonated throughout the house, through the empty rooms. We were alone. The Zennies were at the temple. No clients were scheduled until late afternoon. Slow Hands rested in the dappled morning sunshine. A pleasure dome. And we three, we three proprietors, we three dreamers sat in the midst of our sensuous creation in stunned silence. Mortality had reared its ugly head.

The black worm of extinction had entered our paradise. And all the velvets and silks, and perfumes of Arabia, all the peacock feathers and fur mitts and flattery could not distract or protect us. It could not be ignored or swept away. It had invaded Coralee's body, chewed into her tender vulnerable flesh, and it had to be removed. Immediately. With blood and pain. For it was growing wildly, and if it weren't stopped it would take over its host.

"Is this a punishment?" I whispered.

Simon took my hand, folded it in his. "Only if we make it one," he said.

CHAPTER 15

It was the night before Coralee's surgery. I sat beside her on the hospital bed. She looked so young in the flowered nightgown, her face clean of makeup, blond hair pulled up in a ponytail. "Well, darling," I said, "at least the waiting's over. Sometimes that's the hardest part."

"No, Sarie," she corrected. "I think the hardest part is when the anesthesia wears off."

"Right." I smiled. "Can I get you anything? Videos? Magazines?"

"Not a thing." She lifted a bottle from her nightstand. "Do you know what this is?"

"What?" I studied the purple fluid.

"It's an antiseptic. I had to soap my breasts with it for ten minutes. It's a pre-op precaution, helps reduce infection." She paused. "That's a long time. Ten minutes. I've never touched my breasts, held them for so long." She laid her hand on her chest. "It's a funny thing, I never really liked them. Thought they were too small, too flat. But tonight I thought they were lovely. Soft and warm...and familiar." Her voice choked. "I guess you never really value something until the night before you lose it."

"You'll only be losing a bit of skin and tissue, sweetie. Everything that matters will still be there. You'll still be funny and smart and...beautiful."

"Even if I wake up with one breast gone?"

"We'll deal with that when we have to."

"I've already talked about it with Dr. Webb. There's prostheses. There's reconstruction. They can make it look okay, but the nerve endings will be cut. I won't have as much feeling."

"That will just bring you in line with the rest of us." I attempted another smile. "Would you like me to stay with you tonight?"

"Thanks, Sarie. But it won't be necessary."

"I don't mind. I'd like to. Really. Let me call Harry." I reached for the phone.

Coralee stopped my hand. "I've already got someone to spend the night."

"Who?" I asked. Who could be closer to my sister than I was?

"He's in the lounge waiting. Would you go get him?"

I walked quickly down the short corridor and found Simon pacing in the small visitors' room. The television set blared unwatched. "Sara, I'm so glad to see you," he hugged me. "How is she doing?"

"Fine, I think, considering the circumstances."

"Yes, she's quite wonderful. Would you mind giving me a hand with these? I think I might have gone a mite overboard." He gestured toward a heap of packages. Aromatic candles. Potpourri. A quilted robe and slippers. A box of videos. A large pink satin-and-velvet quilt and four matching pillows.

I reached for the quilt and pillows. "These are lovely. But do you really want to use them in the hospital? They might get stained."

"We're so used to the duvet, we might not be able to sleep without it."

We. There was that word again. Did he mean they had similar duvets...or...

As soon as we entered the room, I saw Coralee's face light up and Simon's mirror that illumination, I knew the answer.

Of course they were sleeping together. They lived in the same house, inches away from each other. Cooked together. Gardened together. Decorated together. Ran the house together. Of course they made love together. Slow Hands was literally a hotbed. How could they not have been infected by the love bug? But then why had Simon given me that massage, and why had he been so willing to receive one? I felt a great rush of jealousy, fiery and ignoble. My sister, one of the three people I loved most in the world, was going under the knife, and I was angry at her.

I brought my attention back into the room. Coralee had slipped into the quilted robe and slippers, lit a scented candle. She and Simon were sorting through the videos trying to decide among "their" favorites. "Which do you fancy, Sara," he asked. *"Annie Hall? Casablanca? The English Patient? When Harry Met Sally?"*

What difference did it make what I fancied? I wasn't going to be watching them, was I?

"I prefer the oldies," I said. "But maybe that's because I'm one myself."

They smiled at my attempted wit, not rising to it or refuting it.

"Well." I dropped the pillows on the foot of the bed. "If there's nothing else you need, I'll be going now." I kissed Coralee on the forehead. She reached out and held me tight. The way she melted against me, her familiar cinnamon smell, she was my baby sister again. And I felt awash with shame.

"Good luck, sweetie," I whispered, my voice choked with tears. "I'll be here when you get out of surgery." I nodded at Simon and beat a hasty retreat.

I climbed into the car, pulled out of the parking lot, rolled up the windows and conjured up my wise woman, Mom.

How can I be so selfish? I railed. So carnal? Corrie is going under the knife, and all I can think about is myself, my horny needs. My crush on Simon. My wanting to "get some." I am despicable.

That isn't all you're thinking about, I hear Mom's voice. *You care about Coralee. You've done everything you can. It's all right to be ambivalent. We are complex creatures. That's what makes us human. Now remember, what are you to do?*

Let the unacceptable feeling speak. Speak from its point of view.

Good. Remember that it doesn't speak for all of you. Just for one part. Let it rip.

He likes her better than me, I wailed. He never looked at me the way he looks at her. They're in love. I can tell.

So?

So...I don't want to lose him.

Lose him?

Lose the feeling.

And what feeling is that?

You know what I'm talking about.

It's been a while. Remind me.

Giddy. Juicy. Young.

Mom hums, *"Some enchanted evening, you will see a stranger..."*

We sing together for a bit.

"Fly to his side and make him your own...."

"Or all through your life you will dream all alone."

Ah, yes, but not exactly true for you. You are not alone. You have Harry.

I love Harry, Mom. But my husband is no romantic stranger.

Isn't that's why you love him?

Yes, of course. I loved him for his familiarity, his dependability, for his lack of mystery. Even the things that drove me crazy about Harry were comforting. Our annoyances were grooved, our arguments choreographed. He might not be Fred Astaire, but I was no Ginger Rogers. I could follow him. But still...

Speak from the unacceptable feeling, she reminded me.

Okay, okay! Screw it all! I want to be swept away.

Sure, so why not? But does it have to be Simon who does the sweeping?

Yes, it has to be Simon. He's captured my imagination,

invaded my pores. Like Thomas, but more so. I love to
hear his voice, touch his lean swimmer's body. I love to
have him serve me food, pour me wine. I love to problem solve together. The dexterous way we handled Les
and Sandy. The plan we concocted for Ralph Rater. Over
the three months we've been running Slow Hands, we've
built a relationship. I don't want it to end.

Well, what do you suggest?

Give him up? No! Steal him away from Coralee? Not
likely! Then what? Share! Of course, isn't that what sisters do? There's enough for both. That's what you used
to say, Mom. "Take turns. Or I'm taking that toy away."

Good girl. Enough already. Let me go home. I'm tired.

Mom, wait. Coralee is going to be all right, isn't she?

I hope so.

Don't you know?

I'm dead, darling, not psychic.

But I'm so worried.

*That's why God invented marriage. When times get
rough, you circle the wagons. Go home and see your
cowboy.*

When I arrived home, my John Wayne was waiting for
me in the living room. He had stopped at The Mandalay,
an excellent Burmese restaurant, braved the nearly im-
possible parking situation and brought home an array of
our favorites: coconut chicken soup, mango prawns,
mushu pork. Wendy spooned them into our good dishes;
Harry opened a bottle of chilled Chardonnay for us and
made Wendy a very light wine spritzer.

It was Friday night; I covered my head with a lace

scarf and lit the Sabbath candles. "Let's hold hands," I said, "I want to say a prayer for Aunt Coralee."

Harry's hand was warm and strong, Wendy's cool and delicate. This tight little circle that I cherished and had taken so much for granted. The world is a dangerous, uncertain place. Earthquakes and fires. Terrorists and crashes. Heart attacks and cancer. When everything falls away, all we have is each other. I looked from one loved face to the other. My husband. My child. Coralee needed that, too.

I didn't sleep much that night, waking up every few hours with a dry mouth and racing heart. I alternated between guzzling water and going to the bathroom. I finally lifted the blanket in which Harry had buried himself and curled against his side, waiting for the dawn. Listening to Harry's deep regular breathing comforted me. I remembered Coralee's favorite toy. Mom had bought it for her when she was three, when Coralee had to spend a night in the hospital to get her tonsils removed. It was a fuzzy brown teddy with a tiny motor placed in its chest. When you held it to your face, it ticked at the same rate as a mother's heartbeat.

"I wish she still had that bear," I said.

"The Heartbeat Bear?" Harry asked. I nodded. Of course Harry knew about the bear. In a long-term marriage you speak in shorthand from a shared memory bank. Sure, you know what he's going to say before he says it; but he also knows the word you mean when you forget it. Right then, I longed to tell Harry about the true nature of Slow Hands and even about Simon. I hated keeping things from him. During that crazy time with

Thomas it was the dissembling, the evasions that pained me even more than the possible infidelity.

But how could I tell him about Slow Hands? His wife, mother to his child, upstanding therapist, pillar of the community running a brothel...for other wives, mothers, pillars? I sighed deeply, feeling the weight of my secrecy and burrowed into his arms. He kissed the top of my head. "She's going to be all right, Sarie. I'll make us some coffee, we'll read the paper, and then it'll be time to call the hospital."

The smell of Harry's Viennese Blend lured me from bed. I took the section of the paper that he handed me but read nothing except my horoscope. "Libra...an unexpected event turns out to be for the best although it may not seem that way now." I read it out loud to Harry even though I knew he put no faith in it. Harry was a scientist, a pragmatist; he believed in what could be proven. I didn't really believe in horoscopes myself, but I still consulted them. This morning, I read Coralee's as well. "Pisces...rough waters this week, little fish, but if you keep on swimming and never mind the waves, you will reach the other shore." Like all oracles, it could be read several ways. What other shore?

Sipping my coffee, I phoned the hospital and waded through the interminable labyrinth of recordings until I finally got the nurse on the surgical ward. Coralee was out of the operating room, in recovery, and I could talk to her doctor.

"This is Dr. Webb," a warm, deep voice said.

"I'm Coralee's sister...."

"Oh, yes, Sara. She's told me all about you."

"How is she?" I asked.

"Doing well. She's still a bit groggy, but she should be ready for visitors by this afternoon."

"Did you..." I stammered.

"I'll let her tell you all about it herself," he said and rang off.

Visiting hours began at one. I bought an armload of yellow daffodils, half a dozen country-and-western CDs and a giant box of chocolates. Harry had to take care of an emergency dry socket, and Wendy had a soccer game, so I was alone. I opened the door to Coralee's room gingerly. She was awake, propped up on a stack of pillows. She managed a smile when she saw me and tried to stretch out her arms in greeting, but the slightest movement made her grimace.

I lowered myself carefully onto the side of her bed and stroked her hand. "Hurts a lot?"

"Only when I move," she said.

"Then don't," I said. "Tell me what you want and I'll get it."

"A hug," she whispered.

I leaned forward, laying my cheek against hers. "You feel warm," I said and placed my lips against her forehead.

"Mom's thermometer," she said.

I laced my fingers through hers. "Want to talk about it?"

"Didn't Dr. Webb tell you?"

"Just that things went well."

I waited. There was a long silence. We glanced out the window, watching the branches of the bare trees sway in the wind, and just breathed together.

"They called it a bilateral subcutaneous mastectomy," she said.

I swallowed hard. "What does that mean?"

"It's like scooping out a cantaloupe...you remove the pulp and keep the rind. So they scooped out the flesh and kept my skin and nipples and then filled the cavities with implants." She paused, attempted a smile. "You know, sort of like stuffing a mushroom. My specialty."

"But why?" I asked.

"When they did the biopsy on my left breast, it was just over the limit for a lumpectomy. Then they checked the right breast, and it had abnormalities as well. I was awake. Dr. Webb gave me a choice. They could remove the lumps, and I could come in every six months for another mammogram and another possible lumpectomy for any suspicious growth. Or I could be done with it, once and for all. I chose peace of mind over my mammary glands." She gave a little hiccuping laugh. "Do you suppose it's the Zennies' influence?"

"Peace and harmony, could be," I said.

"They did it all at once. Out with the old. In with the new. Saline. Like the sea," her voice wavered.

I remembered a thirteen-year-old Coralee, in a summer beach cottage Mom had rented, proudly lifting up her T-shirt so I could see her budding breasts.

"They're pretty stiff right now," she said. "They're still bandaged. And they're numb. I can't feel a thing. But Dr. Webb says they'll soften, and some of the nerve endings will come back. The main loss is the milk ducts. They had to remove them, so I won't be able to nurse a baby." She paused. "It's funny, I never thought of nursing a baby before. In fact, I never thought of having a baby before."

"But now you do?" I asked.

"I don't know," she mused. "Maybe? I always thought I'd have all the time in the world. It's amazing what a little brush with death will do. Two brushes, really. First Mom, now this. It kind of makes you realize what's important. What really matters." She leaned back upon the pillows, fatigued. "Could you put on some music?"

We were listening to the last track, a typical Chekhovian tale, a missed moment, about a man trying to muster the courage to approach an attractive woman at a neighboring bar stool, and when he finally does she's gone, when Simon entered.

He went immediately to Coralee's side, took both her hands in his. "Thank God it's over," he said.

"I lost them," Coralee whispered, "both of them."

"I'm so sorry," he said, his voice choked with tears. "You'll miss them."

"So will you," she replied. "You liked them."

"Yes," he said, "they were beautiful. But what's behind them is much more important." He bent and kissed her forehead. "You. I love you."

Coralee sighed sleepily. "That's good, Simon. But I have to rest now." She yawned and stretched, grimaced as the stitches pulled, and closed her eyes. Simon tucked the covers gently around her. We watched as her breathing became slow and quiet.

A nurse entered, checked Coralee's pulse, made a notation on the chart. "She'll be out for a couple of hours," the nurse said. "Don't worry about her. We'll be checking her frequently."

"Want to get some coffee?" I asked Simon.

"I'm afraid I have no appetite," he said. "And I want to be here when she wakes up."

"Sure," I said, "I understand. See you back at Slow Hands?"

"Could you take over this afternoon?"

"I'm seeing patients," I said.

"The Zennies can do it, then. Jonathan's second in command. He knows the drill."

"I'll give him a call. You'll be there tonight, right?"

"I'll do my best." He turned back to Coralee, tenderly brushing the damp hair from her brow.

I walked out into the parking lot and couldn't remember where I had parked my car. When I finally found it, I couldn't locate my keys. When I found the keys I took a wrong turn to my office. When I got to the office, my first patient had canceled, which was a good thing, as I was much too agitated to be of help to anyone.

Coralee and Simon were lovers. They had been for a while. And today he had said he loved her. That was a great thing for Coralee. But what did it mean for the future of Slow Hands? And what did it mean for mine?

CHAPTER 16

Three days later, Coralee came home from the hospital. She called me that morning from Slow Hands. "Come on over, Sara. I want you to see the unveiling. Dr. Webb has removed the bandages."

I drove to the market, picked up a lavish basket of fresh fruits and exotic berries, and sped over the bridge to Berkeley. I let myself into the house and was greeted warmly by Jonathan. "She's doing great," he said. "She's upstairs in Simon's room. It gets the morning light."

Coralee was propped up on the pillows bathed in sunlight. I sat down on the side of the bed and embraced her gingerly. She drew me closer. "I'm still pretty tender," she offered. "But it feels so good to hug you." She smiled. "Ready?"

"Sure." I took a deep breath and watched as she slowly opened her nightgown.

Her skin was blue with bruises; the stitches were swollen black tracks, but her breasts were round and high and adorned with Coralee's own proud pink nipples. I placed my fingers in my mouth and whistled. Coralee laughed out loud. The wolf whistle was Mom's gift; she had painstakingly taught it to us both, rationing its use to hailing taxi cabs and acknowledging rare beauty.

"You like them?" Coralee asked.

"They're gorgeous," I said.

"And they'll never sag. Dr. Webb said I'll have the perkiest boobs in the old age home."

"I'm jealous," I said.

"Don't be." Her face darkened.

"Just kidding, sweetie."

"Don't be mad at me, Sara. I have something I have to tell you." She buttoned her nightgown.

That lead-in is never good; I sat up straighter.

"It's about Simon and me."

I was sure I knew what was coming, but my psychological training had taught me the virtue of patience. Let the information come to me. Let Coralee tell it in her own way. Don't make assumptions. Listen with an open mind.

"It's not anything we planned," Coralee began. "It just happened."

"What's that?" I asked, my tone measured, noncommittal.

"Simon and I are in love."

"I could see that at the hospital," I said. "That's great." I was thinking fast. That condition would end my budding flirtation with Simon, but it shouldn't have to affect Slow Hands. I was so lost in my thoughts that I barely heard Coralee's next statement and had to ask her to repeat it.

"And we're planning to get married," she said.

"Wow, that is big news," I gulped. "When did all that happen?"

"It's been growing. We've gotten closer every day. And then this," she said as she touched her breasts. "It's a real wake-up call—when the chips are down, all that matters is the people you love." She smiled at me tenderly. "And right now that means you, big sister, and Simon." She leaned back against the pillows. "So are you okay with this?"

"I guess so. I mean...sure...have you set a date for the wedding?"

"As soon as we can get it together. And we want you to be the matron of honor and Harry to be the best man. I can't wait for Harry and Simon to meet. And the Zennies as ushers and The Group as bridesmaids."

"The whole extended family," I said in an attempt at levity.

"We're definitely going to miss them," Coralee said.

"Miss them?" I echoed blankly.

"After we've gone," she said. "Sara, you do realize that Simon and I will be leaving Slow Hands."

"But...but why?" I stammered.

"It just isn't the place we want to start our new life."

"What new life?"

"We want to open a restaurant, build it from scratch, design it, decorate it, plan the menu. You know what a great cook Simon is. And the concept, Sara, the concept is a gem."

"I can hardly wait to hear it."

Missing my irony, Coralee rushed on. "Food for love. 'If music be the food for love, play on.' From Shakespeare. Simon came up with it. And everything on the menu will be an aphrodisiac...oysters, asparagus, chocolate. So what do you think?"

Abandon me and Slow Hands to open a lousy restaurant! I was furious. I was devastated. But one look at Coralee's flushed cheeks and shining eyes filled me with confusion. She hadn't looked this happy in years. I couldn't burst that balloon, not after all she had gone through. My thoughts were racing. If Jonathan took over Simon's role, and I filled in on Coralee's duties, perhaps the rest would fall into place. The first precept of Zen is that the only constant is change. "If that's what you and Simon want," I mustered, "we can manage."

Coralee let out a mighty sigh. "Oh, thank you, Sarie. I told Simon I had the best sister in the world."

"Did Simon think I would object?" I asked.

"To quote him, 'She's going to blow a gasket.'"

"Well, I guess he doesn't know me very well," I said.

"Not the way I do." She smiled. "So when do you want to see the lawyer?"

"What lawyer?"

"You know, Mom's lawyer."

"Why should we go see John Duffy?"

"So I can get my money out," she said.

"Why do you need your money?"

"To open the restaurant, of course."

"Wait a minute," I cried. "You and Simon are not just leaving Slow Hands, you want to close it."

"Sarie," she said evenly, "we want to do nothing of the kind. We're happy to have you keep running it. Alone or with a new partner. Whatever. We don't even want a percentage, even though we both helped to establish it. All I want is my half of Mom's inheritance."

"Oh, that's all is it?" I snapped. "Well, you can't have it."

"It's my money, Sara."

"You know the conditions of Mom's will. A joint business or no dough."

"We followed the dictum, we opened the joint business. And if it's mutually agreeable, we can now dissolve it."

"Well it isn't," I said. "No way."

"Sarie, please." Her voice softened. "Don't make this difficult."

"I will not dissolve this business. It's too important."

"To whom?" she asked quietly.

"To my patients. To women's liberation, and," I confessed, "to me."

"Yes, I know," Coralee said. "Simon said you and he were getting very close."

"It's not just that. Simon's a great guy. I admit I was attracted to him. We flirted a bit. He gave me a wonderful massage, but Slow Hands is bigger than me and Simon. And it's bigger than you and Simon, too. We've begun a revolution, something Mom would have been proud of. Since the beginning of time women have lived to please men—now it's time to even the score. It's our birthright. Desire. Passion. Sexual fulfillment. I am not going to give that up for another stupid theme restaurant."

Her face flushed angrily. "Is that what you think about Food for Love?"

"There are lots of places for a woman to be well fed,

Coralee, but where else can a woman be well satisfied? And on her own terms," I retorted. "I can understand that you and Simon want to open a restaurant, but why can't you still be part of Slow Hands?"

"For two good reasons, Sarie. Love and money. Simon and I want to love each other exclusively and we haven't a dime."

"Take out a loan," I said.

"We can't. Our credit's maxed out."

"Well, you'll just have to wait then."

"We're not willing to wait. We want to start our life together, buy a house, have a baby. The one good thing this cancer has taught me is that all we ever have is time. And I want to make the most of it. All I want is what you already have. A husband. A child. A home. Come on, Sarie, say you understand."

I did understand. I knew how much Coralee loved Wendy, what a comfort it was to her being with me and Harry after Mom's death. What Simon's presence had meant to her healing. "I'm not stopping you from leaving. Or from marrying Simon. Or from having a baby. But I won't let you destroy Slow Hands."

"This is all about money," she said bitterly.

"You made a commitment. You signed an agreement."

"I know," she cried. "And now I want out. Please, Sara."

I was shaking but adamant. "Damn it, Coralee," I shouted. "Be reasonable. The business has real potential. The Zennies are flourishing. The Group is healing." And, ignominious though it was, I was still curious about where my own experimentation might lead. "The answer is no."

Coralee's eyes filled with tears.

I turned and fled the room before I might be tempted to back down.

CHAPTER 17

I waited nervously, but Coralee didn't bring up the subject again. I consulted John Duffy and was assured that there were no loopholes; neither of us could get our money out as long as the business was extant. I had no intention of closing its doors, not after we had come so far. So Coralee and Simon continued to live at Slow Hands just as they always had, and the house ran beautifully. The rooms were filled with fresh flowers and log-stacked fireplaces. The food and drink were sumptuous and plentiful. The Zennies smiled, and The Group glowed. The only change was that Coralee now shared Simon's upstairs bedroom, and they used her former bedroom as a study. Yet somehow I was sure I had not heard the last of this. I knew my sister well enough to know that she hadn't given up.

The weeks wore on through an exceptionally cold and rainy month, and then in February, as is often the case in California, a warm front gifted us with balmy weather, and the plum and cherry trees blossomed overnight. Coralee, Simon and I were sitting in the dining room around the refectory table going over the books. Simon served us each a steaming cappuccino, a pistachio biscotti and a tangy passion fruit-and-mango granita he had just concocted.

"Molto bene," I said.

"Mille grazie, signora," he answered and bowed from the waist.

"Next best thing to being in the Piazza San Marcos," I said.

"Funny you should mention Venice—that's where we thought we would go for our honeymoon," Simon said. The froth of the steamed milk dotted his upper lip. My hand went up instinctively to brush it away, but Coralee was there first and deftly scooped it into Simon's waiting mouth. And as he licked the froth off her finger, I felt my stomach churn. I was swept with confusion, melting warmth for their happiness, followed by deep sexual longing.

"It's the most romantic city," Coralee said. "We thought we'd start there and then Rome, Florence, maybe Lake Como."

"When?" I asked.

"April," Simon said. "Winter's over and not too many tourists. And by then Coralee will be off her meds and have a clean bill of health."

Coralee had handled her surgery so well I had almost forgotten about it. She was energetic, back to her photography and aerobics. And whenever I asked, she replied that she was great, not to worry. It seemed she wanted to

put the surgery in the past, just as she had the unpleas-
antness about leaving Slow Hands. I was grateful that
both crises seemed over.

"Congratulations. So when are you going to tell everyone?"

"How about Valentine's Day? Seems appropriate,"
Simon said.

"We thought we'd have a party," Coralee added. "For
the Zennies and The Group. And it might be a good time
to invite some new members."

"Sure," I said, "as long as we keep it low-key and word
of mouth. I can ask The Group to bring a few guests."

"They've been begging to bring their relatives and
friends," Simon said.

"What's the theme going to be?" I asked.

"Masked ball, à la Venezia," Coralee said and reaching for a portfolio added, "here are the invitations."

It was a photograph of a man and woman, in silhou-
ette, climbing into a steaming hot tub wearing nothing but
elaborate feathered masks. I recognized Coralee's perky
new breasts and, I imagine, Simon's similarly perky
organ. I opened the invitation and there in elaborate calligraphy was the summons. "An exotic erotic happening.
February 14. Beginning at 9:00 p.m. Slow Hands. By invitation only. Come as your favorite libertine. Be prepared to live out your deepest sensual fantasies. Romantic
Food. Stimulating Drink. Titillating Entertainment."

"You're coming, of course?" Coralee asked.

I usually spent Valentine's Day with Harry. But we
could go out to dinner before, I reasoned, and I could stop
by later. Harry was used to my checking on the board-

inghouse at odd hours. At the beginning, Harry had been curious about our venture, asking to visit, but I had staved that off by declaring it not yet ready, and he was being his usual patient and, more likely, distracted self. "Sure," I said, "I might be a bit late, but I wouldn't miss it for the world."

It appeared that The Group shared my sentiments. In fact at the next therapy session that was all they talked about.

"I always hated Valentine's Day. I wouldn't open the mailbox," Laura confessed. "All I did was buy three pounds of chocolate truffles, gorge and purge. But this year, it's my favorite holiday."

"I was supposed to be in Denver on a deposition," Mary Ann said, "but I canceled it. Look, I told them, I have a life. And it's true. For the first time."

Grace opened a large shopping bag and pulled out an elaborate headdress, all black sequins and bugle beads attached to a black lacy veil. As she slipped it on, it transformed her. "Mata Hari, *c'est moi.*"

"Guess who I'll be?" Terry said. In a throaty whisper, she sang, "Happy birthday, Mr. President. Happy Birthday to you."

"Marilyn," I said. I remembered seeing the movie star in a video in that flesh-colored mermaid dress, crooning birthday greetings to the young, virile president of the free world with whom she had just made love. "People say she's trashy," I had said to Mom.

"Moral indignation is just envy with a halo," Mom had mused.

"Do you remember that picture of Marilyn?" Grace

asked. "The one from *The Seven Year Itch* in the white halter dress?"

"The one with her standing over the grate with her skirt blowing, up," Laura added.

"And she's trying to hold it down," Terry laughed, "but not really."

"Arthur Miller had a fit," Mary Ann sighed. "Or was it Joe DiMaggio? What's wrong with those guys? They marry the sexiest woman in the world, and then they try to tame her."

"She was a modern day Aphrodite," I said. "Our goddess of love."

"I remember this one picture," Grace said. "She was entertaining the troops in Korea. The photographer shot her from behind. She's standing with her legs wide open, her arms outstretched, and you can see the faces of thousands of soldiers going absolutely bonkers."

"Makes you proud to be a woman," Terry said.

"But she was desperately unhappy." Laura gulped her diet soda. "She had no self-confidence. She suffered terrible stage fright. She lived on tranquilizers, and she committed suicide."

"That was forty years ago," I said. "If Marilyn were here today, her life would be different. That was before women's lib and before Slow Hands."

"That's right." Terry smiled. "If Marilyn had Jonathan, she would never have had problems with self-worth."

"She needed a Zennie to appreciate her mind," Laura added.

"And her soul," Mary Ann said.

"We are very lucky women," Terry pronounced. "And

we are breaking new ground. I don't know about the rest of you, but I'm feeling pretty good."

"That's great, Terry. What about the rest of you? Can we go around the group," I asked. "A weather report?"

Laura was next. "I came into therapy because of my eating disorder, and I realized thanks to you and The Group and Slow Hands that I had a pleasure disorder, a perfection disorder...that food was just a symptom. Life wasn't something to be afraid of. Life was a banquet and all those riches were my birthright. And I was worthy of them."

"I thought I was too old for love," Grace said. "When my husband left I felt that was the end of my life as a woman. I looked in the mirror, and all I saw were wrinkles and sags. I thought that no one would ever want me again. And now, I know," she said, "if you want to be young forever, break the mirror."

"Or see yourself through the eyes of a young, appreciative lover," Mary Ann said.

"It's all perspective," Laura added, "attitude. It's our mind that makes something good or bad. Our judgmental, fault-finding mind that focuses on what's missing, what's wrong."

"Sound like we're all getting a dose of Zen pillow talk," Grace said.

"So all we have to do is quiet our monkey minds," Terry said.

"And be fully present," Mary Ann added. "Be in our bodies. Be with nature. Know that death is always on our right shoulder, and the saddest thing is to die without having fully lived."

It seemed an opportune moment to bring up Coralee. "Well, speaking about the impact of a brush with mortality, I'd like to share some happy news about Simon and Coralee." I paused for effect. "Guess what? They are planning to get married."

The moment of easy silence that greeted my announcement clearly told me that it came as no surprise. Had Coralee informed them? Or was the love affair obvious, and only I had been blind to it?

"They are such a lovely couple," Laura sighed. "I hope they get married while I'm still thin."

Grace smiled. "I wonder if we'll be invited?"

Mary Ann's dark eyes flashed. "They'd damned well better include us. We're their best customers."

"Not for long," I said. That got their attention. All four women leaned forward, fully alert now. I felt a small rivulet of satisfaction at possessing at least some information they didn't already know.

"You mean they're going to leave Slow Hands to enter monogamy?" Terry asked.

"Oh, that's terrible," Laura said. "The place won't be the same without them."

"And that's just half of it," I blurted.

"What do you mean?" Mary Ann demanded.

Since I had already revealed more than I had originally intended, I decided to tell it all, to share the worst case scenario. "Coralee wants to cash in her share of the business." Granted Coralee had not brought up the issue recently, but if I knew my sister, she was strategizing right now, scouring legal precedent, consulting psychics, whatever it took.

This was the perfect opportunity to protect Slow Hands. The Group had a vested interest in our enterprise and could be counted upon to be discreet; I plunged ahead.

"So what I thought we could do is to divide her share in four equal parts." I was thinking out loud now but confident I was on the right track. "The investment is quite manageable, and you'd each get a fair share of the profits."

There was a long nonplussed silence. Grace was the first to speak, her voice dulcet and measured as always. "It's not that I'm not interested, Sara. It's an honor to be asked. It's just that my capital is rather tied up right now."

Terry quickly agreed. "Me, too, Sara. No cash flow. The market is terrible."

"I've still got my student loans to pay off," Laura demurred. "And I can't touch my trust fund."

Mary Ann just smiled. "I love Slow Hands, but I never mix business with pleasure."

"I see." I kept my expression even, but I was in turmoil. I thought they'd be fighting for the chance to buy in. But when it came to money, as Mom used to say, all bets were off. So it became even clearer that I could not agree to Coralee's breaking our partnership. The survival of Slow Hands depended on our staying together. And Mom would have wanted that, I reasoned. After all, those were the explicit instructions of her will. Although I did hear Mom's nagging whisper, *A restaurant is also a business, Sara.*

It's not Slow Hands, I silently said.

Self-interest or generosity? It's a tough call.

Food for the body or food for the soul, Mom?

I turned back to the group. "Thank you all for considering the offer. But please don't feel any pressure. Slow
Hands will continue as usual. See you all next Monday
at the Valentine's Day Party. The Exotic Erotic Ball."

CHAPTER 18

More chocolates and roses are sold on Valentine's Day than all other holidays put together. And Lord help the man who forgets; women never do. When I was in the third grade, I had dutifully punched out Archie and Veronica valentines and written the name of each child in Miss Rooney's class, boys and girls alike, in block letters on the small white envelopes. Democracy reigned. Even when Wendy was in grade school, progressive though it was, the rule was either you brought Valentines for everyone or you didn't bring any at all. Through the generations, bureaucracy tried to protect the tender heart. But it never worked. Obligatory affection never worked. The recipient always saw through it, for the essence of self-esteem was being chosen for oneself.

I decided to make Harry's mother's meat loaf for dinner. Meat loaf à la Mildred. Harry still thought his mother was a divine cook, a composite of Julia Child and Erma

Bombeck. I would not disabuse him of the notion that *The Joy of Jewish Cooking* revolved around canned mushroom soup, miniature marshmallows and dried onion flakes. Three ubiquitous ingredients that lent their synthetic presence to an array of dishes.

I poured out half an envelope of the dried onion into a bowl, added a beaten egg, a few pours of bread crumbs, a few squirts of ketchup, blended them to form a thick brown paste and mixed them by hand into the ground meat. I remembered the first time I had made meat loaf à la Mildred in the tiny kitchen of our first apartment, a basement studio in the upper Bronx. Harry and I were both in graduate school.

As a wedding gift Mildred had given me, along with Harry's baby book, a metal flowered box filled with index cards, each card neatly printed with a recipe. Each recipe was headed by Harry's Favorite...as in Harry's Favorite Jell-O mold, Harry's Favorite Potato Salad, Harry's Favorite String Bean Casserole. Most contained at least one of the holy trinity of additives.

In those days I followed recipes as if I were conducting a science experiment. I used pyrex measuring cups and nested measuring spoons and rubber spatulas. I had made meat loaf à la Mildred on our first Valentine's Day. I planned it as a surprise. When I heard Harry's key in the door, I ran into the bathroom. He sniffed loudly. "Mama's meat loaf," he cried happily. I flung open the bathroom door, naked except for a tiny apron, "Bet your Mama never served this."

That was a long time ago, but it still made me smile. All I remember was that we were ravenous afterwards and ate the burned meat loaf straight from the pan.

Maybe it's always like that at the beginning. Exciting. Playful. Lusty. And then you get used to each other for good and for bad. I remember the fights, the sulks, the freezes. We don't do that anymore, and I don't miss it. We've become each other's best friend, but when I first met Harry he drove a motorcycle and wanted to sculpt marble in Carrara.

Where is the girl who dared to wear a tiny white apron that barely covered her crotch, and where is the boy who jumped over the couch to tear open the strings? Well, at least this time the meat loaf would be a winner.

I set the table with a lace cloth, dusted it with candy hearts and in the center placed red beeswax candles and an extravagant vase of blush pink tulips. Do the act and the feeling will follow. Set a romantic table and perhaps the appropriate emotions will flow. I had high hopes for a gracious family dinner until the door was flung open, and Wendy stormed through the house and ran up the stairs.

Clearly, things had not gone well for her on this Valentine's Day. "Hi, honey," I called, just to acknowledge her presence. To honor her privacy, I kept my tone neutral and said nothing more. She would come down when she was good and ready, and the worst thing I could do would be to force the issue. She'd been like that since she was in diapers. She had to work things out herself, and then when she was in control of her feelings and had a point of view, she would be willing to talk about it. In that way, she was just like her Aunt Coralee. No wonder Coralee understood her, sometimes better than I did.

I speculated on the cause of her distress: grades, girlfriends, some boy. Sometimes it could be as small a cause as her skin breaking out or losing a basketball game, but usually it was romantic rejection. The wag who said it was better to have loved and lost than never to have loved at all should have been pilloried. Those rejections left their mark; you pulled out the nails but the holes were still there. I remembered every boy who turned me down, dropped me, chose another. It made me more gun-shy of the next encounter, and in self-protection, I retreated. Isn't that what I had done with Thomas? Left him before he could leave me? And with Simon? Had there been opportunities, subtle invitations that I had ignored, out of fear of getting hurt?

And yet I dearly wanted that headlong rush into desire where nothing else in the world mattered but that man— his eyes, his mouth, his hands. It made me feel so alive. Without it there was a Grand Canyon between my heart and my head.

I wiped my hands on my apron. I had resurrected the filmy white one from my honeymoon days, only this time I had tied it over my jeans and sweatshirt. I wondered if Harry would notice. It was Wendy who made the first comment as I climbed the stairs. She had just emerged from the bathroom, face freshly washed, eyes still puffy. She slipped by me into her room, fell upon the bed. The open door was my invitation to enter. I sat down beside her.

"How come you're wearing an apron?" She poked an inquisitive finger at the ruffles.

"Kind of a joke," I said. "Just something silly that once happened between Dad and me."

She lifted her head with interest. "Like what?"

"It was a long time ago," I said.

"Tell me." She rested her head on my lap, closed her eyes. "I need to hear something funny."

So I told her. When I had finished, she popped open her eyes and let out a whoop of laughter. "You should do it again," she said.

"I don't think so," I demurred. "The apron won't begin to cover half of what it used to."

"Don't worry about me. I'm not even going to be here."

"You're not going to be here for dinner?"

"I'm going to Angie's with all the other rejects. We're going to rent horror movies and pig out on junk food."

"So...that guy..."

"Dave...the babe...weaseled out of the dance."

"Why?" I asked.

"Who knows?" she said. "He found someone he liked better. Someone prettier. And don't tell me I'm pretty, because I'm not."

"You have beautiful eyes and hair...." I began.

"And lousy skin, and I look like a beanpole."

"You look just like your Aunt Coralee at your age. And isn't she beautiful?"

"Now," she admitted grudgingly.

"She always was, and so are you."

"Right." Her tone was rich with irony. She grabbed her sweater and headed for the door. As I watched her leave, jaw set, shoulders hunched, I wished there were a junior version of Slow Hands. An introductory course. No sex but lots of male attention and appreciation.

So Harry and I had Valentine's dinner alone, and I did

wear the apron. Harry didn't remember it; although he immediately recognized meat loaf à la Mildred. But then again, this time I wore the apron over and not instead of my clothes. So you could say I didn't give him a strong enough hint. And Harry, like most guys, needed a lot of hints. He ate two helpings of meat loaf, though, thanked me effusively for the wonderful meal and brought me a nicely prewrapped box of vanilla-scented bath salts. Harry dutifully remembered the holidays, and now that I had asked him not to frequent chocolate shops, I had a bathroom cabinet filled with mimosa soap and mango moisturizer and sea island sponges. Harry kept me clean and smelling like the tropics.

As I served the cheesecake, store-bought but topped with fresh strawberries, Harry glanced through the paper and noticed, as if by surprise, there was a Golden State Warriors game tonight.

"Do you mind if I watch?" he inquired. "It's a really important game." They all were. No, I said, I didn't mind at all. As a matter of fact, I had a tenants' meeting at the boardinghouse so I was just going to do the dishes and head off.

"I'll do the dishes, hon." He paused, scrutinizing me. "And, hey, isn't that the apron that burned the meat loaf?"

"You remembered," I said.

"You can still set off my fire alarm." He grinned and gave me a big hug.

I returned the hug, planted a kiss on his bald spot and felt a twinge of guilt. Perhaps this was a night to stay home. But the party was just one evening, I reasoned, and Harry was forever. I waved a cheerful goodbye and promised to be home by midnight.

I had already stashed my costume in the car. I had rented it in the Castro, at a place called Uncle Mame, that billed itself as the ultimate in leather fantasies. I had chosen the most modest of the dominatrix offerings, and even so, I was grateful that the outfit came with a full mask. My superego would be concealed so my id could fly.

I drove the few blocks to the darkened branch library and parked beside it. Slipping out of my daytime clothes, I slithered into my black latex cat suit, fastened the silver chains under my breasts, laced up the thigh-high patent leather boots. In the accessory bag I found a two-foot braided leather whip. I couldn't wait to try it out. Flinging open the car door, I leaped out on to the sidewalk. "Submit, dog," I cried, cracking the whip. I heard a thud and wheeled around to see a black lab fall to the ground and present his belly. The dog was immediately joined by its owner, Julian Moore, the librarian. "I'll do anything you want," he squealed with pleasure. I jumped back into the car and roared away, shaking with laughter. I couldn't wait to tell Harry. Julian Moore was such a prig; he kept *Lady Chatterly's Lover* under lock and key.

Then I remembered I couldn't tell Harry. That was one of the unsuspected deprivations of this "double-life"; I couldn't tell Harry the funny bits or the sad bits or the happy bits. I was used to sharing my life with him; it was a strain trying to remember what I could and couldn't say. Associations were tricky, and I found myself frequently censoring a thought or deflecting it midway; deception was energy depleting. Would there ever be a time when I could tell Harry? Would he understand? Not likely. Accept? Never. I was too attached to Slow Hands to endanger it. It was my secret, and I would pay the price of keeping it.

I could hear the music blasting as I parked the car. Fortunately it was mellow body-soothing reggae that made you want to shake your moving parts. The door was unlocked and I let myself in. Simon and Coralee had outdone themselves. The house was a veritable theme park of love. Candles were everywhere, short and tall, bedecked with ribbon, dozens of flower-shaped scented votives floating in vases and punch bowls. The walls had been draped in red velvet swags and the ceiling festooned with billowing pink chiffon to resemble Scheherazade's tent. The buffet table was laden with the most succulent morsels, silvery oysters and mushrooms topped with pecans and strawberries dipped in heavy chocolate, all finger food, all to be fed to one another. And as I glanced around the room, people were doing just that. Devils and angels, knights and ladies, nuns and priests were slipping up their face masks to reveal broad smiles and open waiting mouths.

A favorite teaching tale sprung to mind. A parable about Heaven and Hell. In Hell there are two groups of people seated at each side of an enormous banquet table laden with a sumptuous feast. They are starving, but the food is too far to reach with their hands and their only utensil is a spoon with a two-foot handle. They can reach the food, but they cannot bring it back to their mouths, so they sit in frustration and hunger. In Heaven, the scenario is similar except that the people are blissful and well fed. And, instead of trying to feed themselves, they feed each other.

I felt a tap on my shoulder, turned to see a fat pink shrimp dangled before my eyes. I opened my mouth obediently and the shrimp was waggled forward. "Choo-choo, here comes the train pulling into the station." It was Mom's feeding mantra. It brought back memories of the breakfast nook and Mom spooning cereal into Coralee's waiting rosebud mouth.

I munched the shrimp and hugged my sister. "Place looks great and the party is really swinging. Happy Valentine's Day, sweetie." I pulled away and held her at arm's length to admire her costume. She wore a belly dancer's swirling diaphanous skirt and a silver mesh bra that displayed her new breasts to great advantage. Her face and hair were wreathed in a shimmering veil. "You look beautiful," I said.

"And you look bitchin'." She laughed. "So is this the real Sara, out of the closet at last?"

"One of them," I said. "There's probably a few more alter egos where this one came from. It's amazing what happens when you let your imagination loose." I surveyed the room. "And it looks as if I'm not the only one. Do I know these people?"

"You sure do. That's Jonathan and Grace as the princess and frog."

I carefully scrutinized the princess. "Really? I didn't think Grace was that tall."

"That's Jonathan," Coralee said, "Grace is the frog." She proceeded to go around the room, identifying the Zennies and The Group. There were also another dozen guests invited by The Group and the staff, all dancing and drinking and taking turns on the assorted amusements.

Everything had been customized for the occasion: Pin the Tail on the Donkey had been converted to put the finger on the G spot; bobbing for apples had been transformed into a sea of baby pacifiers in a tub of milk. Pots of chocolate and strawberry body paint abounded. A piñata in the shape of a giant penis was being thoroughly whacked by giggling party-goers. Not in the best taste, I suppose, but definitely Dionysian in its revelry.

I thought of how every society needed festivals to let off steam. Even the Catholic church knew that before the deprivation of Lent, the excess and release of celebration was necessary. I had heard that in Germany, any child conceived during Fasching, the period of Carnival, was automatically legitimate. In indigenous cultures there were times when sexual taboos were released, feast times when people ate and drank and made love with abandon. Somehow we had tapped into this ancient tradition. If Wilhelm Reich was correct, we might be doing wonders to reduce anger and violence. An orgasm a day keeps the National Rifle Association away.

Sipping a glass of champagne, I wandered about the room enjoying the revelry, the bubbling laughter, the music. After a few minutes, I gave up trying to identify the bantering, flirting couples bending toward each other in ease and pleasure. It was the very anonymity that gave the evening its grace and timelessness. It was the dance of life. Tonight we were forgetting our cares and histories, our roles and personalities, our decorum and limitations. Tonight we were like children who run and tumble for the sheer joy of being in motion. This was divine play.

Where was Simon? I wanted to share this thought with him. I scanned the room, but in the mixture of gender, the brilliant costumes and glittering masks, he was not readily evident. I was just about to call his name when I heard the doorbell ring. The door had been open when I arrived; someone must have locked it. I walked to the door and held it open. A man and woman stood on the threshold, both in police costume, but unmasked. "Welcome," I said, "come join the fun. But forgive me, what's the outfit got to do with romance?"

In answer, the woman reached into her pocket and pulled out a badge. "Vice Squad," she barked.

The man intoned, "You have the right to remain silent, anything you say may be used against you...."

"Okay, I get it, very clever." I beckoned them in. "Come on in, have a drink." Then I couldn't resist, in my best Mae West voice, "Are those billy clubs you've got hanging there or are you just glad to see me?" And as I playfully reached for the man's belt, he wheeled me around and snapped a pair of handcuffs on my wrists. I screamed in shock and suddenly the house went quiet.

"That's her. She's the one." I saw Ralph Rater's full moon countenance appear over the shoulder of the male cop. "And her sister and all those...perverts. Arrest them," he shouted. He raised his fists, punching the air, his face livid. "They're destroying the morals of America. Them and those foreign wimps in bathrobes, with their flower arrangements and creepy chanting. This once safe, respectable, God-fearing neighborhood is going straight to hell. My customers are afraid to come here anymore, afraid of the contagion of this Sodom and Gomorrah."

"I don't know what he's talking about, officers," I said quickly. "There's nothing going on here but a Valentine's Day Party. You're welcome to see for yourself."

By this time the encounter had made itself known and we were drawing a small crowd of costumed revelers. Unfortunately, I noticed, many were in states of partial undress.

"You see how they carry on," Ralph shrieked. "And that's just the start of it." He reached into a plastic bag he was carrying and extracted a video. He held it out from his body as if it were radioactive, his face wrinkled in disgust. "This is what they do...upstairs. And they—" he pointed a shaking, accusatory finger at me "—pay for it."

I stared at the video in his clenched fist. The label was neatly typed, Opening Night...Slow Hands.

"Where did you get that?" I cried. "That's private property." I turned to the woman police officer. "He must have stolen it."

"I wouldn't set foot in that house of ill repute." Ralph raised himself to his full Lilliputian height. "It was mailed to me," he sniffed, "in a plain brown wrapper."

Coralee and Simon were standing beside me now, in stunned silence. "There's been a mistake, officer. It must have been delivered to the wrong house." I addressed my pleas to the male officer as the woman seemed particularly disapproving. I couldn't figure out whether it was envy or contempt that curled down the corners of her mouth and locked her jaw. She looked like a queen-size woman eyeing a sylph in a miniskirt. She wouldn't wear it, but she didn't want anyone else to, either.

The male officer, whose badge read J. Costanza, seemed mildly amused. He kept glancing at Simon and the boys with a scrutinizing look. I could almost hear him telling the cops back at the station house "...and they get paid for it. Can you believe it?"

I interrupted Officer Costanza's reverie. "That video was for the private use of the participants. It was not meant for public viewing. I'd like it returned, now." I held out my hand, but Ralph retreated and hid the video behind his back.

"Sorry, ma'am," Officer Costanza said, "but that's police evidence now. I'll have to ask you to come down to the station house."

The female officer, S. Gonzalez, continued, "We have an arrest warrant for a Sara Russack and Coralee Halprin, co-proprietors of Slow Hands, an alleged house of prostitution. Will you come willingly or do we have to use force?"

"We're coming." I spoke between clenched teeth. "But please, get me out of these handcuffs, they're killing me."

"Why'd you grab my belt?" Costanza snapped.

"I'm sorry, Officer, I was just trying to be friendly."

"Keep your hands to yourself," he commanded, unlocking the cuffs. Rubbing the circulation back into my wrists, I grabbed my coat, and Coralee and I obediently headed for the door. Simon tried to follow us, but he was stopped by Officer Gonzalez. She brandished her billy club at him, snarling, "We'll deal with the likes of you later."

The party had ground to a halt. All the merrymakers stood watching our arrest, their faces reflecting a spectrum of feelings ranging from shock to sadness to concern about their own fate. The Zennies were the calmest, their meditation practice preparing them for "all life is change." The Group, however, was not faring as well. They were still my clients, and the sight of their therapist being arrested was a jolt. They looked absolutely betrayed. Somehow they had not connected Slow Hands with nefarious doings, but more with a kind of New Age healing. But now it was clear that the state viewed these activities quite differently and it was possible, even likely, that Slow Hands would be exposed and they along with it. I tried to think of some words of comfort; as I was hustled out the door, I shouted, "Millay."

"Did you say melee?" Costanza growled.

"Millay," I corrected. "Edna St. Vincent."

And as the door closed, I could hear Simon recite her defiant words.

"My candle burns at both ends
It will not last the night
But oh my foes and oh my friends
It casts a lovely light."

And she did, I thought. She "walked her talk" and so did we.

CHAPTER 19

Coralee and I were booked, fingerprinted, and since we had no prior criminal record, we were released under our own recognizance and told to show up for an arraignment two days hence with a lawyer. It was sobering, disturbing...but perhaps not devastating. It was only eleven, early enough perhaps for me to get back home without Harry realizing anything had gone amiss. But first, I needed a cup of coffee...badly.

There was an all-night diner across the street from the station house. As Coralee and I seated ourselves in a vinyl booth, I glanced across at the only other customer staring at his unfolded newspaper. "Straight out of Edward Hopper," I murmured, "depressing."

"More like Magritte," she said, "surreal."

"I know," I sighed, "the whole thing." I signaled the counterman and since he showed no sign of movement, shouted, "Two cups of java."

"Java," Coralee said. "Very Philip Marlowe."

I waited until the scowling, pimply-faced counterman banged our two mugs of oily coffee on the table before speaking. I held the mug in both hands; its warmth was comforting. "I'm sorry, baby," I said. "Sorry for getting you into this."

She took a sip from her mug and grimacing, put it back down. "What do you mean?"

"Oh, I was just thinking if I had listened to you and sold the house when you wanted to, none of this would have ever happened."

"But you wouldn't hear of it." Coralee played with the rings the mug made on the stained Formica top.

"I know, but I never dreamed anything like this would happen," I said.

"Neither did I," she said softly. "Believe me, Sara, if I did, I would never have done it."

"Opened Slow Hands in the first place you mean?" I asked.

"No, not exactly."

"Then what?"

Coralee looked past me, then down at her hands, then back at the door, anyplace but in my eyes. My heart sank. I recognized the gestures of evasion. They had been the same since she was a little girl playing with my forbidden Barbies. If confronted directly, she could not lie. As soon as she made eye contact, her guilt would be revealed. And then the crime would be uncovered, not by her confession, but by my deductive reasoning. And usually she was relieved to be found out.

This time wasn't very different. The video. It had to be

the video. The thought had briefly crossed my mind during the arrest, but I had thrust it away. Such betrayal! I took a deep breath. "So that video didn't get to Ralph Rater by mistake, did it?"

"No," she said.

"You gave it to him?"

"I brought it into the photo shop to be duplicated and I wrote his address on the return envelope."

"By mistake?" I asked, my voice betraying the hope that maybe she hadn't meant to sabotage our venture.

"No." She lifted her head, looking me square in the eyes. "I wanted him to have it."

"That right-wing bigot! That monster of mediocrity! That sexual saltpeter! How could you?"

"How could you refuse to give me what was rightfully mine?" she retorted. "How could you withhold my half of Mom's inheritance? You knew all she wanted was security for me. And I would have had that with Simon, with our restaurant. You weren't looking out for me. You were looking out for yourself."

Her words rang true. "You still didn't have to turn us in," I cried.

She downed the bitter coffee as if it were hemlock. "I didn't know they'd arrest us."

"What did you think they'd do, give us the good citizenship award?" I shouted.

"I thought they'd give us a warning," she said miserably.

"Oh, sure, after you gave them that tape? How many rooms were in it?"

"All four."

"Oh, great." I could feel my bile rising. "If it were only

one or two we could have said it was a wild party. But four! What were they doing?"

"Everything." She smiled for the first time since the arrest. "Everyone looked so happy."

"Well, once upon a time, so did I. Now what? What the hell do we do?"

She signaled to the counterman for a refill of coffee. "We ask Mom's lawyer."

"John Duffy is not a criminal lawyer."

"Well, we're not criminals," she reasoned. "And, anyway, he's the only one we know. Let's start there."

"All right," I said, not knowing what else to do, "I'll call him first thing in the morning."

"Don't worry, it's going to be all right," Coralee said. "Remember Mom's favorite fortune cookie...'Expect miracles.'" She waved to the counterman to call a taxi. And to my amazement, he pulled a cell phone out of his apron pocket and did it.

Coralee dropped me home on her way back to Slow Hands. The house was dark when I let myself in. It felt safe and welcoming, my oasis, my cocoon. I threaded my way upstairs; when life gets hard all we want is the familiar. Why had I ever embarked in this rash adventure of Slow Hands? What on earth had possessed me? I walked past Wendy's room, heard her soft sibilant breathing. What if she found out about this? She was at the age where my mere existence was an embarrassment. What havoc would this bring? This had to be contained. No one must know about it. Not even Harry. We'd talk to the lawyers and pay a fine. As long as we kept it out of the papers, we'd be all right.

As I tiptoed into our bedroom, Harry turned over to

face the wall. "Are you up?" I whispered, but there was no answer. I hurried to the bathroom, flung off my coat and realized I was still wearing my dominatrix gear. God, what a spectacle! I rolled the costume into a ball and threw it into the hamper. I crawled under the covers, longing to curl up next to Harry but afraid to wake him. My last thoughts before I fell into an uneasy sleep were of Slow Hands. We'd certainly have to close it now. And despite the awful events of this evening and the possible dire consequences, I felt a sharp pang of loss for the pleasures of the place and for the warmth and healing it brought to the people who frequented it.

I met Coralee at John Duffy's office the next morning at ten. I had reached him just an hour before and, to my surprise and appreciation, he had canceled his morning conference to see us. Although it had only been a few months since we were last there, everything looked different, starting with the reception room. The men's club décor of old leather, burnished wood and green hunting plaids had been replaced with gleaming steel and Plexiglas tables, with oval-shaped sofas and in-your-face pop art. The receptionist wore Versace and a crew cut, presenting a trendy mixed-gender message.

When she ushered us in to Duffy's office, we barely recognized him. Gone were the Brooks Brothers pinstripes, the silk paisley tie, the clipped graying tonsure. In its place was a slimmed down, hip vision in a white Armani double-breasted suit, open-necked black shirt, aviator shades, and collar-length hair. At least he had the grace to look a bit embarrassed.

"How about some coffee?" he offered and poured us some from a gleaming high-tech Italian espresso machine. "My wife orders it directly from Rome." Proudly, he presented a framed picture of a young redhead, her slender but curvaceous body displayed to perfection in a clinging black silk sheath.

Of course, I thought, men always had the option to reinvent themselves through the new woman on their arm.

"Congratulations," Coralee said, "I hope you two will be very happy."

John Duffy smiled, "We three. I'll be a father around, would you believe it, Labor Day."

Paternity, the fountain of youth, I thought. And now that women had access to all that biotechnology, we could do it, too, but somehow we weren't as eager. The realities of bearing and rearing a child were more concrete for us and more demanding. On the other hand, romance, a beautiful and attentive young man, a replay of courtship, that was supremely inviting. Almost irresistible.

I hoped that, in the flush of his own second honeymoon, John Duffy would understand the emotions that led us to create Slow Hands. And maybe, just maybe, he could help us find a way to keep it.

"Okay, ladies," John Duffy said, reaching for a fresh legal pad. "Lay it on me."

And we did. Coralee and I took turns, weaving the narrative, filling him in on all the details from our finding the house, to engaging Simon, to bringing in the Zennies, to opening night with The Group, to last night's arrest. By silent agreement, we left out the part about

Coralee's breast cancer and her subsequent wish to end our partnership. It seemed tangential to the business at hand.

John Duffy listened carefully, his eyebrows lifting as we described the range of activities at Slow Hands. "You two have certainly given a new meaning to customer service," he said. "But from what I've heard in the divorce courts, I imagine you've got quite a niche market." He lowered his glasses, the better to meet our eyes. "I'm not a criminal attorney, mind you, but I can give you a first opinion."

He then proceeded to lay out the arguments both for and against our case. "They obviously had a search warrant, and they had evidence, the videotape. The tape demonstrates that sexual activities had transpired in the house. The police officers were eyewitnesses to a party in progress with a number of participants who appear in these lewd tapes. The house, where the party was happening and the tape had been shot, is owned and run in partnership by you two. The women pay a monthly fee to belong to the club, Slow Hands, which is domiciled in said house. The men, who live in the house, enjoy free room and board. Is that correct?"

"That's right," I said. "Pretty incriminating?"

"Somewhat," he agreed. "Now let's look at the other side, shall we? There is no evidence either preceding the evening of the arrest or during that time that any illegal activities were occurring. There was no solicitation and no exchange of money for sexual activities. All activities were engaged in by mutually consenting adults. There were no minors involved. No force, no coercion, no illegal drugs. Is that correct?"

"Yes." I sighed with relief. "It sounds much better that way."

"Let's hope that's the way the judge sees it." John Duffy said, tapping his manicured nails thoughtfully on the desk. "You really kept this place going with so few clients?"

"We were willing to subsidize it for the first few months," I explained.

"We were just about ready to expand the membership," Coralee said.

"But it was all by word of mouth," I said. "We never advertised. We weren't in it for the money. We were content to just meet the mortgage payments."

"And the Zennies didn't need a lot. They've all taken vows of poverty," Coralee said.

"But not chastity?" John Duffy gibed.

"They practice loving kindness," I said.

He stifled a smile. "Is that what they call it these days?"

As he escorted us to the door, he added a note of caution. "Keep a low profile until the arraignment. Suspend all operations and don't on any account speak to the press."

"How would the press know anything about it?" I said to Coralee as we entered the elevator.

"And why would they care?" she added as we exited the building.

As we entered the street, I felt the blinding light of a flashbulb. "Sara, Coralee, over here," someone shouted. "Hey girls, give us a smile."

We were surrounded by reporters, pencils in hand, camcorders, microphones. Shouts of "Here they come, make way for the Berkeley madams." "Say, Coralee, what did you put in your monks' begging bowls...Viagra?" "Hey, Dr. Sara, is that what Freud meant—is that what women want?" One of the reporters, a young woman in denim overalls, held up her press badge, the *Guardian,* San Francisco's liberal voice. "We're on your side. Legalize prostitution."

The crowd pressed in on us. I felt a hand on my shoulder. I wheeled to pull it off and looked into the grim face of John Duffy. He propelled me and Coralee back into the building. "We have no statement at this time," he shouted at the pack.

"How did they find out about it?" I asked him as he ushered us out the back.

"There were a lot of people at that party last night," he said as he opened the door of his waiting limo.

As I sank back into the thick leather upholstery, I reflected upon the mythic theme of the knight in shining armor. Women's lib had urged us all to disavow such options, but right now, the rescue felt wonderful, timely and needed. Thank goodness for upstanding competent men like John Duffy, even if he had a trophy wife. And who was I to pass judgment on his choice of that juicy redhead? Hadn't I done the same thing when given the opportunity? Moved toward youth and beauty? Don't we all want a taste of that, especially when our own youth is gone? I glanced out the window. A few of the reporters were shouting questions and brandishing their cameras as we sped past.

On the far corner stood a bearded man in a cassock carrying a placard with a blowup of the cover of this morn-

ing's *Chronicle*. Exclusive, the headline shouted, Berkeley Bordello Bust, above a large picture of Ralph Rater
holding an American flag.

"I guess that answers my question," I said.

"He certainly got the word out," Coralee added. "Big
time. Sorry, Sarie, I never thought it would be this public."

"It's all right," I said and in some perverse way, it was.
Almost a relief. I had been living this double life for too
long. Now I just wanted to get home and talk to Harry. I
wanted to tell him everything. And together, we would
tell Wendy. If I was lucky, my daughter would someday
forgive me.

I asked to borrow John Duffy's cell phone and dialed
Harry's office. I had left so early that morning we hadn't
yet talked. Ruth-Ann, his dental assistant, answered the
phone. She'd been with Harry since he opened his practice; he threatened to quit if she did. Ruth-Ann recognized
my voice from my first hello.

"The doctor's with a patient," she said coolly.

"This is really important. Can you interrupt him?"

"Can he get back to you?"

"Will you just please tell him I'm on the line?"

"Sara," she said, slowly choosing each word, "he explicitly said that he is not to be disturbed by anyone. Just
leave a message."

I stared out the window of the limousine, the passing
streets blurred by sudden tears. Never, in the twenty years
that Harry and I had been together, had he been unavail-
able to me. I always came first. He would drop everything
to talk to me, to be with me when I needed him. That sup-

port was a given in my life, like air to breathe, or ground to walk on.

Coralee saw my stricken face as I returned the cell phone. She took my hand. "What did he say?"

"He won't take my call."

"Oh, sweetie." She took me into her arms. "I'm so sorry."

The genuine caring of her voice melted the last of my reserves, and the tears I had been holding burst forth in a torrent. I laid my head against her shoulder and sobbed. "Oh, my God, Corrie. What have I done?"

She held me and gently rubbed my shoulder blades. "He's just trying to figure it out, that's all. Men are from X, women are from Y. He has to go into his cave for a while. We're the ones who want to talk about it...right away." She paused. "Maybe, if you're real lucky, he won't want to talk about it at all."

"No one's ever that lucky," I rued.

"If anything happens to you two, I'll never forgive myself," she said.

"What!" I cried. "You think he's going to leave me?" In my wildest moment of self-pity, I hadn't imagined that. It was unthinkable; Harry and I were with each other for life. I had taken those vows seriously, "To love, honor and cherish till death do us part." And somehow, no matter how it might appear, I had always honored those vows. Slow Hands was about something else. It had nothing to do with the permanence, the everlastingness, the through-thick-and-thin, the parenting, the householding, the through-sickness-and-health that Harry and I had. And now that it was threatened, I saw just how precious it was, how dearly desired. And I understood why Coralee wanted to forge that indelible bond with Simon, wanted to make a home, make a baby with a man she loved. Slow Hands was icing on the cake, but a true partner was the staff of life. Oh, God, I thought, I had been a latter day Marie Antoinette telling my starving sister to eat an éclair.

It was my turn to comfort Coralee. "Harry and I are going to make it through this. We've made it through lots of things that were tougher than this," I said, although at the moment I couldn't think of any. "Just tell me one thing, why Ralph Rater?"

"If there was any other way, I wouldn't have done it," she said. "But after the cancer, things seemed so clear. I couldn't wait any longer."

"Did Simon agree?" I asked.

"He wanted us to get married and start the restaurant as much as I did but, no, he wanted me to tell you. He wanted me to give you a warning."

"Why didn't you?"

"Because I know you better than he does, Sarie. If I told you, you would have found a way to talk me out of it." She brushed away a tear from my cheek. "Now, I wish I had."

John Duffy's chauffeur pulled the car to the curb in front of my house. John leaped out of the front seat and opened the passenger door for me. He gave my shoulder a brusque pat. "I'll send my car for you Friday morning for the arraignment. Meanwhile, stay close to home."

"Thank you," I said. "You'll let me know what your fees are. We're a bit cash drained now, but..."

"It's *pro bono*. Just consider it part of the estate follow-up." He cracked a small smile and looked heavenward. "Well, Yvonne, you always said your girls had guts. Now they're going to have a chance to prove it." He slipped back into the car and the chauffeur peeled off in a screech of rubber.

I let myself in the front door. The house was heavy with silence. I couldn't believe it was less than two hours since I had left. Two hours that had changed my life. I walked into the kitchen, brewed myself a cup of tea, searched the counter for a note from Harry. We often left each other messages, domestic ones, like "Pick up Wendy" or "We're out of milk" or "Theatre tonight," often signed with love. But when was the last time I wrote, "You were terrific this morning"?

In fact, when was the last time Harry and I made love? Suddenly I was awash with remorse. I wanted to wrap my legs around him, lean my head on his furry chest. I wanted to climb into our big double bed and pull the covers over our heads until it all went away. I wanted to return Mom's legacy. Like the terrible fable I had heard as a child. "The Monkey's Paw." You wish for something extravagant and get it with grisly results.

And yet, what about Browning? "A man's reach should exceed his grasp or what's a Heaven for?" Too much poetry, I chided myself, I have ingested too many romantic ideas and look where's it's gotten me. I needed solace and the quickest way I knew was hydrotherapy. I turned on the faucets full blast in the tub, opened my new vanilla bath salts and decided to go the full treatment; I needed it. I inflated my bath pillow, got out Wendy's rubber ducky, lit a bevy of aromatherapy candles, all promising

some version of serenity. I turned on the transistor radio
to what I thought would be classical music, although at
the moment it was a commercial, and climbed into the
foaming fragrant tub. I sank to my neck in the welcome
heat and felt some of the tension and despair evaporate.

But not for long. Instead of the dulcet tones of Vivaldi
or Mozart, I heard contemporary rock followed by the
New York nasal voice of, "You found me. I'm Dr. Debbie Dawson. Doctor Debbie. D-E-B-B-I-E. Let's take
our first caller. Jim, welcome to the program." Somehow
I had misdialed and gotten the local talk station. I glanced
helplessly at the radio. It was out of reach. I would have
to get out of the tub and I had just gotten in.

I adjusted the pillow under my head, leaned back and
listened. Maybe Doctor Debbie would be good for a few
laughs. Every now and then I listened to her in the car. I
disagreed with most of her positions. She was an arch
conservative, vehemently anti-abortion, anti-premarital
sex, calling live-in partners shack-up sluts, claiming ho-
mosexuals as sick. The only thing I admired about her
was her certitude. She never wavered, was doggedly con-
sistent and firmly convinced of her own righteous
opinion. Based on what, a degree in physiology and a
counseling certificate? I had more training and experience and I flailed around in self-doubt, always seeing the
other side. Oh, no, I didn't want to be Doctor Debbie; I
just wanted some of her conviction.

"Hello, Jim," she repeated.

"Hello, Dr. Debbie. Thank you for taking my call," said
a throaty male voice. "I'm a little upset today."

"How can I help you, Jim?"

"Well, I guess you've heard about the Berkeley Bordello Bust."

I can't believe it, I thought. This fast!

"Can you believe those old broads?" she chuckled. "What kind of a woman has to pay for sex?"

"My ex-wife, Dr. Debbie."

She snorted with laughter. "So what's your problem, Jim? Want to send her a bill for past services rendered? Just kidding."

"My problem is what to tell our daughter, our grandchildren, our neighbors? The minister? We still go to the same church."

"Just hold your head up high and go about your business," she advised. "You are not responsible for the actions of your demented ex-wife."

"But, Dr. Debbie, I feel responsible. I may have driven Teresa to it by leaving her."

Oh, God, it was Terry's alcoholic ex. "Don't flatter yourself, bozo," I shouted at the radio. "She looks ten years younger."

"All you can do is leave her to the law. Now stay on the line, Jim, I want to send you my Doctor Debbie's Ten Commandments CD and matching T-Shirt. And for you listeners out there, and there are currently thirty million of you, please call and fax us your opinion about this abomination. What does it say about our society when women solicit sex with...monks! So, let's hear from you folks...label your correspondence...Paying For It." She paused for a commercial for megavitamins and came back on the air, chortling.

"Our phones are ringing off the hook. Please limit your

comments to 'yes, I approve' or 'no, I don't' and one descriptive sentence."

Suffice it to say, the nays had it. Maybe because only like minds listened or maybe there was some censorship at work. Dr. Debbie doesn't cotton to dissent. The calls were rapid and rabid.

"Lock up those dames for life."

"Tar and feather them. Scarlet letters, all around."

"Revive the stockades. Union Square at high noon."

"I'm praying for their poor husbands and children."

"I don't believe in divorce but if there were ever grounds for it, the Berkeley Bordello would be it."

"Isn't there a Pope or something over those Buddhist guys? Shouldn't they be excommunicated?"

"Some of those dames are over fifty? What are they... nymphos?"

When Dr. Debbie cut to a commercial for security systems, I emerged from the tub and slowly toweled myself dry. The talk show phone calls had been unnerving. Those callers were angry. And a number were women. Somehow I never expected women's outrage.

I felt my stomach growl. Stress made me hungry. I padded barefoot into the kitchen, opened the refrigerator and peered inside. On the top shelf were my "good foods," the low-fat litany...unflavored yogurt, cottage cheese, carrots and cukes, balsamic vinegar. I looked down at my naked body, my rounded stomach, the jiggly thighs and breasts. I didn't want low-fat anything. I wanted pleasure. And if pleasure meant a few pounds, so be it.

I bent down and surveyed the bottom shelf. Harry's leftover lunch. Half a Reuben sandwich. My idea of heaven. I opened the top slice of seeded rye and reveled in the colors, the texture and aroma of the red corned beef marbled with thin veins of pearly fat, the silvery pep-percorn-studded sauerkraut and the glistening thousand island dressing. And next to it, also from Max's Deli-catessen, a huge chocolate-covered macaroon. It was still wrapped in its axiomatic napkin...Max's Is a Bad Place for a Diet. You've Got a Mouth, Use It. If Anyone Asks You Is Everything All Right, You Get Your Meal for Free. Food with an attitude. I cracked open a bottle of Harry's Dr. Brown's cream soda. I usually relegated myself to diet sodas. Harry, bless him, never worried about calories. He was interested in taste, in flavor. He was gentle with him-self about the few extra pounds he had gained over the years, and, I thought with gratitude, understanding about mine. To Harry, I still looked like the same girl he had married, although that girl's wedding gown was a size eight.

Where was Harry now? Probably in the office. Duti-ful, responsible. He had braces to fit, teeth to straighten, patients to see. But what was he thinking? Feeling? It was a long time, I realized, since I had wondered about that. Normally Harry and I would have breakfast together and over a mouthful of toasted bagels read each other tidbits of the news, half listening. Then a perfunctory kiss and out the door until dinnertime. It was as if he were frozen in time until I heard his key in the lock. But now, Harry was an unknown—mysterious, unpredictable. I felt a quiver of fear, unsettling but distinctly exciting. Harry had suddenly become what the physicists called a quark...a strange attractor.

I took a healthy bite of the thick Reuben, a deep slug of the bubbly cream soda and sighed. No matter what the future brought, at this moment I was fully present...feeling the soft leather seat against my naked bottom, the smooth wood beneath my hands, watching the dust motes dance in the sunlight, chewing and swallowing with gusto. Some guilt, yes. Some worry, yes, but I had rediscovered pleasure. Reinhabited my senses. And I had done that for myself and for Coralee and for The Group. "And that, sweetheart," as Mom would say, "ain't chopped liver."

CHAPTER 20

I was curled up in bed trying to watch the eleven o'clock news when, with great relief, I finally heard the garage door open. I had received a message on our answering machine from Ruth-Anne that Dr. Harry had a dinner meeting, and he wanted me to know that Wendy would be spending the night at a friend's. Had Ruth-Anne's voice always been so unctuous? I visualized her, standing behind Harry's dental chair, her auburn hair coiled in a neat chignon, her pale Irish skin dewy and unwrinkled, fresh as the crisp white uniform that billowed above her formidable breasts. Those breasts that grazed Harry's arm as she handed him some devilishly sharp instrument. Ruth-Anne! She'd always been in love with Harry, and now was her chance.

I listened to Harry's footsteps on the stairs. I knew how many there would be. I counted them, thirty steps in all, and there he was at the bedroom door. He entered the room, holding his jacket and tie. I waited for him to drape them over his desk chair as he always did. For years I had been after him to hang his clothes in the closet, to keep the desk neat, but eventually I had grown accustomed to the six-inch pile of papers, to his shoes on the floor, the suit thrown over the chair, the coins from his pockets spilling onto the rug. It attested to the presence of Harry, just as much as the waft of Old Spice, the old jokes, and the familiar peck on the lips of greeting.

But this evening there was no kiss. No undressing. He went straight to the dresser, pulled out a pair of pajamas and headed for the door. "Good night, Sara."

"Wait a minute," I cried. "Where are you going?"

"I'm sleeping in the guest room."

"Why?"

"Do I have to spell it out for you?"

"Yes, you do." I climbed out of bed. "Please, Harry, we need to talk."

"No, Sara, *you* need to talk. I have nothing to say."

"But, Harry, I can explain."

"I'm sure you can. But it's too late."

"Too late. You mean..." My throat closed; my words were cracked and shaky. "You want a divorce."

Harry stood there for a long moment, chewing his lower lip. He only did that in moments of great stress. His mother had shown me a nursery school picture of a tow-headed Harry in a sailor suit, gnawing on his lower lip. "That was the day his brother was born," she had said. "Harry always had trouble sharing."

"Harry," I repeated. He seemed to be in a trance. "Do you want to divorce me?"

He stared straight ahead.

"Harry, say something. Please," I begged.

He took a deep breath. "You know what the worst thing about this is?"

There were so many choices. "The sex?" I ventured. "The arrest? The public humiliation?"

"No," he said thoughtfully, "though they're all valid. The worst thing, the only unforgivable thing. The thing I thought you would never do."

"What?" I cried.

"Lie to me. Live a double life. For months. I feel like such a fool. I believed you. Believed that you were running a boardinghouse. A nice respectable boardinghouse. You and your sister. And all those evenings when you told me you were going to renters' meetings and welcome teas you were really pimping, pandering...running a whorehouse. While I was eating takeout," he cried, "what were you taking in?"

"Nothing, Harry, believe me. It was all business. I did not sample the merchandise."

"Young studs running half-naked around the house, and you weren't tempted?"

"I didn't say I wasn't tempted. You'd have to be saint not to be tempted. Everybody gets tempted. What about you and Ruth-Ann?"

"Ruth-Ann? Ruth-Ann, my assistant?" He pronounced it like Teresa? Teresa of Avila?

"Yes, that Ruth-Ann. How many are there? She's always been crazy about you. She acts as if she owns you. I've seen the way she leans over to hand you all those picks and drills."

"What about the monks? What about their 'picks and drills'?"

"No. Actually, the only man at Slow Hands who appealed to me was Simon."

"Who's he?"

"Our general manager."

"The one that Coralee is going to marry?"

"That, too," I said.

"You girls, Yvonne always said you were competitive."

"What about you, mister? Mildred said you asked her to give your baby brother back to the hospital."

"Noblesse oblige," he admitted. "I was first, and I wanted to stay first." Harry held my gaze, his face white and earnest. "Am I still first?"

"First and always," I said.

There was a long moment of silence as he took that in. Then he stood and left the room. When he returned, he held a large yellow pad and a handful of sharpened pencils.

"All right, then," he sighed, "let's sit down and figure out how we're going to get you and your sister out of this mess."

"Harry," I whispered, "you weren't really thinking of divorce, were you?"

"Murder, yes, divorce, no." An ironic smile. "Now let's begin at the beginning, shall we?"

Two hours later, the pencils were worn down and so were we, but we had a detailed history, a financial record and, most importantly, a defense strategy. My gratitude toward Harry came flooding over me, thick and warm as desire. This was what marriage was about. Loyalty. Continuity. Forgiveness. And as I sat next to Harry, the husband of my youth, father of my hopefully not estranged child, I had a strong sense of knowing I was in the right place.

"The hardest part of marriage is the day-to-day," I said. "Keeping it fresh. Not taking it for granted."

Harry met my gaze. "I guess I've been on automatic pilot."

"I was talking about myself."

"At least you shook things up," he said. "You didn't just settle."

"For what?"

"For boredom. For same old, same old. You took some action. You moved toward what you wanted. Variety. Excitement."

"Am I hearing you right?" I shook my head as if to clear it. "Are you telling me that you understand why I opened Slow Hands? And why—" I gulped hard "—I might want to sleep with another man?" I waited for his answer, my hands sweaty, throat dry, but oddly light. It felt wonderful to share this, to be so truthful. And somehow I knew that he would not be hurt by this, for what I was confessing was not my wish alone, but the wish of many women and many men. And from the look in Harry's eyes, maybe, upon occasion, a wish of this particular man.

"Have you ever wanted to sleep with another woman?"

"Sometimes."

"Ruth-Ann?"

He looked uncomfortable. "Maybe."

"And did you?" I asked.

He was silent, busying himself by straightening the yellow pages.

Oh, God, I thought. Why did I ask that? If he told me, I'd have to tell him about Thomas and Simon, and what good would that do? "I don't need to know," I said quickly.

"Good," he said, "because I wasn't going to tell you."

And it was good. The mystery. The not knowing. It made Harry more alluring that he could desire and be desired by other women. And that dalliance, real or imagined, could never imperil our marriage. Because a transient affair, a fleeting romance paled beside a committed partnership. One was a rose. The other a sequoia.

I looked at my Harry, thinning hair, stubbly jowls, wrinkles and love handles, in the ruthlessly clear light, and I was awash with tenderness. This man would be with me in sickness and in health, whether rich or poor, young or old, right or wrong...until death do us part.

So, Sara, I could hear Mom's chuckle, *our old buddy Soren Kierkegaard got it right.*

And this time instead of keeping the dialogue to myself, I turned to Harry. "You know sometimes I talk with Mom in my head."

"Really?" he said. "What does she say?"

" 'There is only one attribute that makes a man lovable and that is faith...absolute faith in marriage.' "

Harry laughed. "Not the most flattering portrait but probably true."

"So now, what about Wendy? How do I tell her? What has she got absolute faith in?"

"That you love her," he said.

"And do you know how much I love you?" I reached for his hand. "You're my rock. My anchor. What would I do without you?"

"Did it ever occur to you, Sara, that I don't want to be a rock or an anchor? Some large insensate thing? That I'm more than that?"

"Of course you are," I said.

"I know I'm not handsome," Harry continued, "but I've tried to make you happy."

"You've made me very happy," I protested.

"As a *man,* Sara."

"Oh, God, Harry, come here." How could I not have realized his needs were no different than mine? This familiar man was more passionate and more complex than I had ever given him credit for. This new openness was very erotic. I was incredibly turned on. I pulled him toward me, slid my hand down the front of his pants, felt the warm responsive flesh beneath the cloth.

Surprised, he kissed me roughly, his hands tearing open my robe, seeking my breasts. He knelt upon the floor, pulling me down with him. He caressed my breasts, parted my thighs. I gasped as he moved downward, his mouth burrowing, his tongue like silk.

I pulled him up toward me, ground my hips against his, flung my legs over his back. This was the way it once was between us, I thought. Then as he entered full inside me, I stared into his wild eyes and thought...no, it had never been like this. I came in a series of rising peaks and lay, wet and spent, moaning gutturally in Harry's arms. As I closed my eyes, I thought *Chez* Russack will never be the same, and I was never happier.

CHAPTER 21

Coralee and I prevailed on John Duffy to handle our case. Criminal law wasn't his specialty, but he was smart and savvy and still had a strong loyalty to Mom. We were lucky to have him. He managed to set the arraignment for the very next day. We pleaded not guilty to charges of lewd behavior and running a house of prostitution, and a trial date was set, with unusual alacrity, for the next month. Since we had no priors, no bail was set. Coralee and I were free to go about our normal activities. The residents of Slow Hands could remain living there, at least until after the trial, but it was, of course, closed for business.

Now I could concentrate on my biggest concern, my daughter. Wendy had spent the night at a girlfriend's, hadn't told us which one, and the multiple messages I had left on her cell phone had gone unanswered. "This is Mom, please call as soon as you get this." "I'm worried about you, call me." "Don't be like this, Wendy."

Finally, I took a different tack. It was Saturday. "Hi sweetie. How about lunch today? One o'clock at Zuni's? I miss you."

I had no idea if she would come. Too anxious to stay at home, I got to the restaurant half an hour early. I had reserved my favorite table, set off by itself, next to an expansive window that framed the sunlit bustle of Market Street. It was a table that encouraged talk. I realized, as I waited for her, that I almost never took my daughter to lunch; that ritual was reserved for colleagues and friends. And yet, who more important to have this special time with?

I ordered an iced tea and then another. The waiter filled the bread plate twice. I gazed out the window at the eclectic mix of Brooks Brothers corporate types, hip techies, and the shopping cart brigade of the homeless. At first I didn't recognize her, noticed only a tall figure striding purposely down the street, covered from head to toe in baggy black jersey that did nothing to disguise her fresh young beauty.

It wasn't until she came closer, just before she ducked into the open side door of the restaurant, that I saw, with a start, that it was my daughter, grown into a woman. And for my sins, all I could think of was *Fiddler on the Roof.* Song lyrics, the Shakespearean sonnets of our times. I admit it; I weep every time I hear "Is this the little girl I carried? Is this the little boy at play? I don't remember growing older. When did they?"

My daughter frowned as she scanned the restaurant, then spotting me, walked quickly to the table. I rose to hug her, but she avoided my embrace by immediately taking her seat and reaching for the menu.

"Hi, sweetie," I began. Then at a loss for words, "Did you find the place all right?" About as original, as "Nice day."

"You said it was the west corner—it's not."

"You know me, not much on directions." I could hear the apology in my tone. Enough of that. I straightened my shoulders. "See anything you like? They're famous for their Caesar salad."

Wendy shook her head. "Raw egg? Haven't you heard about salmonella?"

"Sometimes you have to live dangerously." It was out of my mouth before I could assay its innuendoes.

"And sometimes you don't," she shot back.

Just as well, I thought. The only way out is through.

"I guess Dad told you all about it," I began.

"About what?"

"About our business. Aunt Coralee's and mine."

"You mean that whorehouse, yeah. But then again, he didn't have to say much. You were on the front page of the *Chronicle*. Not to mention Larry King. And Dr. Debbie. Goddamn it, Mom, you even made *Doonesbury*."

"I know, sweetie. I'm sorry. I never meant for it to go public."

"It wasn't exactly a low-profile occupation. You broke the law."

"Only in California," I protested.

"Oh, great. That just happens to be where we live. That just happens to be where I go to school. Do you know what it's like for me to walk down the halls of Lowell now? Do you?" her voice rose alarmingly.

The waiter used that as his cue to enter the conversation. "Can I get you ladies something to drink?" I ordered a martini straight up and Wendy, San Pellegrino without ice. I ordered the hamburger and Caesar salad; Wendy ordered the pasta primavera, no oil or butter. I was raising a purist.

The waiter took pity upon me and brought the martini immediately. I wished I could administer it intravenously but contented myself with a long icy gulp. Some people found proof of the divine plan in waterfalls and forests, I found it in martinis and taxi cabs.

Wendy sipped her mineral water, then folded her hands and waited in silence.

I chewed the gin-soaked olive reflectively, buying time. "Well, where to begin...?"

"Cut to the chase, Mom," she said sullenly. "What's going to happen now?"

What's going to happen to me? she meant. I remembered that the only aspects of parents' lives that kids are interested in are the parts that affect them. They come into the world as helpless little bundles of rampant narcissism, a trait which escalates through adolescence and shows no sign of abatement until they become parents themselves. And yet we love them fiercely, starting from that first drooling toothless smile.

"I'm not sure what's going to happen," I said. "We'll have to wait for the trial. You know about trials?"

She poked a fork into her steaming pasta. "White asparagus," she pronounced approvingly. "Al dente, too." She dug in hungrily. "Not too bad. Sure I know what a trial is. Like what else is on TV? Lawyers and doctors." She grinned. "I learned how to do open heart surgery. Want to see?"

I laughed out loud. I had my daughter back. At least temporarily. For the first time that afternoon, her eyes looked into mine. Those chocolate-brown eyes with the gold flecks, same eyes as Mom. I remembered placing Wendy, still wet from the delivery, in Mom's arms, and Mom's tenderly stroking her rosy cheek, whispering, "Welcome little girl. Now you get to cause your mother all the aggravation she caused me."

I took Wendy's hand. "So, darling, what's the worst thing that can happen? What are you really worrying about?"

She eyed my Caesar salad. "Does that have anchovies in it?"

"Only in the dressing."

She reached over, took a leaf and munched it. "I bet this has a thousand calories."

"It's just lettuce," I said.

"Yeah, right. What about the dressing, the cheese, the croutons?"

I eased the plate away. "Then don't eat it."

She pulled it back. "Keep it in the middle." She speared a crouton, popped it into her mouth and framed her question around it. "So, like, are you and Dad going to get a divorce?"

"No, of course not. What ever gave you that idea?"

"Because...like...why else would you have opened that house?"

The *why else* was too complicated to explain over lunch. And at any rate, that wasn't really the question. I told her what she needed to know. And it was the truth.

"Your Dad and I love each other and we love you. We are married for life. We are married no matter what."

"Then why aren't you nicer to him?" she said.

"What?"

"You know what I mean. Sometimes you just kind of ignore him. Like he's not even there."

"I don't think I do that...." I stumbled for words. What else had she noticed?

"And I just want you to know," she said sternly, "if you two ever do split up, I'm staying with Dad."

Her steely gaze was like a blade through my heart. "That's never going to happen," I said.

"Good," she said, "now which one do you want to share...the pot de crème or the lemon tart?"

CHAPTER 22

The next month went by swiftly, filled with household duties, family meals and my clients, who, for the most part, continued to keep appointments. In fact, some seemed pleased to have a therapist in the news. And even that visibility swiftly died down when our sins were upstaged by an imbroglio about city workers getting sex change operations on state benefits.

The morning of the trial, I woke with a heavy fog in my head mirroring the one swirling outside the window. I turned to Harry for comfort, but his side of the bed, though still warm, was empty. I could hear the shower running, and in a minute Harry padded out naked, furry, looking like a benevolent bear. I held out my arms beseechingly, and he sat on the side of the bed and gave me a big damp hug. "It's okay," he said, in his best dental chair manner, "it'll only hurt for a little while."

"Are you going to be saying that when they strap me into the electric chair?" I asked.

"You're entitled to a last meal. Come on and get dressed, I'm taking you out for breakfast."

"Where?"

"It's a surprise."

Although I closed my eyes on the drive, I could smell the sea as soon as Harry reached the Great Highway. The Cliff House. It was where Harry had proposed twenty years ago, where he had planted my engagement ring in a glass of champagne and I had been so undone I had almost swallowed it.

"Remember my ring...?"

Of course he remembered. "It would have worked its way out eventually," he mused. "Most everything does."

Harry had reserved "our" table, the one looking out directly on Seal Rock, although the seals had long gone to better feeding grounds. They now barked hungrily at the hordes of tourists on Pier 39. We ordered our favorite breakfast: fresh-squeezed orange juice, blueberry pancakes, Canadian bacon and double cappuccinos.

"Or is it cappuccini?" I asked as the waitress walked away.

"See, you're feeling better already. Now look out at the ocean," he commanded. "Look at the waves pounding the rocks. The tide comes in. The tide goes out. This, too, my darling. This too shall pass."

He waited until the waitress placed our frothy juice glasses before us, a few floating seeds attesting to its authenticity. "And here's a little bit of oceanic peace you can imbibe."

I stared at the pill. "What is it?"

"Just what I give my squeamish patients before I tighten their wires."

I accepted the pill with gratitude, and we ate the rest of our meal in companionable silence. I don't know whether it was the tranquilizer or the carbs or Harry's forgiveness, but an hour later when we arrived at the courtroom, I felt as if I were quilted in bubble wrap.

We walked into Courtroom 25, the court of Judge Lillian Kramer. I took my place next to Coralee on the front bench. John Duffy had dictated our dress code, and we were both in dark suits with long skirts and low heels. He looked quite sober himself in a gray pinstripes. He nodded briskly to me and pointed to a tall dark man. "Joe Manus, the D.A.," he whispered. I studied Manus; he looked lean and hungry.

"All rise" the bailiff announced. I felt a wild impulse, shades of *Laugh-In,* to break into a bandy-legged run and shout, "Here come de judge." I turned around and caught Harry's eye. He grinned and mouthed my errant thought. So this is what it felt like to be in synch. Clear the channels and it becomes possible. I had once read that the Australian aborigines could read the minds of a fellow tribesman twenty miles away. Our minds are open, they told the amazed anthropologist, because we have nothing to hide.

Judge Lillian Kramer was a small, meticulously groomed woman with a wary expression. Her instructions to the court were succinct. "In the case of Russack and Halprin versus the state, both parties have agreed to waive a jury. Correct?" Both lawyers nodded. "Will the defendants please stand?" Coralee and I rose. I noticed with dismay that the bubble wrap was beginning to peel away, especially around my knees. Coralee was pale, her forehead beaded with sweat. She turned to the back of the room, smiled wanly at Simon who blew her a discreet kiss.

"John Duffy for the defense, Your Honor." Duffy's voice was low and sure.

"And the prosecution?"

"Joe Manus." He sprang to his feet, looking as if he should be on a basketball court, big hands and fast moves.

"Will you be introducing witnesses?" Judge Kramer asked.

"Yes, your Honor." John Duffy consulted his notes. "We will be introducing Grace Davis, a client of Ms. Russack's and a key holder of Slow Hands Spa, and Simon Bartlett, personnel manager of Slow Hands Spa."

"And for the prosecution, Your Honor, the state will be calling to the stand Police Lieutenant J. Costanza of the Vice Squad and Mr. Ralph Rater of Moral Majority Movies and Clean, Well-Lighted Videos."

"The court is now in order." Judge Kramer rapped her gavel. "Proceed."

Coralee and I exchanged a glance. She gnawed at her cuticle, looking grim. I felt strangely calm, as if this were happening to someone else. It was all so familiar. I was a fan of courtroom dramas. The arguments would be presented, evidence revealed and a verdict decided. Case closed. Tune in next week. Only now I couldn't change the channel. It was my life that was being examined, prosecuted and judged.

"Recite the charge," Judge Kramer instructed.

As the bailiff presented it, the judge removed a pair of gold-rimmed glasses from a hard-bodied leather case and began to slowly wipe each lens with a soft chamois cloth. She was a careful woman. I bought my reading glasses at the dime store and tossed them into my purse. That's why she was behind the bench, I reflected, and I was in front of it.

"The charge is that Sara Russack and her sister Coralee Halprin are accused of running a house of prostitution at 69 Grove Street in Berkeley, California. Pimping is a felony crime in California as listed in California Penal Code 266 H, and if found guilty, they are subject to a state prison sentence of three to five years."

"Three to five," Coralee gasped. We had heard the charge before at the booking, but it hadn't seemed real.

"Please stand," the bailiff barked. "How do you plead?"

We stood. "Not guilty," I said, my voice unnaturally loud. Coralee answered in a dry whisper, close to tears, "Not guilty."

John Duffy placed his hand on Coralee's and kept it there through Joe Manus's opening.

Manus made his way forward in the slow and deliberate manner of a tracker forging a path through a Brazilian rain forest. Clearly, this was a strong man about to do a difficult and onerous task. "Your Honor, the State has more than enough evidence to prove that the defendants, the Halprin sisters, were the owners and proprietors of a house of prostitution located at 69 Grove Street, a mere fifteen-minute walk from Sather Gate of the University of California, Berkeley."

"Objection, Your Honor." John Duffy rose. "Irrelevant. What does the University have to do with this?"

Joe Manus sharpened his invisible machete. "It is to establish the pernicious influence of a house of ill repute in the vicinity of impressionable under-age students."

"Are these the same under-age students who get drunk every weekend and download porn off the Internet?" Duffy murmured.

"I was referring to the female students," Joe Manus said unctuously. "We have here an unprecedented situation. We can usually rely on the fair sex to set a moral example, to tread the higher ground so to speak. But when we find mature women, one a mother herself, wallowing in the mud of sexual squalor—"

"Objection. Prejudicial," Duffy protested.

"Sustained." Judge Kramer leaned forward. "Skip the rhetoric, Mr. Manus and get to the point."

Joe Manus squared his shoulders and spat out the next sentences as if they were pieces of rotten meat. "The State will prove the Halprin sisters are guilty of employing male prostitutes and collecting their earnings. They are guilty of pandering."

"Thank you Mr. Manus. Mr. Duffy?"

John Duffy walked slowly toward the bench, his face smooth and calm. He was countering Manus's histrionics with supreme repose. His tone was uninflected, as if the judgment had already been made, as if the case were so self-evident that it merited minimal concern.

"We will prove, Your Honor, that the house in question, 69 Grove Street, was a residential facility which the defendants generously donated to the Loving-Kindness

Sangha for the use of Zen students. They accepted no money from the Sangha or from the students. To help defray costs for the facility, since my clients are not wealthy women, they established a women's health club on the premises, known as Slow Hands Spa, to which they sold monthly and annual memberships. The defense will prove that since no money changed hands for sexual services, the charge of pandering is absurd. We will ask that all charges be dismissed." John Duffy strode back to his seat.

It was Joe Manus's turn, and he called his first witness, Ralph Rater. Ralph had dressed his best this morning, a green polyester suit that was two sizes too small, a once white dress shirt and a bolo tie. His hair was plastered to his skull, and he reeked of floral aftershave.

After he was sworn in, Judge Kramer asked him if Ralph Rater was his real name.

"Yes, Judge," he said proudly. "It used to be Raymond Rappaport, but I had it legally changed when I discovered my calling."

"Your calling?" the judge prompted.

"Creating a smut-free world, Your Honor. Vanquishing video vice. Slaying scatological slime. Would you like to be on my mailing list?" Rater asked, whipping out a card.

Joe Manus quickly intervened. "Mr. Rater, will you describe to the court the contents of State Evidence A, the video you received?"

"Certainly." Rater was all business now. "It was exactly one month ago. I heard the lid shut on my mailbox, and I ran down the stairs. I was expecting the latest animated Bible stories, and I could hardly wait to preview them. I put the first one on, and let me tell you, I could not believe it." At this point he rolled his eyes heavenward. "Shades of Sodom and Gomorrah. Talk about your Armageddon. I was shocked."

"Can you tell us what was on the video?" Manus purred.

"Fornication, that's what. Men and women fornicating. Fornicating in broad daylight. *In fragrante delicto.*"

"That's *flagrante*," Manus quietly corrected.

"And the worst part," Rater continued, "was these people weren't some actor-type porn stars. These were ordinary people. Normal citizens. I recognized them."

"And who were they, Mr. Rater?"

"One of them is sitting right there." He pointed an accusatory finger at Jonathan. "But, believe me, he wasn't wearing no robe."

"And the women?" Manus continued.

"Hooches, some of them old enough to be my mother. I've seen them trooping in and out of that house at all hours of the day and night. Carrying on like the whores of Babylon and—" he drew himself up in righteous indignation "—they took my parking space right in front of my own house."

"And when you discovered the content of the tape, Mr. Rater," Manus said, steering him back on track, "what did you do then?"

"I dropped my whole bowl of M&M's, that's what I did. They rolled all over the floor, too. Let me tell you, I'm still finding them."

"And after you had tidied up, Mr. Rater, then what?"

"Then I called the Vice Squad and reported that filthy tape and that house of ill repute to Lieutenant Costanza."

Rater folded his arms high upon his chest and nodded with satisfaction. "And the police took it from there."

"Thank you, Mr. Rater," Joe Manus said, "no further questions."

The judge glanced at John Duffy, who sailed forward.

"Just one question, Mr. Rater, please name your three favorite movies."

"My favorites or my bestsellers?"

"Whichever you prefer," Duffy said.

Rater grinned, showing gray feral teeth. "They're the same," he chortled as if crying *checkmate*. "*Miracle on 34th Street*—the original of course, with Maureen O'Hara. *It's a Wonderful Life* and, my all-time favorite, *The Sound of Music*.

"*The Sound of Music?*" John Duffy queried.

"The greatest movie ever made," Rater declared and then in a Pavlovian response, sang in a surprisingly pure tenor, "'The hills are alive with the sound of music, with songs they have sung for a million years.'"

"Thank you," John Duffy said.

As the judge asked Rater to step down, I looked quizzically at Duffy. "Just wanted to establish a level of taste," he whispered. "And battiness."

Joe Manus called Lieutenant J. Costanza to the stand. Costanza told about getting the search warrant based on the evidence of the tape. He then described the bust.

"We decided to knock the house over. When Mr. Rater told us about the preparations for the Valentine's Party it seemed perfect, so we organized Operation Cupid."

"Can you tell us, Detective, what you found when you entered the house at 69 Grove?" Manus asked.

"The party was in full swing," Costanza sniggered, "so to speak. In the large downstairs living room, people were dancing and drinking and there was kissing and fondling. We went upstairs and checked out the bedrooms."

"And what was going on there?" Manus asked.

"Hard to tell." Costanza shook his head. "Mostly people were talking real soft or sitting real close, looking into each other's eyes. And, oh yeah, there was foot massage going on. Very kinky."

"Did you find anything else? Any concrete evidence?" Manus prodded.

"You mean the book?"

"I submit the following ledger as State's Evidence Exhibit B," Manus said.

It was our accounts book, a simple lined notebook.

Manus handed the book to Costanza and instructed him to read the entries on the day of arrest. We kept a list of attendance, the names of the guests and the names of staff who were in attendance. He read out the roster in a loud, clear voice. First The Group: Laura Singleton, Grace Davis, Mary Ann Larsen, Terry McGuire. So much for privacy.

Then Costanza read out the list of our male staff, first Simon and then the Zennies.

"And briefly, Lieutenant Costanza, what other notations of significance did the ledger contain?" Manus asked.

"It listed the cash flow. Money in, money out. It listed the expenditures of mortgage, taxes, utilities, linens, food. And it listed the income."

"Which was?" Manus pressed.

"The monthly dues these women paid for...what's a genteel way to put it...being serviced."

"Objection," Duffy was on his feet, "prejudicial."

"Sorry, your Honor." Costanza smirked. "What they paid for...services."

"Your witness," Manus said.

"Lieutenant Costanza," John Duffy's voice was steely, "regarding this ledger, did you see any notation that money changed hands on the night in question, at the Valentine's Day party?"

"No, but..."

"And did you observe any explicit sexual behavior that night?"

"Well, no, but I saw plenty of—"

"Thank you, that will be all."

Lieutenant Costanza stepped down from the stand, and Duffy called Simon to be sworn in.

Clad in a tweed jacket and knit tie, he looked very much the archetypal academic he had once been.

"How long have you been a resident at 69 Grove?" John Duffy asked.

"For four months," Simon answered. "Since its beginning."

"And can you describe your responsibilities there?"

"I train and manage a staff of four. And co-manage the logistics of running the house."

"The logistics?" Duffy probed.

"I oversee the catering and housekeeping, along with Coralee Halprin. I used to be in the restaurant business."

"And the staff that you manage, what are their functions?" Duffy continued.

"They provide the spa services," Simon said succinctly.

"And those are?" John Duffy paused expectantly.

"The emphasis is upon education, Eastern culture and philosophy," Simon explained. "The resident staff gives classes in Zen flower arrangement, feng shui, sumi brush painting, meditation. And upon request, provide shiatzu massage."

"And, Mr. Bartlett—" the judge peered down from the bench "—will you define shiatzu massage for the court?"

"Certainly your Honor. It can be described as pressure point massage. Deep touch to balance the chi...or life force."

"And, where is this pressure applied?" Judge Kramer asked.

"To any of the meridians in the body, your Honor. It's rather like acupuncture."

"And just what is the implement that is used?" the Judge asked.

Joe Manus sniggered, "The big head or the little head?"

Simon ignored the interjection. "No implements, Your Honor. No tools." He allowed himself a smile. "Just touch."

"Can you tell us the qualifications of the staff, Mr. Bartlett?" John Duffy asked.

"They are all long-term Zen students and lay priests."

"Lay priests," Joe Manus snickered. "You got that right."

Judge Kramer rapped her gavel, although her eyes registered her amusement.

"To continue," John Duffy said, "how was the staff renumerated?"

"They received complementary room and board."

"And nothing else?"

"They received the gift of time," Simon said, "that most valuable commodity of all. Time for their spiritual practice. Time to invite the soul."

"Objection," Joe Manus cried, "spare us the poetry."

"Overruled," Judge Kramer said. Then, "Now, how does that verse go?" she mused. "'If I had but two coins, I would use one for a loaf of bread and with the other...'"

"'I would buy hyacinths,'" Simon supplied, "'to feed the soul.'"

The judge and Simon exchanged a brief smile and so did Coralee and I. It was the first time since that awful fight that I felt my sister return to me, complete and unimpeded. I reached out my hand, and Coralee took it in both of hers. "Welcome back, big sister," she whispered. "I missed you."

Judge Kramer rapped discreetly and the trial resumed.

Joe Manus rose for the cross examination. "And just what was the source of your income, Mr. Bartlett?"

"It was the same as the Zen staff. Complementary room and board."

"And what about additional expenses? Bus fare? Haircuts? Breath mints?"

"There was a slush fund."

"The Halprin sisters *kept* a slush fund. For their *kept* men," Manus interjected.

"Objection," John Duffy said.

"Beg your pardon," Manus said. "They supplied expenses for their...what is the proper term? Slow Handers?"

John Duffy called his last witness. Grace was elegant in a jade silk dress that softly outlined her round full breasts and fell just below her knees, revealing a still spectacular pair of legs. Clearly, this was a woman who didn't need to pay for male company.

After being sworn in, she identified herself proudly as a full-time homemaker, a mother of four and grandmother of eight—her tone dropped sadly—recently divorced. That inflection was eloquent; no doubt her ex was a cad.

Under John Duffy's skillful questioning, Grace traced the history of what led her to membership in Slow Hands. She began with the therapy group. I was warmed and gratified by her comments on what a caring and astute clinician I was and how I was in no way responsible for her suicide attempt. She sought my gaze as she finished her testimony. "In fact, it was Dr. Russack's intervention that gave me back the will to live."

"And just what was that intervention?" John Duffy queried.

"The establishment of Slow Hands. And not just for me but for every woman lucky enough to walk through those portals. It was a truly healing experience. I would like to put on record some brief comments from the other three members of our founding group. If I may?"

"Proceed," said the judge.

Grace opened her purse and removed a small state-of-the-art tape recorder. She pressed a button, and the courtroom was filled with the joyous laughter of The Group. Then each spoke.

Laura told of the trials of her eating disorder and finally

learning to love her body through Alberto's careful ministrations.

Terry told of the depression that menopause had brought and how Barney had showed her the pleasures of being "a green and juicy crone."

Grace spoke of the misery of being left for a younger woman and how her confidence was rebuilt by Jonathan's worshipful attentions, how he became both her mentor and her protégé.

And finally Mary Ann talked about relearning the value of body time over clock time, of billing and cooing over billable hours.

When Grace turned off the tape, there was silence in the courtroom. People seemed in a bit of a trance, reflecting, perhaps, on how they themselves had spent the last week. I thought of the adage that no one's tombstone bore the motto, I wish I had spent more time in the office.

Joe Manus broke the silence with a very direct question.

"Tell me, Mrs. Davis. Did your mentor-protégé relationship with Jonathan involve sensual acts?"

"Among other things, yes." Grace smiled in remembrance.

"Sexual acts?" he asked.

"Yes," she said.

"And did you pay for these acts?"

"They were part of the monthly dues," Grace answered.

"So that's what you were paying for, among other things?" Manus probed. "Sexual acts?"

"They were optional," Grace answered. "They had to be completely voluntary and mutually desired."

"Are you telling us that sex was not the main agenda?"

"Intimacy was the main agenda, Mr. Manus," Grace said, "and mutual pleasure the only goal. Sometimes that took the form of reading poetry aloud, sometimes of a foot massage, sometimes of sitting together in silence."

"And sometimes of sex," he persisted.

"When it evolved naturally from what preceded." She leaned forward in her chair, striving to communicate with Manus, to help him understand. It was difficult, like building a bridge between two species. She spoke slowly, "Sex can be a healing sacrament. At Slow Hands we honored that."

"The only thing you honored was lust," Manus scoffed.

"That's right," Grace countered, "a lust for life."

"Thank you," said Manus. "That will be all."

"Mr. Duffy?" the judge inquired.

"No further questions," Duffy said.

Manus waited until Grace had taken her seat before turning to the judge.

"Your Honor, we have an open and shut case here. The evidence of the explicitly sexual videotape combined with an accounts ledger is definitive. Clearly this 'spa' is a cover for a brothel. Whorehouse. Bordello. And the fact that the gender is reversed and that here, so to speak, the woman is on top, does not change the nature of the crime. The State asks that these sinister sisters be sentenced to the maximum penalty the law allows and that they serve their five years in state prison without parole." Manus sat down without looking at any of us.

It was John Duffy's turn to close the argument. He was on high alert; I could almost see the synapses firing.

"Your Honor, we do not question the truth and relia-
bility of the evidence presented. The videotape accurately represents some of the activities that occurred at
Slow Hands. The ledger accurately records the monthly
dues that members pay to partake in the myriad aesthetic,
health and spiritual benefits of the spa.

"However, what has not yet been discussed is the
deeper purpose of this refuge, this place of healing. Sara
Russack, the founder and CEO of Slow Hands, is a registered marriage and family counselor. She has been in
private practice for over twenty years specializing in
women's issues, particularly mood disorders, depression
and orgasmic dysfunction. Based on her expertise, research and deep commitment to her clients she devised
a method and a safe place where their emotional needs
could be met, where their self-esteem could be restored,
where they could achieve or regain a full sense of their
womanhood, of their full potential. Sara Russack and
Coralee Halprin founded a sangha, a community for
women and filled it with loving, attentive men. In medical terms, we would call their staff sex surrogates, in the
Slow Hands Spa model they are called men of compas-
sion or purveyors of loving-kindness.

"Rather than put these women in jail, I suggest we en-
shrine them along with such other pioneer benefactors of
women as Margaret Sanger, Susan B. Anthony and Gloria Steinem."

There was a moment of silence in the courtroom, a
tribute to the theatrical passion, if not the convincing

logic, of John Duffy's speech. Judge Kramer rose. "Counsel and defendants meet me in my chambers."

Manus and Duffy walked swiftly to the back office; Coralee and I trailed behind. I wondered if this was our last day of freedom. As we entered Judge Kramer's chambers I was surprised to see its paneled walls decorated with an extensive display of hand-carved wooden spoons. Each spoon handle was carved differently, a courting gift given by a man to his beloved. "You collect love spoons," I said. "I bought one myself when I was in Wales."

"It's my grandmother's collection," Judge Kramer said. "She had a wide circle of admirers when she was a girl." She gestured toward a picture on her desk of a dewy-eyed young woman with waist-length blond hair. "Granny Thomas," she said fondly. "And here she is at my daughter's wedding."

I examined the woman in the second picture, white-haired, but still beautiful.

"All that male attention stopped once my Grandfather died," Judge Kramer continued. "She told me once, 'I have people to call me Mom and Granny and Mrs. Thomas, and even Katherine, but there's no one left to call me Kat.' I think she would have liked Slow Hands. I wish it were around when she was." Judge Kramer looked at the D.A. pointedly. "Will the defendants wait outside while counsel confer?"

It took less than twenty minutes by the clock, but I went to the bathroom twice and Coralee worried the cuticle on both thumbs to the bleeding point. Finally the bailiff ushered us back. Judge Kramer's demeanor was stern. "In the case of the State versus Russack and Halprin regarding the felony charge of pimping and pandering, I find the defendants—" she paused dramatically "—not guilty."

Coralee let out a long held breath.

Judge Kramer continued. "Regarding the misdemeanor charge of operating a house of prostitution," she paused again, her gaze seeking first Coralee, then me, "I find the defendants guilty as charged."

"Oh, no," I cried. Coralee put her arm around my shoulders.

The Judge continued. "It has been proven in a court of law that sexual services were provided for money at 69 Grove in a house owned and operated by the defendants. Operating a house of prostitution is illegal in the state of California and punishable by fine and jail sentence. Now while the court in no way condones such an operation, the court also believes your intention was neither lewd nor mercenary, but perversely humanitarian. Therefore I will suspend your sentence and put you on two years' probation provided that you cease operating this establishment immediately."

Coralee let out a whoop of joy, and I felt a rush of relief. "You two girls have gotten away with murder," Mom would have said. "Sometimes it's better to be lucky than smart." And we were very lucky. We could have been in the slammer for five years.

After we left the judge's chambers, we stopped in the hall outside the courtroom to thank John Duffy. "What do we owe you?" I asked.

"Consider it a token of appreciation for a brave feminist venture. Berkeley is going to miss Slow Hands." He gave us each a warm handshake, hoisted his briefcase and strode off. We listened to the crisp echo of his heels until the sound died away.

Finally Coralee spoke, "I'm going to miss Slow Hands, too."

"But you're the one who wanted to close it," I said.

"I needed my half of the money, but I liked Slow Hands, and I loved working with you."

"You did?" I said.

"Absolutely. Seeing each other every day. Building a business together."

"And what about Simon? You weren't jealous?"

"A little. But Simon's out of the massage business now," she said firmly. "But there'll be other guys."

"Other guys?"

"You heard John Duffy. Slow Hands is too important to let die. It's an idea whose time has come."

"We can't reopen, Corrie. We've got a record now. We'll wind up in a cell with a toilet that won't flush."

"You can't reopen in California," she said. "But there are other places."

"You'd really be willing to start again? Be my partner?"

"Not me, Sarie. I'm going to have my hands full with the restaurant. And," she rested her hands on her stomach, "with a baby."

"You're pregnant?" I cried. "Since when?"

"This morning. I hope. But don't worry. You'll find a new partner."

"I'd never find someone I'd know and trust well enough."

"You'd be surprised," she said. " 'Sometimes the result of all our wandering is to return home and know it for the first time,' " she said, quoting T. S. Eliot. She smiled mischievously. "Bet you didn't know I knew that."

CHAPTER 23

Harry and I decided to celebrate the end of the trial by resurrecting our old Wednesday night ritual. When Wendy was little and I was preparing dinner most nights, we had declared Wednesday as cook's night off. I would make fancy hors d'oeurves, and Harry would devise some new and lethal cocktail. Wendy would get a peanut butter sandwich and a video, while Harry and I would get slightly looped and cuddle on the couch. When I started to work evenings, the ritual lapsed. Tonight I wanted to reinstate it.

So Harry mixed us a pitcher of his margaritas grandes, rimmed the glasses with Kosher salt, and I bought two pounds of jumbo prawns. "Jumbo shrimp," Harry mused predictably, "an oxymoron."

And instead of censoring him for the cliché, I was warmed by its familiarity and joined him in his old comic routine, "Like military intelligence."

"Like open secrets," he chortled.

I took a deep slug of my margarita, so cold it made my teeth ache. "Talk about open secrets. Did you know?"

He slowly licked the salt from the rim of his glass. "I knew something was going on, I just didn't know what."

"What did you think?" I asked, really wanting to know. I didn't want anything hidden between us anymore.

"I was afraid you were having a love affair." He met my gaze. "I'm glad you weren't."

"I wasn't." I finished my drink and held out my glass for a refill. "But if I had slept with one of the Zennies, would that have bothered you?"

He dipped one of the prawns into the cocktail sauce, chewed it reflectively. "Horseradish," he said, "lemon juice and what else?"

"Cayenne."

"Great," he said. "Yes, it would have bothered me. But I could understand it."

"You could?"

"We're complex people, Sarie. All of us. Not so much an animal as a zoo. We've all got multiple personalities. What makes us think we can be all things to one person? We can't."

"But we can be the most important person in the world to each other." I took his hand. A dentist's hand, so well scrubbed, the nails short and straight. "You are that to me."

"And you, Sara Jane Russack *nee* Halprin, are that to me." He stroked my hand. "So what's the next step, honey bunch? Where do we go from here?"

I speared a shrimp with my free hand, popped it into my mouth. "Back to normal, I guess."

"Maybe not," he said.

I felt a clutch of worry. "You think we'll be in trouble because of the publicity, that our practices will suffer?"

"I was thinking maybe we don't want to go back. Maybe we want to go forward."

"Forward where?" I had the feeling that Harry, counter to form, was way ahead of me.

"You put so much of yourself into Slow Hands. And it did such good, I don't think you'd be happy going back to 'talk' therapy. It'd be like going back to black and white after Technicolor. Back to the typewriter after the computer. I think you should have a chance to dream the dream onward."

"Like how?" I asked.

"Like how about Nevada?"

"Nevada?"

"It's legal," he said. "What about we reopen in Nevada?"

"We?" I said. "What *we?*"

"You and I," he said.

"But Harry, you're an orthodontist."

"I've been one for twenty-five years. But I'm getting tired of all that blood and pain and messing around with nature. I'm getting tired of those white jackets. I'm getting fed up with teeth. I think it's time for a change. I could help you set up the new Slow Hands, and then I'd have time to pursue my new hobby."

"What new hobby?"

"Who knows? Learn Italian? Sing Verdi? Sculpt? Grow

cacti? Hang glide? Yeah, I've always wanted to hang glide. Must be the closest you can come to being a bird."

So Harry wanted to be a bird; I had no idea. I grinned at him, noticing how broad his shoulders were, how well muscled his arms. My ex-motorcycle bad boy; I moved in closer.

"I've got lots of ideas for us," he said. "The Zennies will like Nevada. The desert is excellent for meditation—clean air, silence, major sunsets. Land is cheap. We can build a great spa. It's not that far from San Francisco. The Group can fly in for the night. We'll have to expand our clientele base, but that won't be a problem with the Internet. Slow Hands.com(e)! We can even franchise it... Amsterdam. Berlin. Copenhagen."

"Harry, you really mean this? You want to reopen Slow Hands and be my partner?"

He reached into his pocket and held out two airline tickets to Reno. "We leave on Saturday."

I hadn't realized until that moment how much Slow Hands meant to me. "Oh, thank you, darling. That is so good of you. I'm so happy."

"Then why are you crying?"

"I just wish Coralee and Simon could be there, too."

He pulled out another set of tickets. "They're coming with us. No promises but they're going to look at the site. Slow Hands is going to need a good restaurant. People get hungry after a workout." He paused. "So what do you think of Slow Pans?"

"Slow Pans?" I laughed. "Who thought of that?"

"Who do you think?" he said.

"You?" I didn't mean it to sound as surprised as it came out.

"You think that's punny," Harry growled and wrapped his arms around me. "I've got a million of them."

And so he did. My sweet Harry.

"You have reached Slow Hands. All our operators are busy serving other customers. Your call is important to us. Please stay on the line."

"'Believe me, sister, I understand. When it comes to love, you need Slow Hands.'"